A D...
at
Candlewick
CASTLE

BOOKS BY EMMA JAMESON

A Death at Seascape House

MAGIC OF CORNWALL
Marriage Can Be Murder
Divorce Can Be Deadly
Dr Bones and the Christmas Wish
Dr Bones and the Lost Love Letter

LORD AND LADY HETHERIDGE MYSTERY SERIES
Ice Blue
Something Blue
Blue Murder
Black and Blue
Blue Blooded
Blue Christmas

A DEATH
at
Candlewick
CASTLE

EMMA JAMESON

bookouture

Published by Bookouture in 2021

An imprint of Storyfire Ltd.
Carmelite House
50 Victoria Embankment
London EC4Y 0DZ

www.bookouture.com

ISBN: 978-1-80019-761-9
eBook ISBN: 978-1-80019-760-2

"Sweet Nightingale" words first published in Robert Bell's Ancient
Poems of the Peasantry of England, 1857.
"The Song of the Western Men," also known as "Trelawny" written in its
modern form by Robert Stephen Hawker in 1824.
"Roll the Old Chariot Along," also known as "A Drop of Nelson's Blood."

For Pamela and John, with love

CHAPTER ONE

Slawterpooch, Chuggypig, and a Pair of Janners

The gun's barrel jabbed Jemima Jago's rib cage as a low voice growled, "This is it. Hand over your purse, missy."

"Ow! Where'd you find that? Frozen in a block of ice?" Jem's bathing suit, a navy one-piece, afforded little protection against the chilled metal.

Turning from the boat's wheel, she was confronted by the sight of a most unusual pirate. Her friend, Micki Latham, tall and statuesque in a red swimsuit, had added a black tricorn hat, striped sash, and gold hoops to her ensemble. To cap it off, she'd used an old flintlock pistol to poke Jem's ribs. The firearm looked surprisingly realistic.

"Avast!" Micki cried, fully in character now. There were surprisingly good acoustics in the glassed-in wheelhouse of *Bellatrix*—a vintage fishing boat Jem had recently purchased by emptying her savings account—and Micki's shout echoed rather pleasingly off the windows. Not to mention a nearly 360-degree view of the blue-green Celtic sea.

"I don't remember the invitation saying anything about costumes." Jem's eyes flicked to the navigation console, where a bright yellow flyer lay beneath her *Reeds Skipper's Handbook*. A quick scan of the widely distributed invitation confirmed her memory.

First Annual Pirate Extravaganza, Saturday August 7
Pirate Radio Broadcast, 3–6 p.m.

Live Music, 7 p.m.–?
Door Prizes
Kids' Costume Parade
Marvel at the *Jolly Codger*, a real pirate ship!

The ad copy was followed by cut-and-paste images: pirate ships, the skull and crossbones flag, and a treasure chest.

"Nope, nothing about costumes for grown-ups," Jem said.

"Following rules is for boring people," Micki said lightly. "If I'm the only bird in piratical plumage, all eyes will be on me."

Jem couldn't argue with that logic. Sometimes traveling in Micki's wake was entertaining. Her friend tended to pull all the admiring gazes to herself, like flies to a slice of luscious fruit. Jem didn't really mind though. She still considered herself recently divorced, even if the papers had been signed at the beginning of the year and the entire process had been amicable—acknowledgement of a mistake rather than a bitter breakup.

Since returning to her childhood home in the Isles of Scilly, two and a half hours off the coast of Cornwall, Jem had attracted the attention of two very different men. Her goal for the summer was to ignore both of them, focus on her work, and pour all her leftover energy into the great outdoors, as opposed to dealing with the XY set. Sticking close to extroverted Micki helped make that possible.

"Where'd you get that stuff, anyway?"

"Got it off the Tidal Pool Players," Micki said, meaning a small acting troupe on the island of St. Mary's. Her cousin Clarence, a B&B owner with a rich, sonorous voice that was made for the stage, had joined the troupe as a set designer, though he hoped to soon win a speaking part.

"Clarence was in the Empire Theater painting a backdrop and invited me inside for a tour," Micki said. "He said no one would notice I'd borrowed them as long as I brought them back tomorrow."

"The gun, too?" Jem asked, surprised by its authenticity.

"Oh, sure. They have a trunk full of prop weapons. Deactivated antiques. Real knives with dull blades, and gag knives with retractable blades. Swords, too." As she spoke, Micki stuck the flintlock in her sash. The chilled metal barrel made her wince.

"Told you. Why's it so cold?"

"To sneak this stuff aboard without you or Pauley noticing, I hid it under the ice in the drinks cooler. Then I did a quick change when Pauley wasn't looking. I was hoping to startle her. Make her laugh."

"Did it work?"

"Did you hear any laughter?"

"Oh, well." Jem automatically scanned the sea. Although it was an easy passage between their starting point, St. Morwenna, and their destination, Tresco, this was *Bellatrix*'s maiden voyage, which made her feel extra protective. Moreover, from the middle of Friday night until around six a.m., a surprise gale had fallen upon Land's End, the Scillies, and half of Cornwall, lashing trees and topping the waves with white foam. Now, at half-past noon, the clouds had vanished, the sea was mild, and the bad weather seemed like a dream. But as skipper, Jem still had to keep an eye out for other vessels, swimmers, and flotsam churned up by the storm.

"Didn't even take her earbuds out," Micki said. "Just sort of stretched her lips. I wouldn't call it a smile."

"Poor thing." Through the wheelhouse's aft-facing window, Jem saw her friend of many years, Pauley Gwyn, draped over the bench that overlooked *Bellatrix*'s wake. As usual, she was decked out in vintage finery. A boyleg black swimsuit with ruched sides; cat's-eye sunglasses with twinkling rhinestone accents; flip-flops crowned with little black rosettes.

Pauley, an ultra-curvy, alabaster goth in an archipelago full of tanned and trim tourists, never left home without her factor seventy sun cream or her signature blood-red lipstick. But lately her bubbly personality had gone missing, and her face was set in a solemn mask. Six weeks ago, her mum had died. While Mrs. Gwyn had been poorly for years, the loss nevertheless seemed to have shaken Pauley to her core.

"Sometimes I think she'd benefit from a good, long cry," Jem added.

"Hah! A bloke is what she'd benefit from," Micki said. "Oh, don't look at me like that. Not to marry. Just for a drink. A dance. Maybe a snog," she added, grinning. "She told me herself she hasn't been on a proper date in two years."

"Yes, well, you have lofty goals. I'm just glad Pauley finally agreed to come out with us. Until today, I haven't been able to pry her out of Lyonesse House to do anything. Not even grab a pint at the Duke's Head Inn."

Jem was too practical to believe going to Tresco for a pirate-themed festival would do much for Pauley's mood in the short run. But from personal experience, she also knew that to emerge from grief, the first step was to force yourself to rejoin the world at large—even if that meant enduring, rather than enjoying, social gatherings. While you were doing it, it felt pointless and silly, but on the unconscious level, it did a lot of good. The most potent proof that life goes on is to venture out and watch it unfold, even if that means sitting quietly at a party with an untouched drink in your hand.

"Almost there, eh?" Micki asked, eyes on Tresco's southernmost tip. It was growing larger by the moment.

"Yeah. That's Carn Near Quay." Jem scanned the boat slips. Before setting out, she'd rung the boating office to check the number of slips available. The clerk had breezily assured her there were always open spaces. Yet Jem saw no gap in the quay's long row of berthed powerboats and yachts. Tresco, famous for its tropical gardens, seemed especially popular today.

"Ooh, posh one, that," Micki said, pointing at the largest yacht, gleaming white and about sixty feet long.

"You don't think the pirate festival attracted the smart set, do you?"

Micki snorted. "Drove some of them out to sea, more like. I heard there was a council shouting match over the approval. If it doesn't go well, there won't be a second annual festival. Not on Tresco, at any rate. Anyway, hurry up and bring us ashore. I need a wee."

"There are no open slips."

"So find one. Make one. You owe us," Micki said. "You're the one who told a whopper about this bucket having a head. I've had a look. There's nothing there"—she gestured to the deck—"but a bench and an engine compartment."

She wasn't wrong. *Bellatrix* had about twenty square feet of useable deck space, if you ignored the gear heaped in one corner and the engine compartment stuck in the middle. Technically, *Bellatrix* was a clinker, meaning a boat with a wood-paneled hull. Emmets—a Cornish term for tourists—and casual boaters didn't know what to make of it, but older fishermen often waved or tooted their horns. To a working boatman, she was a classic. But she wasn't spacious or up to date.

"I beg your pardon, there *is* a head," Jem said primly. She was still too boat-proud to let slander go unanswered.

"Where?"

"There." She pointed at the wheelhouse's far corner.

"You'd better not mean the bucket under all that grot."

"Oh, for heaven's sake." Jem shifted a pile of books. Wherever she lived or worked, stacks of books cropped up like mushrooms. This particular one included a biography of Sir John Arundell for work, a stargazing guide for pleasure, and her much-underlined first edition of *Jonathan Strange & Mr. Norrell*, for no other reason than she loved the ruddy thing.

"Ta-da!" Jem said, fully revealing the head.

"Jem, love. That's another bucket."

"No, it's not. It's a proper maritime toilet, I assure you."

Gingerly, Micki lifted the lid, had a peek, and dropped it. "That's a bucket. With a lid."

"But there are chemicals inside to neutralize what you put in. Neat and tidy. Come on, Mick. Did you really expect a flushing porcelain throne on a boat this size?"

"No, but I expected an enclosed head. Hidden behind a curtain at the very least. This is out in the open, surrounded by windows!"

Jem shrugged. "Fishing used to be completely male-dominated. Back when they knocked *Bellatrix* together, it was all over-the-side, if you get my drift. That chem-bog was added by the last owner as a selling point."

"Well, I'm not plopping my bottom down in front of God and everyone," Micki declared. "Make landfall. Avast!" She waved the flintlock at Jem.

"Stop that. I'm telling you, every last slip is claimed. Why don't you go for a swim?"

Micki pulled a face. "Come on. I need the ladies'. Or terra firma, at the very least."

"Why? I thought you were a strong swimmer."

"I am. But if you had curly hair, you'd know why I don't fancy getting it wet," Micki said. "Besides, the water feels cold to me. I know you two barely notice, but without a dive suit, I find it comes as too much of a shock."

The wheelhouse door opened and Pauley asked, "Are you guys talking about going ashore?"

"Yes, but Jem says all the slips are full up."

"Tresco hosts conventions every summer," Pauley said. "This must be one of the days. Those vessels won't clear out before noon tomorrow." A lifelong Scillonian, she knew by osmosis things that

Jem, most recently from Penzance, and Micki, born in St. Ives, had to ask around to uncover. "Why don't we circle around to the castle side? Usually there's only a few ramblers taking in the ruins. Maybe not even that, if the storm canceled their plans."

"Good idea." Jem smiled at Pauley. "It's been eons—I'd like to see it again myself. We can drop anchor close to the beach, wade to shore, and walk inland from there."

"So I'm still getting wet?" Micki asked.

"Not your hair."

"Fine."

Pauley's eyes flicked over Micki, taking in the hat, sash, and flintlock. "What's with that get-up?"

"I'm in costume because it's an extravaganza. About pirates."

"Oh. Right. Sorry." Pauley folded her arms across her chest and sighed, that faraway look returning.

Seeing Micki on the verge of telling her to buck up, Jem intervened with a furtive shake of the head. No amount of hectoring Pauley would spark genuine interest in the festival. She'd agreed to come along. She was even choosing to remain half-inside the wheelhouse, propped against the open door, instead of returning to the relative solitude of the aft bench to mope. That was good progress for a first day out.

"Changing course," Jem announced unnecessarily. She had a bit of a bossy streak, and it was fun to be skipper.

"Look at the sea. Crystal clear," Micki said, smiling over the shimmering waters as *Bellatrix* skirted Tresco's southern tip, veering toward the northernmost shore. "But what about those rocks below? There's no danger of scraping one, is there?"

"Nope. They're not as close as they look. The refractive index of water is different than air. Makes things look bigger," Jem said.

Micki let out one of her trademark wheezy laughs, like a squeaker toy on its final go. "I'm going to pretend I understood that."

"Don't be too impressed. She got it from one of those." Pauley indicated Jem's pile of books. "She's dying for you to ask how she knows, so she can produce a sextant or something equally tedious and lecture you on how to use it."

"I don't lecture," Jem scoffed. "Besides, remember that summer when we were ten? We had loads of fun with my sextant, till I lost it."

"Till I buried it."

"What? You slawterpooch!"

"Chuggypig!" Pauley retorted.

Micki, clearly wanting a piece of the action, announced, "You're nothing but janners, the both of you!"

Jem looked around. "Huh?"

"Come again?" Pauley said.

"Never mind. I reckon you have to be a true Cornishwoman to understand that one," Micki said.

"I'm a proud Scillonian," Pauley sniffed. "By the way, Jem, just because I suggested going to the castle doesn't mean I want to hear a speech about the Civil War."

"But actually, the history of the castle's quite interesting…"

Jem waited, but her attempt at a leading statement went completely ignored. Micki and Pauley began checking the contents of their dry bags, which substituted for handbags aboard *Bellatrix*. A dry bag was a waterproof backpack with plenty of inner pockets. They kept mobiles, cash, and dry clothes safe from the sea. Jem had purchased a color-coded set of three: red for her, green for Micki, and yellow for Pauley.

Micki's was stuffed to the gills with items like her sundress, which doubled as a cover-up, a beach towel, a motorized personal fan, and a bottle of tequila. Unable to cram her pirate accoutrements into it, Micki stuck them into Pauley's, which was half empty. Jem's was almost as overfilled as Micki's, containing her swim goggles, snorkel, and fins, plus the usual personal essentials. In the islands, you never knew when your dive kit might turn a good day into an adventure.

As Micki fussed with her hair, twisting her billowy dark curls into a crude topknot for wading, Pauley appeared to watch a gig rowing crew as it passed the boat, their oars dipping in perfect unison. Jem enjoyed gig rowing—she'd done plenty of it in her younger years—and wondered if she might join a team next year. She still hadn't decided if she was moving back to Penzance next month, which would make her work life easier. Or if she would give up her mainland flat and settle permanently back in the Scillies. Either way, *Bellatrix* was the key. She could either commute to Penzance and the Courtney Library as needed, or she could take to the sea every weekend, visiting her friends in the Isles of Scilly whenever she wished.

As they headed north past New Grimsby Quay, Tresco's changeable coast transformed from white sands to muddy rockpiles. Granite slabs jutted up dramatically, like a giant's broken teeth. Trees, homes, and evidence of modern life vanished. Studying the shore was like peering through a magic spyglass at the days of wooden sailing ships, when Britain's Royal Navy ruled the seas.

Although over three hundred years old, Candlewick Castle still looked strong and viable as a military fort. Technically, it was a ruin. Nevertheless, its round tower, constructed from the stones of a nearby royal castle pulled down by Parliamentarian forces, stood tall, gun ports pointing at the bay. As a girl, Jem had visited frequently. Although the site was owned by English Heritage, there was no entry fee and no poncy gift shop allergic to the presence of unaccompanied children. She'd loved climbing the castle's staircase, a perfect place to reenact the swashbuckling sword fights of *The Princess Bride*. As for the round tower's gun deck, it was ideal for flying kites, tossing stones, or just leaning over the parapet and watching the waves.

Jem dropped anchor not far from the channel between Tresco and its island neighbor, Bryher. The channel was deep in places, and after the storm it was too deep to wade. By using *Bellatrix*'s echo sounder, Jem found a spot close to the shore in only three and a half feet of water.

Micki, determined to face her fears, was the first overboard. She slid in by degrees, holding on to *Bellatrix*'s gunwale until she was sure the water was shallow enough to stand up in.

"It's cold!"

Pauley came next, her rhinestone sunnies and flip-flops stowed safely in her yellow dry bag. She, too, chose to enter carefully, the better to protect her recently colored magenta hair. It stood out vividly against the blue-green water. As Jem looked down at her friend, she wondered idly if the International Space Station was passing overhead. If so, the astronauts were probably marveling over that hair.

"It's fine!" Pauley contradicted Micki, wading confidently toward the shore.

Before disembarking, Jem's final task as skipper was to shut down *Bellatrix*'s diesel engine. As for the keys, she left them in the nav console. Traditional piracy wasn't an issue around the Isles of Scilly, and anyone who stole a replanked clinker fishing boat wouldn't get far. In the fiberglass and plastic world of recreational boating, Jem's vessel was virtually unique.

Hoisting her red bag, Jem gave its zips and pulls a quick once-over. She knew her valuables were secure, but she did it anyway. Over the course of her thirty-three years, Jem had learned to respect the sea's power. It liked to invade secret places, stealing what it could and corroding the rest. It was why she'd worn a life vest throughout the serene voyage to Tresco. When she'd bought *Bellatrix*, she'd promised herself to never put convenience or ego over safety on the water.

The red bag was indeed sealed up tight. Removing her life vest, Jem slipped the bag's straps over her shoulders, wriggled to make sure they were secure, and dropped over the gunwale into the sea. The water didn't feel cold to her, only refreshing.

It didn't take long to reach the shore. At first glance, the heritage site appeared completely deserted of tourists and ramblers. It looked so peaceful and inviting, Jem almost wished they didn't have a festival to attend. In her opinion, this was a perfect day for swimming. The sky was a hard summer blue, empty of anything but the occasional wheeling gull.

Peeee-you! Peee-you!

Jem almost jumped out of her skin. Micki and Pauley, emerging from the surf, pointed at something a few meters inland from Candlewick Castle.

The storm had covered the shore in tidewrack: bits of seaweed, driftwood, dead fish, and broken shells. Inland, where clumps of gorse and heather grew, a large black and brown bird with a powerful hooked beak and a big wingspan was settling down to peck at something.

Buzzard, Jem thought, drawing up beside her friends. As they watched, the formidable creature plucked a struggling crab off its prey and sent it flying. Jem squinted to see what it was pecking at so excitedly. Had the storm washed up the corpse of a seal or some other marine mammal?

With another *peee-you!*, two more buzzards touched down, landing heavily, like a pair of Army Chinooks. The first bird, offended by this encroachment, dug into the feast, probably hoping to do a takeaway. It tugged on a thick white tube with bluish mottling. The tube, which appeared to be wearing a shiny metal bracelet, terminated in fingers and a thumb.

"Oh, no," Jem breathed.

"I know. Let's give those buggers a wide berth," Micki said.

"I don't mean the birds. Can't you see what they've got?"

Pauley shaded her eyes to study the scavengers. They'd fallen to pecking at one other, *peee-you*-ing and beating their wings in rising fury. "Looks like a pile of clothes. Pink shirt and khaki shorts."

"It's a dead body. A human body," Jem said.

Micki and Pauley swapped glances. Their response came in perfect unison:

"Again?"

CHAPTER TWO

A Death at Candlewick Castle

"Do birds that big attack people? I've never heard of them killing anyone. Dogs, maybe," Micki said.

"I think it's safe to assume the body was dead when the buzzards found it," Jem said.

"Ooh, listen to you. Solve one murder for the police and now you know everything. Are those things Golden Eagles? They look like cousins to pterodactyls," Micki retorted. "Tear out your throat with one great peck. Or the swipe of a foot."

"Golden Eagles are in Scotland. These are buzzards," Pauley declared with the confidence of a lifelong resident. "The worst they'll do is spew vomit."

"You're joking."

"I'm not. Apparently they've worked out the one thing humans can't abide."

"I think we need to get over there and make absolutely sure the person is dead," Jem said, though she had no idea how that blue-white, unresisting arm could still be attached to anything living. "But I'd be lying if I said those birds aren't intimidating."

Micki and Pauley made no suggestions, only watched Jem expectantly. It seemed they were waiting for her to decide their next move. She wasn't entirely surprised. In unfamiliar or threatening circumstances, she had a tendency to launch herself into the breach. An incident involving a certain London bag-snatcher who got himself chased down and kicked in the shins sprang to mind. Still, despite spending her formative years on St. Morwenna, which had involved plenty of wildlife encounters, Jem's knowledge of buzzards was scant. Being a Special Collections Librarian didn't require much wrangling of birds of prey.

"I say, find your mobile and ring Hack," Micki said, referring to Sergeant Hackman, the recently installed head of the Isles of Scilly police department. "Let him fight off the monsters."

"That could take a while. Maybe an hour, if they're off dealing with nuisance emmets or drink driving," Jem said. By "nuisance emmets" she meant overexcited holidaymakers, usually young men, who treated the Isles of Scilly like a no-holds-barred party in Benidorm. The Scillies were known for peace, quiet, and natural beauty, not uni students gone wild. As for "drink driving" around the islands, that mostly meant inebriated boaters. Only St. Mary's had proper roads and cars, and by mainland standards, just a few.

"Ooh, look at him go." Dark eyes widening, Micki watched as the largest, most dominant buzzard, determined to make his competitors give ground, tore into the corpse with fresh determination. "This is awful. Somebody will want to give that poor bloke a proper burial."

"Then I'd better call. Hope I can get signal here." As Jem shrugged off her dry bag to retrieve her mobile, sunlight bounced off the mini-compass attached to a zipper pull. Just as the dominant buzzard's head shot up suspiciously, the reflected light hit his pitiless yellow eye.

PEEEE-YOU!

"Shit," Jem said.

"I still have to wee!" Micki cried.

"Oh, bloody hell." Balling her fists, Pauley lowered her head like a pretty goth bull and ran full tilt at the birds. "Slawterpooches! Chuggypigs!" she bellowed, waving her arms as she charged each in turn.

Two of the raptors beat a clumsy retreat, winging skyward as if they'd suddenly remembered how dangerous and unpredictable *Homo sapiens* could be. The dominant buzzard reared up, revealing an intimidating meter-wide wingspan, but Pauley's charge didn't waver.

"Oi! Janner! Away with you," Micki cried, running toward the biggest bird.

"Yeah, you ruddy janner!" shouted Jem, hard on Micki's heels. She still had no idea what "janner" meant, but it sounded rude if you yelled it loud enough.

Apparently, the dominant buzzard thought so, too. As Jem and Micki reached Pauley's side, it sprang into the air, *peee-you*ing furiously. Before disappearing over the sea, it got the last word, bombing the rocks with a splatter of white as a final insult.

For a moment, the three of them watched the buzzard's retreat, giddy with triumph. Then Jem rounded on Pauley.

"Is this how it will be from now on? Every time there's trouble, you'll just tuck your chin and run straight at it?"

"If it's bird trouble, yeah," Pauley said, unrepentant. She was grinning, truly grinning, something Jem hadn't seen her do in weeks.

"All right. Bird confrontations are fine. But bad guys are different. Especially when they have guns."

"Oh! The *smell*," Micki said in a strangled voice.

They'd stopped a few feet short of the body, still half-hidden by gorse and heather. But a gust of wind carried the stench of death to their nostrils, burning their tongues with the taste of something unspeakable.

"Nope, nope, nope." Micki turned away. "If you need me, I'll be in the ladies." Marching toward a nearby pile of granite rocks, she disappeared behind it.

"There's no law that says we have to get up close and personal with the body. We just need to notify the police," Pauley said, trying to cover her nose and feel inside her dry bag at the same time. "I'll give Hugh Town Police Station a ring."

The smell was so revolting, Jem was tempted to retreat into the cleansing freshness of the sea, or perhaps climb the round tower of the castle and wait on the gun deck until the proper authorities arrived. The first corpse she'd found had been in far better shape, and the circumstances leading her to examine the crime scene had been uniquely compelling. This was a tragedy, but it had nothing to do with her.

As Pauley brought out her mobile, another glint of sunlight, less brilliant than the flash that offended the big buzzard, caught Jem's eye. There was stony rubble all around the castle, but in the midst of it, she spied what she thought was a round bit of glass among the heaped brown stones.

Jem located her flip-flops and put them on. Not especially tender-footed, she didn't mind walking through mud, but granite rubble could cut like knives. Besides, although Tresco was beautifully managed and English Heritage sites were typically litter-free, that didn't mean someone hadn't recently brought wineglasses to a picnic. No matter how often emmets were warned not to take glassware or crockery onto the beach, they kept right on doing it, leaving broken shards in their wake.

As Jem passed the body, she spared it a sidelong glance. That bluish-white arm was connected to a man every bit as horribly pale. He looked like an uncooked giant prawn. She had a quick impression of his clothes—typical leisurewear, a knit polo shirt and cargo shorts. The thing that most stood out, perhaps because of his general pallor, was his socks—the black mid-calf style that usually went with trousers and wingtips. He wore no shoes. In the bottom of one sock was a hole, presumably from where the birds had been at it.

Ugh. Disgusted, Jem turned back to the nearest rubble pile, trying to pick out the circular bit of glass she'd seen. The shape's perfect symmetry intrigued her, although it was probably nothing more than the snapped-off foot of a broken wineglass.

"I'm on hold. Naturally," Pauley huffed, mobile on speaker so the music was faintly audible. "Ten quid says Hack, PC Newt, and PC Robbins are all eating lunch together with their mobiles on silent."

"Probably," Jem admitted. She resisted the temptation to stick up for Hack. A recent transfer from Exeter, Hack was introducing basic efficiency and professionalism to the islands' small police force, which had languished under the old chief's irresponsible management. As he'd explained to Jem, these changes were fundamental, and couldn't be implemented all at once. He didn't want the small staff, hired by someone who'd only cared about doing as little as possible and getting paid for it, to resign en masse, overwhelmed by a complete overhaul of policies and expectations. Thus, the weekend tradition of a leisurely group lunch had continued. If it rendered the team unreachable for the discovery of a dead body, Jem suspected that pleasant tradition would be next on the chopping block.

Picking her way among the rubble, Jem continued her search for the circular bit of glass. The rocks were remarkably uniform in color, and too sharp for her to get down on her hands and knees. She turned, sharp eyes raking the line of rubble until another glint of sunlight revealed something almost under her feet. Staggering aside so as not to tread on it, she recognized the item at last. A pair of wire-framed spectacles with large round lenses.

"What did you find?" called Pauley, who was still on hold.

"Someone's dropped their specs," Jem said, picking up the eyeglasses by a slender earpiece. People often called modern specs wire-framed, but what they really meant was metal rather than plastic frames, or perhaps the flexible titanium that cost a pretty penny. But these specs were actually constructed of wire that encircled each scratched but unbroken lens. The hinges were a little rusty, and when Jem positioned one lens over a fingernail, it magnified her nail bed's ridges only slightly.

Weak lenses. Definitely vintage, she thought. *And there's no way they've been lying here very long, rust or no rust.*

"Do you think they belong to the dead bloke?" Pauley called.

Before Jem could answer, the hold music on Pauley's mobile ceased and a woman spoke.

"Yes. I see. All three of them are at lunch, are they? What a surprise," Pauley said. "Listen, Carenza, this is serious. You'll have to either ring the pub or lock up and…"

The vintage specs were delicate, so Jem carried them over to her bag for safekeeping. Dumping her sunglasses out of their sturdy case, she tucked the wire-framed specs inside as she listened to Pauley tell Hugh Town Station's receptionist, Carenza Morgan, about the situation.

In a close-knit island community, there was no such thing as an anonymous call to the authorities. Pauley and Carenza had known one another all their lives, so naturally Pauley was filling in her friend on every detail. In turn, Carenza would probably feel empowered to repeat those details to any fellow islander who seemed interested. For tourists, the evening news or a push notification would eventually clue them in. As for the residents of Hugh Town, half of them would know about the corpse at Candlewick Castle before Hack and his constables ever set eyes on it.

"Who knows," Pauley was saying to Carenza. "Maybe he was rambling along the shore and had a heart attack."

"Heart attack? He has no shoes," Jem said, contradicting her longtime friend in a peremptory way she never would've used on anyone else. "I expect he fell overboard, perhaps during the storm, and the tide carried him in."

"Oh, pardon me, Carenza, the great detective has spoken," Pauley said. "Has anyone ever told you that Jem Jago solved a murder last month?"

Carenza's tinny laughter carried clearly to Jem. "Solved a mystery? You don't say!"

Slightly miffed, Jem walked back to the body to further examine it and prove her hypothesis. The stench, while still revolting, had grown more bearable after several minutes' exposure. Maybe she should roll the poor man over? There might be a boater's lanyard around his neck—the sort with a universal kill switch that prevented powerboats from rocketing off in the event their skipper fell overboard. But the idea of touching him made her stomach lurch. Instead, Jem decided to begin by studying the body minutely, starting with his head.

"Jem!" Micki emerged from behind the boulders of her makeshift loo. "What are you doing?"

"Just having a peek."

He was an older man, perhaps in his sixties if his sparse white hair was any indication. His exposed scalp had been pecked extensively, and Jem was glad the raptors had discovered him lying face down. Otherwise, those cruel beaks would've left a mess for whichever poor soul was asked to identify him.

His polo shirt, which she'd taken for pink at first glance, appeared tie-dyed. The collar and one shirtsleeve was red, the other pink. The sides were pink-streaked, but at the center of his back, the fabric was a dingy white.

The hair on the back of Jem's neck stood up. This man had bled to death. That explained why he was so very pale, and already smelled as if advanced decomposition was underway.

Seizing the body by its shoulders, Jem rolled it onto its back. The man's ghastly white face was unmarked; his eyes, thankfully, were half-closed. It took Jem a little while to register those details. In the shock of the first moment, she saw something like a wide, impossible grin. Through the opening in his throat, exposed bone gleamed like bloodstained pearly whites.

CHAPTER THREE

Roller Barbie and a Splash of Paint

"More," Jem said.

Pauley squirted another dollop of hand sanitizer into Jem's open palms. "I'll bet when Hack gets here, he reads you the riot act for moving the body."

"How was I supposed to know the man was murdered?"

"I think the point is, since you're not the police, you're supposed to sit back and let the proper authorities take charge. Besides, if you keep stumbling across murder victims, people will start to think you're bad luck. Poor Micki," Pauley said.

At Jem's shriek, Micki had loyally raced across the beach to her friend's side. Seeing the dead man in his full horror, she'd turned and dashed right back to her makeshift loo. Now the sounds of violent retching drifted over to them, suggesting she was losing not only her breakfast, but yesterday's dinner, too.

"You took the sight of him pretty well," Jem observed.

Pauley shrugged. "Changing adult diapers and mopping up bloody vomit will change your perspective on what's unbearable and what's just unsightly."

Before Jem could think of how to reply, or decide if any answer was helpful, Pauley said, "Sorry. Did I go too dark? I have to stop blurting out things like that."

"Well. Perhaps. But not with me," Jem said stoutly. "Listen, we've already moved the poor man, and Carenza said it would be

another forty-five minutes or so before Hack arrives. Why don't
we look him over one more time? In case there's anything else that
might help with the investigation?"

"This is becoming a sickness with you," Pauley said, a smile
nevertheless pulling at her lips. "You never could resist a puzzle.
Unless this is about Hack?" The possibility seemed to please her.

"Hack?"

"Don't play dumb, you're hopeless at it. I know he's smitten.
And I think you are, too, even if you prefer to hide out in my
library."

"Your library happens to be my job at the moment. Besides, I
wanted to stay close in case you needed me. And no, I'm not trying
to impress Hack. It's like you said. A puzzle." That was more or less
true. This was Jem's summer of self-discovery, doing the work she
loved, spending her weekends on *Bellatrix* and reconnecting with
St. Morwenna after twenty years away. While the idea of spending
time with Hack intrigued her, it directly contravened her plan to
temporarily avoid men.

"Fine, let's play detective," Pauley said. "Honestly, I'd rather do
that than go wait at the castle. You might start reciting names and
dates to do with the Civil War."

"That reminds me. Your famous forebearer, Captain Mortimer
Gwyn, has always been presumed a Royalist, but in the library, I
found letters calling that into question. During Oliver Cromwell's
ascendancy..."

Pauley hurried toward the corpse, forcing Jem to follow. Now
that the shock of that carved-out grin had faded, she found herself
once again scanning the body methodically, with Pauley's observa-
tional powers as an added bonus.

"Do you recognize him?"

"No, thank goodness. I mean, I'm sure he's changed from how he
looked in life, but he's not an islander. He could be a second-homer,

though," Pauley said. "See that logo on the shirt? The crowned griffin and castle? It's Brunello Cucinelli. Italian. Very high-end."

"Trust you to recognize a fashion logo. What about that?" Jem wanted to indicate the dead man's wristwatch without touching the arm, which had borne the worst of the scavenging buzzards' attacks. Plucking a long, slender branch from the storm-borne debris, she used it to reposition the mangled limb so Pauley could examine the watch's face. "Even I know a Rolex when I see it."

Pauley gave a low whistle. "One of the nice ones," she said, kneeling for a better look.

"As opposed to the really ugly Rolexes you see every day."

"None are ugly, but there are degrees of excellence. You can get a stainless steel one for five grand or so," Pauley said. While her personal style was quirky and she preferred to sew her own clothes whenever possible, she'd followed fashion trends since her early teens and still kept up. "This is a gold Rolex Yacht-Master. Fifteen or twenty grand retail, I reckon."

Jem took that in. Someone had cut this man's throat with one deep, devastating sweep of the knife. And after it was done, he hadn't bothered to steal the valuable watch off his unresisting wrist.

As if following her thoughts, Pauley ran her hand over one of the buttoned pouches on the corpse's cargo shorts. There was a distinctly square bulge. "Pretty sure his wallet's still in there."

"Yeah. We'll leave it for Hack." Struggling to ignore the smell and her own kneejerk revulsion, Jem searched the body for any additional clues. Judging by the heavy lines on the dead man's forehead, not to mention the rough texture of his face and neck, he'd been an outdoorsman of the old school variety, unacquainted with sun cream or SPF-factor hats. He'd also been a small man, no more than five foot four, as lean as a strip of jerky.

"Something about his grandad socks tugs at my heartstrings," Jem admitted. "I wonder if his family has missed him yet?"

"Are you two still at it?" Micki called. She appeared to have regained her composure, and was probably determined to hang onto it, because she stuck close by the boulders.

"Sorry, Mick," Jem called.

"Feeling better?" Pauley asked.

"Empty is the word I'd use. I suppose we're instructed to sit tight until the coppers arrive? Fine. But I'm keeping well away from that stink." Hands on her hips, Micki started toward the water. "Maybe I'll take a stroll along the shore."

As Pauley turned away from the corpse, it suddenly occurred to Jem to check the third finger of his left hand, in case he wore a wedding ring. What she found was a torn space where the finger should have been—courtesy of a bloody great buzzard, no doubt.

"Oi! Guys!" Micki waved at them from the beach. "Look at this!"

"Please, God, not another body," said Pauley, looking appalled. Jem tried to feel equally taken aback by the suggestion, but her adrenaline surged. More clues?

*

Thankfully, what Micki had discovered wasn't another victim. Washed ashore a few meters from the castle was a fluorescent orange life vest, a vinyl seat cushion, and a plastic float attached to a length of nylon line. The line was still neatly braided, as it had no doubt arrived from the manufacturer, suggesting it had never been used.

"I'm surprised we didn't see all this from aboard *Bellatrix*," Pauley said. Every item was brightly colored, intended to capture attention even at a considerable distance.

"It wasn't there. I'm sure," Jem said.

"Yeah. The vest came in with the tide just as I called for you," Micki explained. "And what's that?"

Jem looked in the direction her friend was pointing, towards the granite escarpment around the castle. On the surface of the water was a small orange bucket. As they watched, the gentle rollers carried it to the granite wall, where it struck the wet stone and bounced away. This happened over and over again. Each time the bucket connected with stone, Jem heard a faint but distinct tap. Without her binoculars, she couldn't be sure, but the bucket seemed far sturdier than a child's beach toy.

"Might be part of a boat kit. A bailer, maybe."

"Think it's from the dead man's boat?" Pauley asked.

"Could be. Let's get some elevation and look again," Jem said.

*

Entering Candlewick Castle had been made simple for modern visitors. With the addition of stone steps, a low window had been transformed into a door, and there was even a handrail for extra stability. Nevertheless, a sign warned,

VISITORS ARE WARNED TO TAKE EVERY CARE TO AVOID ACCIDENTS

"Did I mention I once sprained both knees in a roller derby tournament?" Micki asked. "Hope they're up to this."

"It's not so steep," Pauley said. "Roller derby? Really?"

"Either there's nothing she hasn't done, or she's having us on again," Jem said. "I haven't quite decided."

"There's plenty I haven't done. And I don't want to cripple myself in this old pile so that I can't do more in the future. Including go dancing next week," Micki said.

"Stick close to me and you'll be fine," Jem said, leading the way. "Is there really such a thing as roller derby in England?"

"Of course. We belong to the International Roller Derby League."

"Don't believe a word of it," Pauley said.

"That there are Englishwomen who play roller derby, or that I did?"

"Either. Pics or it never happened."

"Oh, I have pics. I looked exactly like Roller Barbie in my little shorts and helmet."

Jem and Pauley exchanged bemused glances.

"I'll be finding those pics. Then you'll owe me a pint."

Jem let her friends' bickering fall into background noise as she took in the castle's gloomy interior. True to the cliché of adults returning to childhood haunts, it seemed much smaller than she remembered. The staircase was a particular letdown, quite unlike her embellished memories.

There had been duels with driftwood swords, heart-stopping chases up to the gun deck, and threats to fire the Civil War-era cannons into the bay. One early spring day when Jem was fourteen, a bit too old for make-believe but still indulging in it, she'd led Rhys Tremayne on a merry chase across Tresco's heath and into the castle. It was a day she'd never forget.

Then on the cusp of sixteen, Rhys had emerged from the winter tall and lithe, his blond hair falling almost to his shoulders like his surfer idols. On that day, he'd chased her with a new heat in his dark blue eyes, seizing her by the waist as he caught her halfway up the stairs. Wriggling free, she'd darted for the gun deck. There, cornered by black cannons with her back against the wall, Rhys had loomed over her. She could've ducked under his arm and ran back down the stairs. Instead, she looked him in the eye, seeing him for the first time as a devastatingly handsome boy, not a playmate, and parted her lips for her very first kiss.

"Right! Hard on the knees," Micki complained as they emerged onto the gun deck. It was paved with irregular blocks torn from King Charles's Castle, still considered a Tresco landmark despite the fact the Parliamentarians had stripped it to the foundation. The cannons, mounted on wheeled wooden carts, kept a silent vigil on New Grimsby Bay.

"You should do yoga with me some time," Pauley said. "Good for the joints."

"She *is* amazingly limber…" Jem began.

"For a big girl," Pauley finished.

"For someone self-taught," Jem corrected. As a child, Pauley had been terribly sensitive about her size, always attempting fad diets and severe exercise schemes. Her inability to find off-the-rack clothes that weren't tailored like rain ponchos had sparked her interest in sewing from patterns. Now that they'd reconnected, Jem had been thrilled by Pauley's grown-up confidence. But it seemed that grief had dredged up her old habit of assuming every compliment sent her way must be a backhanded one.

"Okay, true, I am self-taught. Sometimes I think I've gone as far as YouTube can take me," Pauley said as Jem headed for the parapet to examine the bay. "Tresco has a yoga class with a good instructor. Maybe I should… What's that?"

"Where?" Jem scanned the gentle choppy waters. The orange bucket was still knocking against the granite lip just below. Other than that, she saw no flotsam bobbing atop the waves.

"Over here," Micki said, beckoning for Jem to come and see. "It's just lying on the floor. I don't reckon we ought to touch it."

Jem hurried over. Upon seeing it, her first thought was, *murder weapon*.

The item was a short knife, perhaps thirteen inches total, with an eight-inch blade and a five-inch wooden handle. Both sides of the blade were serrated with unusually large, wavy teeth. A mixture of pigments—orange, yellow, and red—had dried on it.

"Could you cut a throat with that?" Pauley asked.

"Dunno. The teeth look rounded," Micki said.

"I don't think it's a kitchen knife. I think it's a tool," Jem said. Using the edge of her flip-flop, she gently kicked the item over. The handle's other side bore the manufacturer's name: Piranesi.

The name conjured up mental images like the mind-bending art of M.C. Escher. But less like a puzzle and more like a fantastical vision of antiquity, filled with mysterious temples, grottos, and crumbling statuary. As Jem struggled to put a mental finger on the memory—a headful of eclectic trivia was, for librarians, an occupational hazard—Micki asked, "Any chance that's a painter's knife?"

"Makes sense. Piranesi was an artist," Jem said.

"Oh, I should've recognized it right away," Pauley said. "Rhys buys that brand. Sometimes when he talks about teeny-tiny details of creating art, I go to my happy place. I enjoy his art, really, but listening to him talk about heavy parallel brush strokes versus vigorous brush strokes sends me right off to sleep."

"So Rhys was up here recently?" Jem asked.

Pauley shrugged. "He's not the only seascape painter in the islands. But he's the best. And this would be a good vantage point."

"You can give it back to him." Picking up the artist's knife, Jem passed it to Pauley, who slipped it into her yellow bag. She was a bit disappointed that their find didn't relate to the corpse, and from the looks on her friends' faces, they felt a bit letdown, too. Maybe she wasn't the only one who liked solving puzzles and clearing up mysteries.

Of course, Jem hadn't led them up to the gun deck in order to scoop up clues helpfully scattered around the ruin. She'd led them to the top of the round tower so they could study the clear waters of New Grimsby Bay.

"Wish we had some binoculars. Too bad there isn't one of those tourist viewfinder-thingies," Micki said.

"Look out there! Something's floating," Pauley said, pointing west. "Could it be an oar? Oh. No. Bit of green sticking up. It's only a tree branch."

"Steady me. I'm going higher," Jem said. As a girl, she'd often climbed on the cannons when there were no adults around to stop her. As a grown-up, that seemed dangerous to the historical relics, so she clambered onto the unrailed parapet instead.

"This isn't what I'd call taking every care to avoid an accident." Micki steadied Jem on her left side while Pauley, who even as a girl had prided herself on being an immovable object, held her from the right.

Scanning the water, Jem searched for a dark shape—one large enough to stand out atop the pale sand bars, yet too regular to be a submerged rock. After a brief search, she found one, situated in the channel almost directly between Tresco and its nearest island neighbor, Bryher.

"There!" she cried triumphantly, allowing her friends to pull her back from the brink. "Pauley, pass me my red bag, will you?"

Unzipping its bottom compartment, Jem drew out her swim goggles and fins. "Sorry I only have the one set, guys. But would you mind keeping watch over the body in case the birds come back? I'm going to swim out and take a peek."

CHAPTER FOUR

Dead Man's Shoes

On top of the granite escarpment under the castle, Jem left her flip-flops on a boulder and slipped on her fins. She was tempted to drop backward off the smooth round rocks into the water, but even if it wasn't a proper swan dive, it would still be head-first. In an archipelago, feet first was always wiser.

Just as she slid into the bay, the round dark head of a seal broke the surf near Hangman's Island, another remnant of England's bloody Civil War. In the Scillies, seals popped up everywhere; the fact that the seas stayed fairly cold suited them well. Jem estimated that the channel was no more than eighteen degrees Celsius, and that was being generous. But even fully immersed, she found the temperature refreshing rather than daunting.

To get to the middle of the channel, she did the front crawl, using long, powerful strokes to warm up. By the time she reached the general region of the shadow glimpsed from above, her heart rate was up and she felt fully invigorated. Soon it would be time to dive.

Hope I can see well enough down there without a torch, Jem thought.

As she treaded water, she took slow, deep breaths, saturating her bloodstream and large muscle groups with oxygen. According to divers and fishermen, the air in the average person's lungs was used up after only six seconds of holding your breath. After that, the body called on oxygen reserves, first from the bloodstream, then from those large muscle groups. The secret to diving wasn't lung capacity, it was cardiovascular efficiency—that, and the ability to keep a cool head as the weight of the water closed in.

Although Jem had a snorkel tube among her gear, it wasn't remotely suitable for what she had in mind. Snorkeling was limited to depths of about twelve inches. The face mask provided a wide, clear view, but even with the tube removed, once she descended to approximately two meters below the surface, the mask would begin to press too hard against her face. For successful duck diving, all she needed was swim goggles and fins.

Duck diving meant going under between ten and fifteen meters without SCUBA gear. Any sort of diving was safer with a partner, but Jem wasn't worried; she didn't intend to mess about or try to set a personal record underwater. She was fortunate that the storm had depressed boat traffic around the island. Had the channel between Tresco and Bryher been filled with pleasure craft, Jem would've needed a partner *and* a dive flag. Otherwise, surfacing might lead to getting run over by a powerboat or banging her head on the hull of a vessel as it passed overhead.

When she felt she'd practiced enough deep breathing, Jem dove under. The channel was still stirred up by the remnants of the storm, the sediment churned up from the seabed rendering the water murky and dark.

A thought occurred to her: Wasn't there a very old shipwreck somewhere near Tresco? The sort with its wooden ribs broken open and covered with pale barnacles? Jem suddenly realized such a wreck could very well be the dark shape she'd glimpsed underwater.

That would be disappointing, she thought. *Then again, as a girl I always begged Gran to let me dive for one of the famous wrecks. She said I was too young. Not to mention too impulsive and irresponsible. And she was right. Oh, well. If I jumped the gun and mistook an*

eighteenth-century wreck for a modern one, at least I'll finally get to touch
the hull of an ancient sailing ship, instead of only reading about them.

Descending with strong, practiced kicks, Jem squinted into the murk. Around three meters down, fins really started to come in handy, maximizing each leg movement and allowing her to travel further while using less effort. She could afford to spend about forty-five seconds searching for the wreck. After that, she'd have to swim for the surface. Assisted by fins, she was using less energy on the way down, and would therefore feel less oxygen-starved on the way up.

And a torch really would've come in handy, she thought, reaching the bottom sooner than expected. At this depth, the channel was a hazy green, the water dense with the microscopic life that drew local plankton-feeders, like basking sharks. Seaweed waved, rippling with the current, and rocks of every shape surrounded her. Most were covered with spongy invertebrates: cup corals, sea fans, and anemones. She brushed one such rock on her way toward a long, dark shadow, startling a fish with repeating stripes. He swam away with an undulating motion, supple as an eel.

That shadow ahead resolved into a recognizable shape just as Jem experienced her first strong physical urge to head for the surface. The sunken boat was a yacht, gray with white detailing and about twenty-five feet in length. Unlike *Bellatrix*, which unkind people called clunky, this was a sleek, aerodynamic vessel built for speed. Had Jem not been several meters underwater, she would've whistled at the aft section's power—five outboard engines that jutted out like a hot rod's exposed engine. With all five of those motors running, the yacht might have been capable of hitting sixty miles an hour.

A sport fisherman's boat. And probably the sort of vessel a man wearing a Yacht-Master Rolex would favor.

It was time to head for the surface. As Jem kicked her way up, she looked over her shoulder and glimpsed the boat's name, painted proudly on the stern. *Family Man*.

Some poor mum and her children are about to get the worst possible news, Jem thought, rising rapidly through clearer waters toward the surface. *Did he take someone out on his boat, only to have them turn murderous out at sea? Or did a stranger sneak aboard, hide below deck, jump out and cut his throat?*

Her head broke the surface. Gasping, Jem willed herself to take deep, controlled breaths rather than wild, shallow ones. As her muscles relaxed and the desperation for air faded, another question occurred to her.

Did the dead man fight for his life? Is that how the yacht sank? Or did the killer sink it himself, to try and conceal what he'd done?

Funny how she'd immediately assumed the killer was male. It was sexist, perhaps, but statistically accurate by a factor of more than ten to one. There were plenty of women in the world who were physically capable of tackling a man from behind and opening his throat right down to the bone. But how many females, even true clinical psychopaths, would choose to commit murder using such a risky approach? Once upon a time, pirates routinely cut throats as part of their vocation, along with yo-ho-hoing and drinking barrels of rum, but modern people tended to quail at gory methods.

Unless it was the act of someone early in their career, working up to the truly dark avenues of psychopathology. The way Jack the Ripper visited the worst atrocities on his final victim, Mary Jane Kelly, Jem thought. She'd seen the photos—what librarian hadn't? Letting her thoughts go down that road served no purpose right now.

I shouldn't jump to the conclusion this is the work of a serial killer. I don't even know for a fact that Mr. Family Man wasn't robbed. Maybe the killer was desperate for money or a fix and settled for what he could grab off the yacht. Maybe he just forgot to scoop up the wallet and watch.

That didn't feel very satisfactory, but with so little to go on, any guesses Jem made about the killer or his motive were only that—guesses.

The recovery rule for duck diving was simple: rest for twice as long as you were underwater. Jem figured she'd been down for about a minute and a half, so she decided to tread water while deep breathing for at least three minutes. Midway through this process, the seal's round head popped up again by Hangman's Island. When it knew it had Jem's attention, it began to showboat, diving low and making a splash. Pinnipeds were great ones for hamming it up when watched.

The second time Jem dove, it was with greater speed and confidence, since she knew where *Family Man* was and how long it would take her to reach it. The yacht was even more impressive on second glance.

Swimming close to the glassed-in helm, she put her goggles right up against a pane to peer into the central console. It was downright luxurious. With its inlaid blond wood, ultra-padded skipper's chair, and huge monitors, the vessel must've cost Mr. Family Man a pretty penny. Without a torch to beam into the nooks and crannies, Jem couldn't be sure, but she saw nothing ominous. Certainly no splashes of blood or a gore-streaked knife.

Before she knew it, her body once again demanded air. Her ears felt wonky, too. Kicking away from the sunken boat, Jem made for the surface. As she rose, a strange pair of seaweed plants caught her eye. They weren't sinuous and gray-green in the murky depths. Rather, they were red and white, the colors spiraled like a candy cane, terminating in odd black bulbs.

Once her head was above water, Jem began another round of deep breathing, pondering what she'd glimpsed. The sight was completely out of context in the seabed, and her brain had tried to interpret it as mutant seaweed. What she'd seen was surely human gear from off *Family Man*. The more she pondered it, the more she thought she knew what it was.

Once certain her oxygen reserves were replenished, Jem dove for the wreck a third time. The water at the bottom was cloudier than ever, thanks to her own movements, and she could only see a few inches in front of her face. Parting a clump of seaweed with her hands, Jem swept gracefully past them, thanks to her fins. A flash of red to her left caught her eye. Kicking around, she saw it: the killer's plan to keep his victim's corpse concealed, at least for a while.

On the seabed sat a large rectangular ice chest, no doubt loaded with ballast to keep it from rising. Red and white boat line had been wrapped around the chest's handles and knotted securely. The end of each line was tied around a pair of black wingtips. All that was missing was their previous occupant, Mr. Family Man. Clearly, he'd slipped the bonds of this makeshift anchor and been swept up near the castle with the tide.

Not really a surprise, given the power of the storm. I wonder if the poor bugger was dropped in the channel before the gale kicked up, or during?

The current shifted, rushing past Jem with the kind of unnatural force that signaled a powerboat was passing. It was probably the Isles of Scilly Police Department's recently acquired rigid inflatable boat, or RIB. Hack and his officers were inordinately proud of their new toy, and took it out at the drop of a hat. Whenever Jem saw them go rushing past, usually to investigate a complaint about drink driving, she heard the theme music from an old TV program her gran liked to watch, *Miami Vice*. All Hack, PC Newt, and PC Robbins needed was pastel jackets and shoulder pads.

As the current changed, the lid of the ice chest rose slowly, revealing its ballast: heaps of boating gear to keep it from sweeping off with the tide.

The killer did well in that respect, Jem thought. *But he should've secured the lid. It bangs against the wingtips as it rises.*

On a second glance at the cords holding the shoes, Jem saw that each terminated in another empty loop. No doubt those had once been around Mr. Family Man's ankles—until the ice chest lid's intermittent rising had knocked the dead man free.

Looks a bit like a fish tank under here, with a bubbling treasure chest, Jem mused, casting her eyes around in the gloom.

A roar signaled the RIB coming around again, faster this time. As the current shifted, a shoe slipped out of its mooring. The motor sound rose, the water whooshed past Jem, and before her horrified eyes, the weighted chest was swept away.

Jem intended to swim back toward the castle the moment she surfaced, but her ears weren't having it. They needed equalizing. Pressing her lips together and pinching her nostrils shut, Jem blew as hard as she could. One ear cleared, but the other remained stubbornly blocked. Two subsequent attempts, the second culminating in a very unladylike honk, were required to get both ears back to normal. As Jem prepared to kick off, she noticed the seal was bobbing near Hangman's Island again, staring at her as if it had never witnessed anything so uncouth.

Everyone's a critic, Jem thought, beginning her front crawl toward Tresco's stony northwest shore. Sergeant Hackman would probably have a few criticisms for her, too.

CHAPTER FIVE

Save a Dance

Jem's identification of the IoS PD's rigid inflatable boat proved prescient. It was beached near the foot of the castle, and three of the Scillies' finest had disembarked. Hack stood close to the dead body in conference with Pauley. PC Newt was jotting down notes as he stood with Micki several yards away, probably upwind from the stink. PC Robbins paced near a line of rubble, speaking to a dispatcher via the personal radio unit on her shoulder.

Jem was just out of the surf, goggles around her neck and fins dangling in one hand, when Hack glanced toward the water and saw her. A slow smile spread across his face. That was a good sign. He couldn't be all that irritated by her snooping, then, no matter how much he might pretend to be.

Excusing himself from Pauley, he started down the muddy shore toward her, black cowboy boots leaving a ragged trail in the wet sand. The boots were one of his many eccentricities. His specs, with their flashy earpieces—hot rod red—were another.

Since taking over command of Hugh Town Station, many islanders had expressed doubts over Hack's idiosyncrasies of dress, while others had chafed under his authoritative style. Leather boots weren't practical for sand and sea, much less slippery decks or stone quays. As for the specs, they had the sort of photochromic lenses that darken in bright sunlight and transition back to clear indoors. Given the islands' many vagaries of light and dark, the lenses were usually smoky, giving Hack a blank, unreadable look. The locals found it off-putting, and considered his refusal to adopt more appropriate footwear downright belligerent. His predecessor, the retired Chief Anderson, had frequently worn socks and sandals on the job.

The old chief's name had come up a lot in recent weeks. While he was on the job, Chief Michael Anderson, better known as "Randy Andy" because of his very public love affairs, hadn't been much admired. He'd avoided actual conflict—issues like permit enforcement, unauthorized dumping, flouting of safety ordinances by shops and roving vendors—while focusing on the low-hanging fruit: gobby kids, littering emmets, and the odd person who looked at him the wrong way.

During Randy Andy's tenure, the council had increasingly resented his lax enforcement of key ordinances, which harmed revenue collection for public works. Meanwhile, regular citizens had grown accustomed to workarounds, like applying directly to PC Newt or PC Robbins for help. Now that Hack had settled in, there was a steady hand on the tiller. He wasn't afraid to enforce the law or issue cautions about illegal disposal, unsafe workplace conditions, or lapsed permits. The council seemed overjoyed. The rest of the community was rather shell-shocked.

"There she is. Ursula Andress out of the sea," he called to Jem, referring to the Swedish bombshell who'd played Honey Ryder in the Bond film called *Dr. No.*

"Hiya, Hack."

It felt a little chilly out of the water, but otherwise Jem was comfortable in her swimsuit. Its modest cut provided plenty of coverage, and he'd seen her in it before, on the night they first met. Her long, tanned legs were arguably her best feature, despite the raised pink scar on her right ankle. It was an ugly mark, her lifelong reminder of a teenage misadventure, but she wasn't self-conscious about it. As for her brown hair, which was all one length and fell unbound to the middle of her back, it was still more or less in place, thanks to her double bun. Being a long-haired person meant finding new ways to keep it under control, and her favorite method, the double bun, had now withstood the rigors of duck diving in the Celtic Sea.

"Pauley filled me in on how you found the dead body. Another murder?"

"Seems so."

"People will talk."

"I'm no stranger to controversy."

That prompted another smile from Hack. Since his arrival, Jem had thrown off the shackles of bad memories and lingering regrets. She'd even managed to forgo much of the standoffishness she'd cultivated during her university and London days. St. Morwenna and the Scillies as a whole had welcomed her back, something she'd once believed impossible. She wouldn't knowingly toss away that rekindled sense of community, not for the world. But she couldn't suppress her curious nature. Besides, mysterious things had a way of happening in her presence. She hadn't gone looking for another dead body, but once she'd found it she couldn't switch her brain back to festival mode, secure in the knowledge it was the law's problem. There was such a thing as being a helpful, concerned citizen, wasn't there?

"Anyway, he's in pretty bad shape," Hack said. "Damn near decapitated. Then came the birds. Must've been brutal. Did you see them take his ring finger?"

"No, but they were playing tug-of-war with the man's hand and arm, so it's a sure bet one of them nabbed it."

"Pauley says she's heard of birds swallowing objects and then regurgitating them. A bony finger, with or without a wedding band, seems like it might come back up. I wonder if it might be lying around here somewhere."

"You could start over by Mr. Family Man and walk an expanding spiral," Jem said. She'd been looking forward to the opportunity to casually make such a suggestion.

"Someone's read up on police search procedures. I'd prefer a grid, if enough people turn up to do it properly." Hack sounded amused. "Why did you call the victim Mr. Family Man?"

"Sorry. It's only because I, erm, happened to dive in the vicinity of the wreck he must've come from." Jem smiled in what she hoped was a casual manner. "It's a twenty-five foot sport fishing yacht. In great shape, apart from being at the bottom of the channel. The name *Family Man* is painted on the side. But I'm afraid your arrival in the RIB messed up the scene." She filled him in on the weighted ice chest and the tethered wingtips, washed away in the powerboat's wake.

Hack appeared slightly dubious, as if the scene she described was too ridiculous to be true, but all he said was, "I'll alert the dive team when they get here. In the meantime, I've had a look at his wallet."

With a blue-gloved hand, Hack removed a clear plastic evidence bag from a pouch on his stab vest. Being fully kitted out under the August sun seemed to be taking its toll; his neck was flushed and a bead of sweat dripped off one of his razor-edged sideburns. The care he took to sculpt those sideburns, as well as his small, neat beard and mustache, was another point of controversy with the locals. Randy Andy was just another average-looking, pot-bellied islander with a penchant for the ladies. Hack was mainland-attractive. He was *groomed*, in the modern parlance, and some people disapproved of it.

Consulting what looked to be one of the man's many bank and credit cards, Hack read, "Herman Thomas Castleberry."

"Is there cash in that wallet?"

Hack raised his eyebrows. Because of his sun-darkened lenses, it was hard to be sure, but he seemed to be going for a stern expression.

"I can't divulge that."

"You just told me his name."

"I was giving you the opportunity to recognize him."

"I saw his face when I rolled him over."

"About that." Hack segued smoothly into what Jem realized was likely to be a more in-depth scolding. "In future, please don't touch or move crime victims unless a police dispatcher or some other relevant authority authorizes you to do so."

"I had to turn him over to check if he was still alive."

He made a scornful noise.

"What's the harm? It's not as if you could dust the area for fingerprints. Besides, you're the one who nicked the wallet off the deceased. Aren't you supposed to wait for a supervisor from Devon & Cornwall to take command of the scene?"

He returned the evidence bag to its pouch. "You've been studying up a *lot*, haven't you?"

"No, but I've been reading procedural mysteries my entire life. You should swear me in as a deputy. *Posse comitatus* and all that."

"That law was repealed in England before you were born, thank God. Maybe it's still in effect in America, but that's their problem. At any rate, all I need from you is to accompany Micki and Pauley to the festival, have a lovely time, and… I don't know. Save me a dance? In the unlikely event I'm able to put in an appearance?"

Pleasure surged through Jem at the suggestion, coupled with apprehension. It was the first time Hack had made any overture beyond friendship to her since he'd settled into his role at Hugh Town Station. This was surely because he was so busy correcting those long-deferred problems Randy Andy had papered over. Not to mention convincing the rest of the locals that he only wanted to reassert good order, not establish a police state. St. Morwennians particularly resented being told what to do.

Of course, if there was another reason it had taken Hack six weeks to get around to asking her out, it was probably because Jem had been hiding out in Lyonesse House's library and slobbering over the old books and papers, as Micki put it. Jem loved getting stuck into that sort of work, and she found it easy to let her fascination with historical ephemera become a stand-in for passion and romance. Heaven knew she'd romanced the library throughout her sweet but sexless marriage to Dean; there was a reason why *Jonathan Strange & Mr. Norrell*, a book featuring a magician's quest to free the lovely Arabella from the land of Faerie, had such a special place in her heart.

Since their divorce, Dean had found himself a new life and a charming boyfriend, as he should have done ages ago. Maybe it was time for Jem to wean herself off the literary laudanum? To spend more time with the handsome policeman standing right in front of her?

But what about my summer of self-discovery? Avoidance of the XY set?

Suddenly that all seemed ridiculous. Some long-dormant desire had flared to life at his suggestion, and Jem suspected it wasn't going back into mothballs without a fight. Hack was fit, nice to look at, and good company. He was only a bit older than her, in his early forties. They were both divorced without kids and without bitterness. In an archipelago where the pallid bulk of Randy Andy could play Romeo, discovering a man like Hack was the equivalent of spying a Spanish doubloon glinting in the surf.

"You manage to show up and we'll dance," she said, smiling. "But do you really think you're likely to get away tonight, with a dead body here and a sunken yacht in the channel?"

Hack shrugged. "You weren't wrong about Devon & Cornwall. They're sending two teams—a murder unit and a special marine diving unit. I'll be lucky if I'm permitted to do more than beg their forgiveness for checking the deceased's ID."

He seemed about to say more, but the mobile clipped to his duty belt chimed.

"Hackman," he replied. "Yes, that's right. Sergeant I. Hackman. Call me Hack if you—oh. Of course. Formal suits me as well." He rolled his eyes at Jem. "I said I. Capital letter I and a full stop. That's my name. Says so on my ID badge and everything."

Micki, strolling to their section of the beach after completing her interview with PC Newt, overheard the latter part of Hack's mobile conversation and whispered to Jem, "If I were him, I'd just make something up. Call myself Isaac or Ian and put a stop to all the ruddy questions."

"He's got a contrarian streak," Jem suggested. The hypothesis had been growing on her for a while, based partly on Hack's refusal to part with his cowboy boots or his transitional specs. It was unreasonable, perhaps, to expect a man to shave off his goatee and pointed sideburns, but the hot rod red frames and tooled leather boots were distracting. Either Hack genuinely loved them and didn't care what anyone else thought, or there was a part of him that enjoyed subverting expectations—which might be a clue as to what got him bounced from metropolitan Exeter to the secluded Scillies.

"I hope we're free to go soon," Pauley said, approaching them with all three dry bags in hand. "I need another application of sun cream. And, if I'm being honest, something cold. Is it too early for a G&T?"

"Are you kidding? Pubs ought to be required to hand them out to anyone who stumbles across a dead body," Micki said.

"But you were just sick."

"Exactly. I need a drink to steady my nerves. It's medicinal. Look it up."

"Could you pass me my bag? I want my cover-up," Jem said.

First, she returned her swim goggles and fins to the bag's bottom compartment. Then she dug into the main compartment, feeling around for the blue cotton sundress that would serve as her cover-up. Her fingers touched her sunglasses case, and suddenly she remembered the wire-framed specs found among the rubble.

"Oh, Hack! I almost forgot!"

He was still on his call, and didn't seem to be enjoying it. Jem pulled her sundress, which was loose and sleeveless, over her head and on top of her damp swimsuit. In half an hour she'd be dry, or dry enough. But two quick searches through the bag didn't reveal her flip-flops. She turned to Pauley and Micki.

"Do either of you have my flops?"

"Did you leave them near the castle? On top of the boulders where you jumped in?" Micki asked.

Pauley groaned. "Why did you tell her? I wanted to watch the great detective tear through all the bags looking for them."

"I think you're perking up, missy."

"Maybe." Following Jem's example, Pauley slipped on her cover-up, a knee-length black dress with ruffles all over, and Micki put on hers, a red sundress that matched her suit exactly.

"Good. Then I reckon today's already been a success, even with a dead body," Jem said. "If Hack ever gets off the phone, tell him the specs we found are in that case. He might want to claim them as evidence. I'll be right back."

Jem wasn't surprised she'd forgotten the location of her flip-flops. Diving down to find *Family Man* had co-opted most of her brainpower. Hack's surprise request for her to save him a dance had hijacked the rest.

The flip-flops were indeed sitting on the escarpment, right where she'd left them. As Jem climbed onto the smooth, blast-scored granite, she was startled by a familiar knocking sound.

The orange bucket!

Going back in the water was a nonstarter; the dive team would arrive soon, and besides, she was already half dry. But if she could snag a bit of *Family Man's* flotsam out of the channel while remaining on the shore, why not?

In this case, the RIB's powerful wake had worked to her advantage. The orange bucket had been washed into a space between two outcroppings of granite. Now it was caught there, ping-ponging off each rock with an audible *ump*. High tide would probably free it, but until then, it could only travel back and forth. Jem knelt down, leaned out until she felt like her shoulder might pop, and plucked it from the sea.

It's a dry canister, she thought, seeing the little bucket's tightly fitting plastic cap. When she shook it, she heard something soft moving inside.

She knew she should march the sealed canister straight to Hack. She'd already moved the dead man's body and performed an impromptu recovery dive, both to satisfy her own curiosity. It would be irresponsible, perhaps even actionable, to keep messing with elements of the crime scene. In mystery novels, it was cute when amateur sleuths like Miss Marple eavesdropped, arranged sting operations, or withheld crucial evidence until they were ready to thrill the reader *and* the proper authorities with their conclusions. Here in the real world, if Jem kept mucking about, she might find herself charged with obstruction.

My fingerprints are already on it. One quick peek won't hurt a soul. I'll look, and then I'll reseal it.

Turning her back to shield her actions from anyone who might be watching, Jem unscrewed the top of the dry capsule and gently tipped out its soft contents. Into her open palm came a clear plastic quart bag full of white powder and three loose hundred-euro notes.

CHAPTER SIX

A Telling-Off

As Jem hurried back up the muddy shore with the resealed canister in her hands, she saw Hack slipping the wire-framed specs into a clear plastic evidence bag. Catching sight of her as he sealed the bag, he smiled, just as he had when she emerged from the channel. But then he spied the orange object she was carrying, and the smile melted away.

"What's that you've got?"

"A dry canister. From *Family Man*, no doubt." Jem held it out to him, but he didn't take it. The expressionless way he regarded her was slightly unsettling, so she added, "It's like our dry packs, only a bit tougher and made to float. Most yachts come with one. People stash valuables in them."

Hack didn't answer. He still didn't reach out to take it. From a few yards behind him, Micki and Pauley watched with interest. Over near Herman Castleberry's corpse, PC Newt and PC Robbins were marking off the scene's inner perimeter with blue and white crime tape. PC Robbins, a petite woman who'd been born in London, was sinking the wooden stakes. PC Newt, whose surname was McDowell but who preferred to go by his first name because he thought it sounded friendlier, was unspooling the tape, wrapping it around each stake. Both paused in their work to observe Jem and Hack, as if scenting a telling-off in the wind.

"Where did you find it?" Hack asked.

"In the sea. Just over there, near the rock where I left my flip-flops."

"Why didn't you call for one of us to come fetch it?"

"I wasn't surprised to see it. It's been there all along," Jem said, making this announcement before pausing to consider how it sounded.

"I see. Why didn't you say?"

"I forgot. I was too busy telling you about the boat."

"Which you took it upon yourself to search for. And examine."

"Yes! Which is excellent, really, because I saw the wingtips tied to the ice chest before *your* current swept them away. Well done, Jem. No need to thank me," she plowed on, thrusting the orange canister at him for a third time. "Just take this. And, you know, maybe have a look inside?"

That suggestion landed like a lead balloon. Hack accepted the canister, but when he spoke, he no longer sounded carefully inflectionless. The telling-off had begun.

"Jem, the IoS Police, as well as the jurisdiction of Devon & Cornwall, are very grateful for the assistance you rendered us back in June. However, when it comes to serious crimes, the most helpful thing any member of the community can do is make a report. Once they've made that report, they should do nothing more—absolutely nothing more—unless specifically instructed to do so by the proper authorities."

"I understand all—"

"Please let me finish," he cut across her, still in that lecturing tone that made her want to kick him in the shins. "In light of your previous service, when I arrived and noted damage to the crime scene, I chose not to remark upon it. Turning over the body was unnecessary, in light of its obvious state. Walking around the nearby area and picking up those spectacles was also potentially detrimental. At most, you should have noted their position and informed us upon arrival."

These statements were absolutely correct, so Jem could only fold her arms across her chest and scowl. "Sorry I walked on your rocks. I'm sure the forensics guys could've scraped loads of clues off all that wet rubble. After the rain and the tide and all that. How awful of me."

"Pauley tells me you put the object in your sunglasses case, and then put the case in your bag," Hack continued, with the air of a barrister winning over the jury. "Please promise me you'll never handle potential evidence that way again."

"Again? Are you expecting more murders in the Scillies?"

"If not murders, crimes. Lawlessness happens everywhere. And if you stay true to form, you'll trip and fall into a crime scene or end up tackling the crook. Promise me, Jem—no more mishandling of evidence."

"I promise," she said, looking at her toes instead of his face. No wonder the locals hated those sunglasses. They capped off his blank copper's look, turning it impenetrable.

"Good. Now. When I take the lid off this canister, what will I find?"

Deciding that keeping her eyes on her toes would seem shady, Jem chose to look Hack full in the face. "I don't know what's in it," she said, throwing in a smile for good measure.

He sighed. Removing his specs, he held them by one sizzling red earpiece. "Say again?"

Jem boldly returned his gaze. "I don't know what's in it."

After what felt like a brief but intense staring contest, Hack put his specs on his head and looked over his shoulder. Immediately, Pauley and Micki became interested in Micki's billowing curls, which Pauley started to braid. PC Robbins redirected her gaze to the dead man, as if he'd suddenly whispered a hint about the case. Only PC Newt kept right on watching, transparently eager to see what happened next, until PC Robbins hissed at him. Then he, too, awkwardly refocused his attention on the corpse, frowning in a way that suggested intense cogitation.

Hack moved closer to Jem and murmured, "Word to the wise. Excessive, sustained eye contact is a classic tip-off that the subject is lying."

"Fine." She sighed, feeling like the wayward child she'd once been. "But after that speech about evidence, and you making me promise and all, how could I tell you I'd opened it?"

"You already told me, by the way you presented the canister. Not to mention how you literally told me to look inside. I've been a policeman for almost twenty years. Your demeanor was wildly suspicious."

"Twenty years, eh? How can that be? You're so young," Jem said, widening her eyes and maintaining contact until he laughed.

"Should've known the first thing you'd do with that piece of information is use it against me. Now. Seriously. What's in the canister?"

"Drugs and money."

"No doubt. Fine. I'll just remove the lid, thus, and see what…" Hack tailed off, staring at the plastic bag full of white powder as the three loose hundred euro notes fluttered to the ground.

"Mr. Family Man, indeed," he muttered, bending to snatch them up before the wind carried them away.

"Think he was doing a deal on the water?" Jem asked.

"'Doing a deal?' Don't you sound like a copper from the telly." Hack chuckled. "Yes, I suppose the victim might have been killed whilst conducting an illegal transaction." Removing more clear plastic evidence bags from his kit, he slipped the items inside and sealed them up. "But it was sloppy work. Unprofessional. Your average killer picks up the valuables and flees the scene. They aren't worried about how things look to the law or when and where we find the body. This is routine for them. A professional perp just goes to ground until the ruckus dies down."

"Whereas this killer left behind his victim's Rolex, wallet, and a canister full of goodies," Jem agreed.

"Not quite full. There's only three hundred in euros."

Jem chuckled. "That's still a tidy sum in the Scillies."

"Not saying it isn't. Only, I'd expect the cash in a roll. Three notes next to what might be twenty thousand pounds worth of blow is a bit odd. Not impossible," Hack said. "But odd. And don't forget the boat. No professional would sink a perfectly good sport fishing yacht."

"I don't know," Jem said. "It's pretty flash. And once the police bulletin went out to all the harbormasters, the skipper wouldn't be able to travel near the coast or put into port without being identified."

Hack looked amused. "Well-reasoned *if* you're a law-abiding citizen. But consider this. The pros have a network of safe harbors. They know where they can take a stolen vessel for depersonalization. A day in dry dock can give a yacht a new lease of life. Or it can be chopped up and resold in anonymous parts."

"Oh. All right. Then I suppose we'll have to wait and see if the boat sank because it was sabotaged, or if there was structural failure."

"We?" Hack still looked amused. Damn the man.

"Fine. You'll have to wait and see. Unless Devon & Cornwall are still treating you like Johnny No Mates."

"They are." Hack sighed. "I used to be a detective. Now I'm a local yokel."

"Then maybe I'll see you on the dance floor tonight. Micki! Where'd you say the pirate ship's due to drop anchor?"

"Near the Old Blockhouse," Micki called.

"Meet me near the Old Blockhouse," Jem said. "Now us civilians will get out of your hair and let the proper authorities take over." Giving him a cheeky wave, she trooped off toward Pauley and the newly styled Micki. Pauley looked quite pleased with her handiwork, and Micki, who had the trick of adopting any hairdo and making it seem made for her, turned her head to show off a neat French braid.

"Pub, ladies?"

"Yes, please."

Linking arms, the three of them set off. As they entered the heather moors that lead to the ruins of King Charles's Castle, Jem threw a final glance over her shoulder.

PC Newt, who still apparently nurtured an unrequited passion for Pauley, seemed downcast. Since her bereavement, he'd respectfully kept his distance, a choice that clearly made him miserable, though Pauley hadn't seemed to notice. His colleague, PC Robbins, was talking to someone via her personal radio. As for Hack, he'd joined his fellow officers inside the crime scene's taped off inner perimeter. Squatting beside the bloodless corpse of Herman Castleberry, he regarded it silently, a blank-faced police officer once again.

*

"Remember, I want a peek at the famous abbey before the festival starts," Micki said as they walked along a two-lane dirt track studded with bits of rubble.

She was walking in the middle of the trio, with Pauley on her left and Jem on her right. Pauley passed along an old stone hedgerow crowned with leafy vines, while Jem walked beside a meadow enclosed by trees and a weathered wooden fence. The meadow's deep green grass, and the leafy crowns of the trees that ringed it, reminded her of the fields of Devon. For such a small island chain, the Scillies offered a variety of landscapes that occasionally surprised even the residents.

A recent transplant to the Scillies, Micki was mostly familiar with St. Mary's, where she worked as a bartender at the Kernow Arms. During her free time, however, she was frequently on St.

Morwenna, where her cousin Clarence ran a B&B. This was her first time on Tresco, the island most associated with upscale holidays, and Jem knew she was keen to explore. Now that she had *Bellatrix* and could run herself and her friends anywhere in the region, water taxi fees and schedules no longer constrained them. She hoped they could soon have an outing to St. Martin. A weekend trip to its vineyard sounded lovely.

"Seriously, how far are the Abbey Gardens?" Micki persisted.

"Remember when we arrived at Tresco? When I said there were no slips available? Remember that pretty stretch of beach we saw, before you insisted I find you somewhere to wee?"

Micki made a suspicious sound.

"Well, the Abbey Gardens are close to that beach. To get there, we should've walked south from the castle. We're heading east, toward Old Grimsby."

"But we just came from Old Grimsby."

"Sorry. That was New Grimsby," Pauley said. "We Scillonians like to keep names as similar as possible. That way if some lost lamb like you ends up in the wrong spot, you'll never know it." She laughed, and Jem joined in.

"You two are mean. It's not my fault I was born with no sense of direction."

"Everyone has at least a little sense of direction," Pauley said.

"Especially in the islands. You always know where the sun is. And at night you can go by the stars," Jem said.

"Maybe you can, Stargazer." Micki seemed to like Jem's childhood nickname, and often used it in company, as if intent on reviving its use. "I'm not kidding when I say I have no sense of direction. Once I dated a fellow who was mad for computer games, so I played them, too. In his favorite, you were supposed to maneuver your little man through medieval villages, collecting quest items and whatnot. I always got turned around in the streets.

I'd forget which shop was which and keep pushing the joystick, sending my little man straight ahead until he plowed off a cliff."

"That, like you competing in an International Roller Derby, is another story I choose not to believe," Pauley said. "Jem, are you trying to lead us to the Island Hotel?"

Jem glanced at her.

"Sorry to break it to you, but it was demolished," Pauley said. "Now there's The Ruin, a beachside café. It's nice, but it tends to fill up on weekends. Let me ring them and see if we can get a table."

The first person who answered at the restaurant informed Pauley she could only make a reservation for dinner, which was still hours away. Being a local had its privileges; when she asked for the manager on duty, she was put through to an old chum from St. Mary's School.

"Hiya, Stuart. Me and two of my mates are hoofing it in from the castle. We're famished and gagging for a drink. If you can find a place for us, I promise we'll sit anywhere. Inside a broom closet, if that's all you've got."

Stuart put her on hold, took himself off to work some hospitality magic, and returned with the happy announcement that there'd been a cancellation. Jem had no idea if this was true, or if Stuart had simply been moved by Pauley's plea to release a table held in reserve for last minute VIPs. Either way, she felt silly for assuming Tresco hadn't changed since her teens, and grateful to Pauley for taking charge.

With a firm destination in mind, they picked up the pace, practically tasting those G&Ts. As they made their way east, the landscape grew more manicured, and posted notices said they were skirting the grounds of Sea Garden Cottages. It was a sweet, unassuming name, but the resort actually turned out to be a sprawling complex with palm trees, a swimming pool, tennis courts, and a flagged path looping around the buildings.

"I hear the sea," Micki said happily.

"Yes. Maybe we'll be sat within sight of a window," Pauley said. "By the way, The Ruin has a good menu, but I say don't bother agonizing over all the possibilities. Go straight for the woodfired pizza." She rubbed her hands together in anticipation.

"I don't know how you can eat after giving PC Newt the cold shoulder," Micki said, apparently ready to retaliate after being teased over her inadequate sense of direction. "Poor little bunny. He kept hopping around, casting sad looks in your direction, but you never even glanced his way."

They'd fallen into the habit of calling PC Newt a bunny rabbit because of his wide-eyed, big-eared, utterly earnest face. He wasn't bad to look at—in his early thirties, he was fit and clean-cut, with a firm chin and a nice smile. But his trusting, one-step-behind manner drove Pauley nuts. Besides, she wasn't keen on men who came on too strong, and ever since she'd arguably saved his life, PC Newt had pursued her like a lop-ear on the scent of carrots. To Jem and Micki, it was amusing and slightly endearing. To Pauley, it was an embarrassment.

"I look forward to the day you stop telling us about men you dated back in the mists of time and bring round your current bloke," Pauley told Micki as they approached The Ruin's triple wooden peaks. "After you break up, I'll bring him up as a topic whenever the conversation lulls. I do hope he's a local. Imagine heading into a place like this, primed for drinkies and a slice, only to look on the porch and see your…" Pauley tailed off, as if abruptly out of petrol.

Jem followed Pauley's gaze to the man who stood on The Ruin's porch. Although his back was turned and he was uncharacteristically dressed in the antithesis of island wear—a suit—he was six foot four with broad shoulders, a tapered waist, and sun-streaked blond hair. She knew him instantly.

"Keep dreaming. I'm a Latham. I don't kiss and tell," Micki was saying. "When you grow up in a big family with everyone's nose in your business, you learn to keep secrets. See that big blond hunk up there? He could be my ex, and you'd never know it from how I… oh. Whoops! Jem, that's *your* ex, isn't it? And doesn't he clean up nice."

Rhys Tremayne gave Jem, Micki, and Pauley what looked like a very forced smile, his gaze ranging over them as he took in their swimsuits, flowing sundresses, and flip-flops. "You three look like fun in the sun. Let me guess—the pirate thingy? Isn't that happening by the Old Blockhouse?"

"We dropped anchor near Candlewick Castle because this one," Micki said, pointing at Jem, "gave up on finding a boat slip."

"Because this one," Jem retorted, "is too precious to swim out for a wee."

"We were assured *Bellatrix* had a proper toilet," Micki said.

"We were sold a bill of goods," Pauley agreed.

"A proper bog on *Bellatrix*? That old clinker?" Rhys laughed. "You're lucky if it's got a fish finder manufactured after 1990."

"I assure you, my fish finder is young and vigorous," Jem said haughtily. "What are you doing on Tresco?"

"Getting married, by the looks of that suit," Micki said.

"Appearing before a magistrate, more like," Pauley said. "But that would happen on St. Mary's."

"I came here to talk to my agent. The one representing me for the gallery showing that's supposed to be next month," Rhys said. "But either Hermie's dodging me again, or he's running obscenely late."

"Hermie? As in, Herman Castleberry?" Jem asked.

Rhys raised his eyebrows. "Yeah. How'd you know?"

"Not coming," Micki muttered.

"We met him on the beach," Jem began.

"Rhys, you've hardly talked about your agent, and never by name," Pauley said. "Were you guys close?"

"Not by a long shot. Why?"

"When I say we met him, I mean we found his body. He's dead."

CHAPTER SEVEN

Old Artists Never Die, They Just Get the Brush-Off

Inside the restaurant, Jem felt a bit underdressed. The Ruin wasn't formal by any stretch, but the staff had a highly professional air and the menu, particularly the wine list, was a cut above. Moreover, many of The Ruin's lunch patrons looked as if they'd turned up to mix business with pleasure. Rhys's choice of a suit and tie made sense in this context. And heaven knew he carried it off like he'd been born in it.

They'd met when Jem was eight and Rhys was ten. Her first impression of Rhys was that he was the most hyperactive, idiotic, mindlessly competitive boy in the world. Every time they were thrown together, he tried to outdo her. If she climbed halfway up a tree to swing from a limb, he had to climb higher and dangle from the topmost branch. If she ran top-speed from one side of the schoolyard to the other, Rhys bellowed, "Time me!" to his little brother, Cam, and ran the same route two seconds quicker. When she got in trouble for nicking a bicycle for an hour-long joyride, he committed a similar crime the very next weekend. Except in his case, the joyride lasted all day, and he capped it off by finding Jem and riding around her in circles to reveal what he'd done—taken the best bike on St. Morwenna, a ten-speed belonging to Hobson's Farm, a flower farm and commune.

Rhys's parents had come down hard on him for that offense, even though the commune members were sanguine about their possessions and shrugged the whole thing off. Something about Rhys's gleeful theft must have impressed Jem at long last. When Rhys's punishment was over, Jem invited him and his little brother Cam to play with her and Pauley at St. Morwenna's biggest freestanding rock formation, Sir Tristan. Rhys and Cam immediately renamed the oddly shaped rock Sir Knob—they *were* boys, after all—but by the end of that day, the four of them had been inseparable.

Have I ever seen Rhys in a suit and tie? Jem wondered, trying not to stare. He'd been a cute boy and a pretty teen—the sort of red-cheeked, long-eyelashed youth that made girls swoon and old ladies dote. But he'd grown into a startlingly handsome man, his light brown hair turning blond in the summer, his eyes a deep, dark blue. As Jem's teen boyfriend, he'd been long and lithe, much like the Fistral Beach surfers he idolized. But adulthood had brought him a rash of personal problems, and recently he'd started lifting weights and soft-sand running as a way to work out his frustrations. The result was a beefed-up physique that filled out his light gray suit, and then some.

I have seen him in a suit and tie. At Cam's funeral, Jem realized.

Once, she'd believed nothing could bridge the gap of sadness and self-recrimination between her and St. Morwenna, much less her and her first love, Rhys. But over the past six weeks, much of that tension had fallen away. For all Jem knew, Rhys might have considered asking her out to have a pint and catch up. But when Pauley's mum died his attention had, of necessity, been concentrated on his longtime friend. And Jem herself had, of course, been spending an inordinate amount of time in Lyonesse House's library, hard at work on the Gwyn Family Collection, even after hours. Her summer of self-discovery, etc. etc.

My summer of dodging Hack, Rhys, and to some extent, myself, Jem thought wryly. Deep down, she'd known that was what she was doing all along. Was it as obvious to Micki and Pauley? Probably. She hoped they'd have the decency not to mention it, though.

After a brief wait in the foyer, The Ruin's manager on duty, Stuart, emerged from the kitchen to seat them. A freckled man with a gap-toothed smile, he greeted each of them in turn, lingering on Pauley the longest. But the presence of Rhys in their midst seemed to surprise him. "I thought you packed it in and went home."

"I was just on my way when I ran into these ladies. They need a chaperone, so it's down to me."

"Well, I'm glad you didn't let Castleberry ruin your entire afternoon," Stuart said, mentioning the dead man's name with a flicker of distaste. "And it's only fitting that you join this party, since it was your table I gave them. Follow me, please."

The Ruin's interior was bright and pleasant, with rough oak paneling and copper pendant lights. To Jem's delight, however, Stuart led them straight through the busy dining room and onto the rustic patio overlooking the beach. The seating was simplicity itself—wooden tables and benches under broad umbrellas—and several patrons had brought along their canine companions. The dogs lolled here and there, soaking up the sun as their humans chatted and ate. The breeze smelled of salt, gulls wheeled across the cloudless sky, and it was all very pleasant, but nothing could compete with the view: white sands leading to shimmering blue waters, with a sailboat in the bay like a cherry on top.

"The Abbey Gardens can wait," Micki told Jem, sliding down the bench to make room for her. Pauley scooted along the opposite bench, settling in the place across from Micki and leaving Rhys in the spot facing Jem. Their eyes met for an instant, and then she reflexively looked away.

When Stuart handed out menus, she pretended to study hers minutely. Under the table, Rhys's long legs brushed against hers. That slight touch sent her heartbeat into overdrive and she turned her body to give herself space. This was ridiculous. She'd been calmer at Candlewick Castle, snooping around Herman Castleberry's corpse.

"May I start you off with drinks?"

Rhys ordered a soda. Jem, who wasn't meant to know he was a recovering alcoholic, was suddenly uncertain. He'd been sober less than a year. Was it insensitive, or even an act of sabotage, to order booze in front of him? Fortunately Pauley, who'd been taken into his confidence, spoke up, ordering G&Ts for herself, Micki, and Jem. She'd been friends with Rhys throughout the twenty years Jem had lived on the mainland. Jem's understanding of him relied heavily on memories of their teen years; Pauley knew Rhys as an adult. If she was willing to drink in front of him, it meant he wouldn't find it an unbearable temptation.

"Abbey Gardens Gin?" Stuart asked, meaning a brand bottled in the Scillies.

"Of course. What do you think, guys? A couple of pizzas to share?" Pauley asked.

There were nods all around. After Stuart picked up the menus and headed to the bar to submit their drinks order, Rhys asked in a low voice, "So you did it again? Found another dead body?"

Something in his tone made Jem roll her eyes. "I didn't go looking for it, it just happened." Speaking quietly so as not to shock and entrance their fellow patio diners, Jem told the story of how they'd discovered the dead man, rescuing his corpse from the post-mortem ravages of buzzards. With frequent addendums and the occasional contradiction from Micki or Pauley, she covered nearly everything: the cut throat, untouched Rolex and wallet, wire-framed spectacles, sunken yacht, submerged shoes, and the dry canister's sinister payload.

Throughout most of Jem's story, Rhys sat stone-faced. Perhaps he'd disliked Herman Castleberry so much, the details of the man's awful end stirred no sympathy, or even prompted any questions. Only when Jem mentioned the dry canister and its contents did he seem interested.

"Here we are. Drinks all around," Stuart sang out, appearing at the table bearing a loaded tray. After depositing Rhys's soda, the G&Ts, and four glasses of iced water, he promised the pizzas would arrive soon, and took himself off again.

"It's not every day the manager miraculously finds you a table with a great view, then serves you himself," Micki said. "Pauley, am I imagining it, or is Stuart rolling out the red carpet for you?"

"He might be. We dated a little, before my dad got sick." Before Pauley had nursed her mum through stage four cancer, she'd helped her father during his own terminal illness. Altogether, she'd attended to her parents for almost thirteen years.

"He clearly hasn't forgotten you," Jem said.

"Maybe not, but he got married a few years back. No one waits around forever," Pauley said, looking downcast again for the first time since chasing away the scavenging buzzards.

"Perhaps it didn't work out," Micki suggested.

"If he still has a wife, that's a nonstarter," Pauley said. "Besides, it's no big deal. Sometimes the planets line up, the moment comes, and you're off doing something else. When that happens, you've missed your shot, and that's that." She picked up her drink and sipped.

Alarmed by her bleak tone, Jem and Micki swapped glances. Rhys, who'd just opened his straw's wrapper, blew through the open end, shooting a slender missile at Pauley's face. He laughed when the paper bounced off her cheek.

"Hey!"

"You should go into motivational speaking," Rhys told her. "Or address an A.A. group. I finally picked up a sobriety token, if I never mentioned it. They're used to tales of lives completely messed up and people bravely carrying on through the wreckage."

Jem tried to look surprised and interested by Rhys's casual revelation; a quick look at Micki revealed that she was trying to do the same. Rhys, clearly not buying it, laughed again. "Come on, you knew. The entire Isles of Scilly and half of Penzance knows."

"We might have heard something…" Jem and Micki muttered.

"I imagine you did. It's fine. What have we got to talk about in the islands except our neighbors?" Rhys poked the straw into his soda and had a sip. "Besides, even if it was a deep, dark secret, I would've known by the way you two watched me order this. People sort of hold their breath until I ask for something non-alcoholic, then mentally award me a gold star. Anyway," Rhys said, turning back to Pauley, "I'm glad you've come round to the fact your life's over. Do they still have nunneries? Not necessarily for religious women. Just shattered old husks that have been sucked dry."

Pauley narrowed her eyes at him, as if stuck without a withering comeback and forced to bombard him with bad vibes.

"Now, as for *me*, when I was at my lowest," Rhys continued in a light, charming voice, "Pauley told me I was only thirty-five and still had my whole life in front of me. We're actually kind of in the same boat. She inherited a property that requires constant maintenance and infusions of cash; me, too. She spent too much time mopping up after her family; me, too. She has yet to take a walk down the aisle; me, too. But for some reason, she expects me to hold my head up and work for something better, while she locks herself in Lyonesse House and watches *Buffy the Vampire Slayer* all day long."

Pauley seemed about to interrupt, but Rhys continued, "The only difference between us that could possibly affect her reckoning is that she's a woman and I'm a man."

"Barely," Pauley said.

"All right, I'm a dude. Point being, you're acting like a product that's past its sell-by date. Stop it."

Silently, Pauley sipped her G&T. Then she put down her glass, pulled Rhys's ear hard enough to make him yelp, and said, "You're not wrong, damn it."

"Everything all right?" Stuart approached their table carrying one pizza; behind him, an assistant in chef's whites carried the other. He seemed hopeful that Pauley was in actual distress so he could solve the problem for her, even if it meant giving Rhys the keys to the street.

Jem and her friends assured him everything was fine. Looking as if he had something more to say, Stuart hovered over the pizzas, making awkward conversation about the view. When Jem and the others gave him no real encouragement, he left them to it.

"So about that canister," Rhys said, directing the conversation back to Herman Castleberry and the *Family Man*. "What did Hack make of it? Does he think Hermie brought a drug dealer aboard and got himself killed?"

"He shut me down pretty definitively when I asked about that," Jem said. Micki and Pauley, who'd already dug into their food, nodded along. "To him it looked like an amateur job. He didn't comment on the brick of cocaine one way or the other. The loose bills struck him as odd, though. Said he would've expected a bankroll rather than a few loose notes."

Rhys seemed to take that in. Tearing off two huge slices of pizza, he demolished them with the unselfconscious speed of a man who never, ever thinks about fat grams. As he chewed, he seemed to come to some decision.

"Ever heard that saying: 'Old artists never die, they just get the brush-off'? Hermie told me my art was a bust. My serious art, obviously. He said I should stick to sunsets and count my blessings."

"You didn't tell me that. When did this happen?" Pauley asked.

"Yesterday. He's been dodging me, but yesterday I ran into him in Hugh Town and made him tell me why the gallery showing still wasn't scheduled." Rhys paused to wash down his pizza with some soda. "I had him cornered, so he told me the truth: I wasn't good enough. I didn't take it very well, if I'm being honest."

"Is that why you scheduled a meeting with him here today?" Jem asked.

"Yeah. He was already on Tresco for an art buyer's conference at the Flying Boat Studio," Rhys said. "Some of those people in the dining room are probably returning to it. Hermie was supposed to pop by and explain again what he accomplished for me as my agent, and what he spent my money on. Because otherwise I was going to sue him, if I could stomach it."

"So you think he was scamming you?" Pauley asked.

"Maybe. I mean, if he got his throat cut on his yacht in the middle of the night, maybe he ran with some dangerous people. I can't believe I ever trusted him." He sighed. "I've been such a bloody muppet."

"Why a muppet?" Jem asked. "I've seen your souvenirs in Island Gifts. You're already a success. Couldn't you branch out to the mainland?"

"I have, a little. A shop in Penzance down by the Promenade sells them, too. I buy the materials in bulk and churn them out on a schedule. It's decent money. Saved me from selling the lighthouse," he added, referring to St. Morwenna's best-known landmark, a squat white lighthouse that sat on the island's highest point. "I even saved up enough to reactivate it."

"Does anyone want that?" Micki asked. "I'm not being negative. Only, certain people"—she nudged Jem—"like to bang on and on about how on St. Morwenna there's no light pollution and it's perfect for stargazing."

"She's right. Cranking it up every night would be a disaster. But for holidays and festivals, the lighthouse's beam would serve as an attraction," Rhys said. "Tour guides have been asking me to get it done for years. Anyway, I figured if the lighthouse drew more emmets, I wouldn't have to spend so much time churning out souvenirs. I could be an artist instead of a craftsman, and take things to a whole new level."

"All that makes sense," Pauley said. "When does the story turn muppety?"

"First, let me explain one thing. The Cornish art community can be a bit sniffy. At least if you're me, and have a reputation for bailing on projects and spending weekends in the drunk tank," Rhys said. There was no self-pity in his tone, just a matter-of-fact accounting of his past. "Plus, I'm mostly self-taught. I don't have the right schooling, I don't have the right friends, and when I was young and dumb, I burned my boats. Once I was finally ready to commit to the work, it turned out no one was interested anymore. Then I met Hermie.

"It was last November. We were at a show in St. Ives. He was buying paintings. Expensive ones. I had my portfolio with me and he looked it over. Then he said that even though he worked mostly as an art dealer, he could offer me an alternate path to break into the art scene. A back door, he called it. I knew it wasn't totally above board. It's not the accepted method of—"

"Just spit it out," Pauley cut in.

"He said he'd act as my agent, but I had to pay him upfront. I needed to cover his travel and expenses while he represented me. He also wanted me to buy a suit, get some studio headshots, buy new business cards, and paint twelve new pieces, all similar materials and themes. Hermie said he'd go up and down the coast, find a respectable gallery, and get me a showing in six months."

Jem asked, "That portrait studio. Did he refer you to a particular one, by any chance?"

Rhys sighed again. "Yes. He just happened to know a place. They designed my business cards, too."

"So Hermie Castleberry got travel money off you. His friend the photographer got a full-service customer," Pauley said. "After you'd spent the winter painting those twelve new pieces, what happened with them?"

"I assumed he'd come view them in person," Rhys said. "You can't evaluate art from an emailed photo. You have to stand in front of canvases to really get whether the image resonates or not. But Hermie told me the email was good enough, and the next step was to crate up the canvases and ship them to an address in St. Ives. He said it was his storage unit."

"At your expense?" Micki asked.

Rhys nodded. "I didn't want to do it. I could've paid Bart the Ferryman to take me and the paintings to St. Ives. You know Bart—always skint and up for a special charter. It would've saved me a mint. But Hermie wouldn't hear of it. Said he couldn't possibly bring them into a gallery wrapped in newspaper like bits of fish. I laid out the money and tracked the shipment to verify it was received. It was—but not at a storage unit. The person who signed for it worked at a place called the Fleaste Hotel."

"Fleas?" Micki asked.

"I think he said fleeced," Jem said.

"Let me show you the place." Pulling out his mobile, Rhys used its browser to load the hotel's website. He passed it around so all three of them could get a look.

"Bit dark," said Micki.

"Bit gloomy," said Pauley.

"It's a dump. Basil Fawlty wouldn't stay there," Jem declared, scrolling down to check something before handing Rhys his phone back. It was as she suspected. Should she mention it, or keep the damning detail to herself?

"Of course, when I saw that, I thought there'd been a mistake," Rhys said. "I rang Hermie and went to voicemail. I left loads of messages. After a week he texted me something like, 'All is well, sit tight and wait, the art world moves slowly.' That's when I started feeling like a muppet."

"I hope you can get your canvases back," Pauley said. "You worked all winter on them. They represent hours and hours of hard work."

"Suppose Hermie auctioned them off to his art collector friends and pocketed all the money? What a bastard," Micki said.

Rhys gave her a smile that made Jem's heart turn over. It was amused, self-deprecating, and grateful, all at the same time. "What a lovely thing to say. No, sadly, I don't think Hermie got rich auctioning off the paintings I can't get any reputable gallery to show. But thank you, Micki, for believing it might be possible. By the way, how many rooms do you think the grotty little Fleaste Hotel has?"

"Twelve," Jem said. "I just checked."

"Yeah. Wanna bet there's now a piece of abstract art hanging in every room?"

Pauley groaned. "No wonder you never told me much about your agent. You know you're never supposed to—"

"—supposed to pay an agent up front, yes, yes, I do know that, but I was stupid enough to do it anyway," Rhys broke in, clearly furious with himself. "I told you, I knew it wasn't right, but I felt desperate. And Hermie seemed so confident, so successful, I thought it was a good gamble. When he asked me to get a suit and headshots, I never thought he was just throwing a little business to a pal. I thought he was getting me ready for the big time. But looking back, it seems like such an obvious scam."

"So… how much are you out?" Jem asked.

Rhys scowled.

"You didn't dip into your lighthouse renovation fund?" Pauley asked, alarmed.

"Forget it," he muttered. "I'd rather not say."

"Oh, love, I'm sorry. It's hard to see through a cheat when your dreams are on the line," Micki said sympathetically. "I'd tell you to sue, but I don't reckon you're likely to get anywhere now that Hermie's gone to the great beyond. But don't pack it in because of one bad experience. Your time will come, I know it will."

The remaining pizza was verging on cold, but still quite tasty. The four of them finished it off, then drained their glasses. The rest of the patio had already cleared. Down on the beach, towels were being spread out and umbrellas were being opened as the mid-afternoon temperature peaked. Most of the sunbathers stayed on the sand or dipped their toes in the surf, but a few brave souls were like Jem and Pauley, happy to swim in the bracing waters.

"I reckon Stuart's eager to prepare for dinner," Micki said, nodding toward the staff inside the restaurant, who were collecting up the lunch centerpieces and sweeping up. "We ought to settle up and let them get on with it."

As if summoned, Stuart chose that moment to return to the patio and present their bill.

"I'll get this one," Pauley announced, reaching across the table for the bill. "You guys can owe me one."

She'd been flush with cash ever since one of the Gwyn family collection's most intriguing finds, a previously unknown poem by Oscar Wilde, had been sold at auction. The upkeep on Lyonesse House would eat it up eventually, but for the time being, she could afford to treat her friends.

Stuart, returning with her change, had an odd look on his face. He seemed to be trying to look sad, or at least compassionately concerned, but his eyes gleamed with excitement.

"I started to tell you earlier, but I wasn't sure how. There's been news," he said, pausing for dramatic effect. "A friend on St. Mary's heard it from Carenza Morgan at Hugh Town Station, so it's as good as official. A dead body has been found." Another pause. "With its throat cut." Pause. "Here on Tresco. By Candlewick Castle."

"Right. Hermie Castleberry. Hang on, there's a kind of symmetry in that, don't you think?" Rhys deadpanned. "Castle. Castleberry."

"And there was a castle logo on his shirt," Pauley said. "Do you think that matters?" She directed the question toward Jem. No matter how much they teased her, when push came to shove, they clearly valued her sleuthing instincts.

"You knew about it?" Stuart looked incredulous. "How?"

"Stuart!" called one of the servers from inside The Ruin's dining room. "Sorry to interrupt, but it's your sister. She says it's an emergency. She says—"

"He's dead," cried the sister in question, surging through the dining room and onto the patio. Blonde and perhaps forty, she was dressed in a shapeless brown maxi dress and sandals. Jem thought she would've been pretty if not for the horror and grief distorting her features. Behind her trailed a tall, broad shouldered, gawky teenage boy wearing a rather shell-shocked expression.

"Georgia." Stuart put his arms around her. "I know. I just heard. It'll be all right, love. Everything happens for a reason. It's true, I promise you, it's true. Maybe… maybe now you can get your life in order, hey?"

CHAPTER EIGHT

The Perfect Man

"Stu!" Georgia wrenched herself out of her brother's embrace. "What a thing to say to me. To Leo!" she added, reaching up to touch her tall son's shoulder. Jem thought he was perhaps sixteen, with a cloud of curly brown hair and spots across his forehead. He was at that stage of adolescence where elbows, knees, and the Adam's apple predominate. Something about his mute dignity, as if he were holding himself together by sheer force of will, made Jem's heart go out to him.

"It's okay, Mum," he muttered in a startling bass voice.

"You're right, I shouldn't have said that. I'm sorry." Stuart was instantly contrite. "I know how much you loved him. And I'm sure he cared for you. Both of you."

"Oh, hon, you've had a terrible shock," Micki said, popping up from the bench. "Let's get you sat down and sorted."

As if they were in her own place of employment, the Kernow Arms, instead of The Ruin, Micki led Georgia and Leo to the table nearest their own. Then she made a beeline for the servers' beverage station, snagging two glasses and a pitcher of iced water. Back at the table, she served Georgia and Leo deftly, whispering, "Of course," as Georgia shakily offered thanks. Then she slipped back into her place, squeezing Jem's knee under the table. The meaning was clear—if she wanted to learn more about Hermie Castleberry's death, now she had the opportunity.

"He can't be dead," Georgia burst out, gripping her water glass as though she might hurl it onto the beach. "We've only been married a year. And he was the perfect man. As unsure as you've been about him, Stu, you have to admit it. He was the perfect, perfect man."

Leo shifted on his bench, sipping his iced water. Somewhere under the wild hair, acne spots, and jutting limbs was the framework of a handsome young man, coming together but as yet unfinished. Jem remembered Rhys's brother Cam, who'd been a bit like that at fourteen, all sharp elbows and knobby knees.

"He was, wasn't he?" Georgia demanded of her son.

"Sure, Mum." Awkwardly, he slung a long arm around her. She looked wan and breakable as she leaned against his broad chest.

Stuart, apparently retreating into the restaurant to avoid answering her question, procured a chair, and carried it onto the porch, situating it next to Georgia's table. Jem wondered why he didn't just sit on the bench next to his nephew and sister. He seemed uncomfortable, even a little guilty, perhaps regretting the times he'd criticized his brother-in-law.

"I, erm, take it the police notified you?" he asked after an awkward silence.

Georgia nodded, sniffing. "I came for the pirate festival. Leo was already here with the Sea Guides on summer camp so I went to get him. Hermie was meant to meet me by the Old Blockhouse. I waited for what felt like forever. I thought he'd got held up in a meeting, or changed plans and forgot to ring me again. He's a very busy man. Terribly successful," she added, as if the habit of bragging about Hermie was too deeply ingrained to forgo just because he was dead.

"You don't have to tell me how busy he was," Stuart said. Nodding toward Rhys, he added, "Nor this fellow. He waited over two hours for Hermie to show up for a business lunch."

"You expected to meet Hermie today?" Georgia asked, focusing her red-rimmed eyes on Rhys as if seeing him for the first time. "Do you own a museum? Or do you deal in fine art?"

Ordinarily, Jem and Pauley would've pounced on those absurdities, but under the circumstances, they maintained their composure. And perhaps Georgia's supposition wasn't so ridiculous, Jem thought, regarding Rhys with fresh eyes. She had to stop thinking of him purely in terms of his teenaged self. Today, in his gray suit and smartly knotted blue tie, he looked every inch the successful businessman.

"Neither of those. I'm just a painter," Rhys said gently. "Your husband was my agent. I'm very sorry for your loss."

"Oh, your agent? Of course. He was so generous with emerging talent." Georgia's eyes welled with fresh tears. "How can he be dead? The police said there was evidence of foul play. I was sure they'd got it wrong, that it was a case of mistaken identity, but they wouldn't let me go to the police station and prove it. Sergeant Hackman said I have to wait until after the forensic team finishes their evaluation. Then I'll be asked to identify his clothes. Does that sound right to you? His *clothes*?"

Jem and her friends looked anywhere but at Georgia's plaintively questioning face.

"You guys seemed to have some inside info on Hermie," Stuart said, turning to them. "Do you have any idea what's going on?"

Jem could have simply lied. To be completely truthful would do nothing but upset Georgia even more. But with Carenza spreading the news in Hugh Town, it was only a matter of time before Georgia learned all the facts. Jem might as well share what she could, as delicately as possible.

"Mrs. Castleberry, the fact is, the girls and I also came for the Pirate Extravaganza. We dropped anchor near Candlewick Castle and waded ashore. We found your husband on the beach."

"But what happened to him? Was he just lying there? In the middle of nowhere?"

Jem said vaguely, "I'm sure the police will figure it out."

"But how did he look? Was he beat up? Stabbed?" Georgia's voice edged on hysteria.

Leo sighed, covering his face with his hands. "This is intense," he muttered.

Jem began to wish she'd pretended to know nothing. Such revelations were probably better left to professionals.

Pauley said, "He was lying face down when we found him, so…" She tailed off, letting the selective truth do its work. "I'm so sorry for your loss. Do you live on Tresco?"

"St. Mary's," Georgia said, sniffling. "Leo and I moved here a few years back from Norwich. We wanted to get away from city life. I thought it would be easy, but it wasn't. It was hard to find a full-time job, and I could only afford a tiny flat. We were barely getting by when Hermie came into our lives. He was a godsend, wasn't he, love?" she asked Leo, again putting a hand on her son's shoulder.

"Yeah," Leo whispered.

"And he treated you like his own, didn't he?"

"Bought me my Xbox. And my bike."

"The perfect man," Georgia whispered. "Some kind of maniac must've come upon him. A robber or a serial killer. There was a murder on St. Morwenna not long ago." Georgia rubbed her eyes and focused on Jem. "Wait. Aren't you Jemima Jago? Special Collections at the Courtney?"

"Yes. Are you a librarian?" Jem asked.

"I volunteer at St. Mary's Library. I do about twenty hours a week," Georgia said. "I've heard the staff mention you, and I saw a write-up about you online. That murder on St. Morwenna—you solved it, didn't you?"

Jem nodded.

"When you found Hermie, did you notice anything that might help the police? Footprints on the shore? A weapon?"

Jem decided to follow Pauley's example and offer a selected truth. "There were a few things washed ashore that suggested a boat sank nearby. I'm a strong swimmer, so while we waited for the police, I dove in the channel between Tresco and Bryher. Sure enough, I found a yacht on the seabed."

Georgia looked blank.

"I found *Family Man*," Jem clarified. "A sport fishing boat, judging by the motors. I couldn't stay down long without proper gear, but why it sank wasn't obvious to me. Sergeant Hackman said a forensic dive team will salvage it."

"A boat. You think Hermie was a passenger on it?" Georgia sounded confused.

"Yes," Jem said, choosing not to go into the missing shoes tied to the ice chest. "Because of his Yacht-Master Rolex, I assumed *Family Man* belonged to him."

"No. Hermie didn't have a boat."

"Yes, he did," Rhys said. "I'm sorry to contradict you, Mrs. Castleberry. But after Hermie became my agent, he gave me a ride on *Family Man* a couple of times. He was quite proud of it."

Georgia emitted a pitiful sound, like a woman breaking under the weight of the impossible.

"He's right, Mum. Hermie had a boat," Leo said, leaning forward. "He was waiting until your anniversary to tell you about it."

"Oh, yes, he had a boat," Stuart agreed. His earlier contrition was gone; now his tone reeked of I-told-you-so. "I saw him on it last month and thought I was hallucinating. He was on the deck in cargo shorts and black dress socks, as always," he added, a sour note creeping in. "When I asked him what you thought of it, he said he'd overspent on the ruddy thing and swore me to secrecy. He didn't want you to know until he'd moved some money around. Which I hope he managed to do before he died, so his legacy to you isn't a load of past due accounts."

"Do you think I really care about the money? Why are you like this, Stuart? Why were you always so negative about him?" Georgia burst out. "Everyone else adored him. He didn't have an enemy in the world. But you've always behaved like he wasn't good enough for me."

"As a matter of fact, I don't—"

"Nonsense! The truth is, I wasn't good enough for him!" Georgia said passionately, fresh tears rolling down her cheeks. "When I came here, I was divorced, broke, a stone heavier than I should have been, and thirty-nine years old. I'm lucky *any* man gave me a second glance, much less a handsome, successful, generous man like Hermie!"

On those final words, Georgia went dead white. She whispered, "I'm going to be sick," and jumped up, hurrying into the now-darkened dining room, no doubt bound for the bathrooms.

For a few seconds, no one spoke. Then Stuart sighed, pinched the bridge of his nose, and said, "The simple fact is, Hermie Castleberry wasn't adored by everyone. I despised him. I think a lot of people did, though they might not be willing to say so, just at the moment." He gave Leo an apologetic look. "Sorry. I know you got on with him."

The boy crossed his arms over his broad chest and looked down at his huge, trainer-clad feet. "Yeah. I did. But you're not wrong. I can think of a couple of people who hated him."

"Who?" Jem asked before she could stop herself. Rhys shot her a glance that said, *Really?*

"Roddy Levitt. He has a gallery in Penzance. Hermie and Roddy used to be best mates. Not sure why they fell out," Leo replied, shrugging as only disinterested teenagers can. "But the last time I asked why Roddy never came around our cottage anymore, Hermie told me to let sleeping dogs lie."

Turning to Rhys with a speculative gaze, Stuart said, "Georgia wasn't wrong when she said Hermie liked working with quote-unquote emerging artists. But over a pint he told me they fell into two groups. The viable clients, whose works he sold or placed with galleries. And the vanity clients, who he charged up front. I asked what he meant by vanity. He said big dreams, small talent, and a willingness to try and buy a place at the table."

Rhys maintained an admirable poker face. Jem, who'd seen his perfectly lovely souvenirs for sale in St. Morwenna's gift shop, but never his serious paintings, was offended on his behalf. Even if Rhys wasn't destined to set the art scene ablaze, that didn't give Hermie Castleberry the right to con him.

"Mr. Franks has been calling our place a lot," Leo added. "Yesterday he left a message and said it was urgent. I kept the recording in the queue for Hermie to listen to when he got back. He travels almost every week, so it's usually Sunday before he catches up on calls and post."

"Mr. Franks as in Jimmy Franks of Franks All Marine?" Rhys asked.

"Hermie used to go fishing with him," Leo said.

"I know Jimmy," Rhys said. "He sends me bodywork on damaged boats sometimes, when his shop's too busy to cope. He's... a fine enough bloke, I guess."

Not precisely a ringing character reference, Jem thought.

Georgia wandered back to the patio looking pale and weak, like someone who'd taken a body blow and was moments away from collapse. "Leo, we need to go home and wait for Sergeant Hackman to call. He said the clothes won't be ready before tomorrow, but I feel certain he'll call before that. This has to be a case of mistaken identity. There's no way Hermie was found dead by the castle. I refuse to believe it."

Rising, Leo went to her side. "It'll be okay, Mum. I'm here. I'll take care of you."

"Let me get you back to St. Mary's," Stuart said, rising. "I know a bloke with a cabin cruiser who'd be happy to give us a lift. I'll ring my boss and get someone to cover for me." Turning to Pauley, he asked, "Would you care to follow us to the front? I'm locking up."

Jem and her friends exchanged glances around the table.

"That's okay," Pauley said. "We'll just follow those steps down to the beach."

CHAPTER NINE

The Jolly Codger

"Poor Mrs. Castleberry," Pauley said as they slowly made their way up the beach toward the Old Blockhouse. The sun beat down on them, but the wind off the waves was glorious. It was past three o'clock, but Jem heard no music wafting toward them. Maybe the First Annual Pirate Extravaganza was late getting underway.

Rhys, who'd taken off his suit jacket and draped it over his shoulder, was drawing looks from the people lounging on towels and playing in the surf. Probably it was the incongruity of a suit on the beach, but maybe it was just him. Good-looking guys like Rhys drew stares wherever they went. Especially in the Scillies, where the pickings were slim.

"You must be boiling," Micki told him.

"I am. This shirt will need a wash when I get home. As for the suit, no worries. Who knows if I'll ever need it again."

"Weren't you just scolding me for self-pity?" Pauley asked.

He shrugged. "That crack about Hermie and his 'vanity clients' hit me right between the eyes. Did you see the way Stuart was looking at me? Like he knew. Even the kid was eyeballing me."

"Don't worry about what a kid thinks. As for Stuart, I reckon he was just fishing for an amen chorus," Micki said. "He wanted you to chime in and say you despised Hermie, too, so he wouldn't look like a jerk to his sister and nephew. Maybe Hermie considered you a mark, or maybe he was just a lousy agent."

"Even if he did see you as a mark, that doesn't mean you can't make it as a serious artist," Jem said. "Stuart said Hermie was shifting money around and hiding a major purchase from Georgia. If he was desperate enough, he might have decided to milk all his clients to the max."

Rhys looked at her in mild surprise. "He did say that. Thanks, Jemmie. Maybe it's only a sop to my self-esteem, but I'll take it." He smiled at her.

"By the way," Pauley said, craning her neck to meet his eyes, since at six-four he overtopped her by precisely a foot, "you *were* right, damn you. The way poor Mrs. Castleberry talked down about herself made my skin crawl. Gross. Maybe I should try to focus on the positives in my life. You three for a start." Pauley smiled.

Something about the way Rhys had lightly said, "Thanks, Jemmie," made Jem yearn to bridge the narrowing gap between them. She still hadn't visited Tremayne Lighthouse, which he used as his studio. As she considered how to make such an overture, Micki stopped dead and pulled her sundress over her head.

"It's too hot for this now. Time to get back into my pirate gear. Give me half a sec," she said, digging into her green bag.

"Pirate gear?" Rhys asked.

"She raided the Tidal Pool Players' wardrobe," Pauley said.

"They'll want it all back straightaway. There's a play next week," he said.

"I know that." Unpacking the tricorn hat, Micki popped it on her head. "My cousin is helping with the scenery. He told me you were one of the players."

Jem turned to stare at Rhys, astonished.

"In the ensemble. It's no big deal," he said, waving it off. "If a play requires a special backdrop, I'll paint it. If there's a part I fit, I'll do a walk-on and say a couple of lines."

"Wow. You've come a long way from the sheep who wouldn't baa," Jem said.

Pauley burst into silvery peals of laughter. "Oh, my gosh, I hadn't thought of that in years. The sheep who wouldn't baa. One line in the Christmas play," she explained to Micki. "One line, and it wasn't even a word, and he couldn't do it!"

"I was eight. I looked out at all those faces in the audience and had a wobble." Rhys shrugged. "I've evolved."

"Good on you. Don't listen to those two," Micki said, tying the striped sash around her waist. "Even Barbra Streisand gets stage fright to this day. What role will you play next week?"

"A character called the Pransome Hence. It's a gag role. I enter on a hobbyhorse, tell the leading lady she'd be lucky to have me, and admire myself in a mirror. Then the monster enters, stage left, and I run away in terror."

More silvery peals rang out from Pauley, and Micki's distinctive wheezy laugh told Rhys everything he needed to know.

"I'm sure you'll be great," Micki said, still smirking.

Micki clipped the huge gold hoops to her earlobes, then dug deeper in her pack, coming up with the flintlock gun. As she did so, something else flipped onto the sand: an item made of wood and metal, stained with dried paint. For a moment, Jem was mystified by the sight of it.

"Oh! Can't believe we haven't given this back yet," Pauley said, picking it up. "Rhys, here's your knife."

Rhys stiffened. "What?"

"Your knife," Pauley repeated, holding it out to him. "We climbed the castle and found this lying on top of the round tower, near the guns."

He made no move to take it. "Oh. Well. I'm flattered, but I'm hardly the only painter in the Scillies. It could be anyone's."

"It's a Piranesi," Jem said. Something about Rhys's change in demeanor worried her. "Isn't that your brand? Pauley recognized the logo."

With clear reluctance, Rhys accepted the artist's knife and studied the handle. "Well. What do you know? I haven't been out to the castle to paint a sunrise in weeks. If it is mine, I suppose it fell out of my bag."

"Aren't you lucky it's come back to you, then? Take it as a good omen for your art career," Pauley said.

Jem wondered if the upkeep around Candlewick Castle had changed substantially during her time away. Although no fee was charged for admittance, it was still managed by English Heritage and carefully looked after by volunteers. She couldn't imagine a small knife, even a blunted one used by painters, would have been left lying around the site for weeks. Surely someone would have binned it.

With Micki kitted out in her pirate gear, they resumed their progress toward the Old Blockhouse. The sound of pop music began floating toward them, as well as chatter and the shouts of kids playing in the surf. As they approached another of Tresco's attractions, the stone fort, a crumbling sixteenth-century military defense overlooking New Grimsby Harbor, a family came toward them. They marched with a picnic hamper, blankets, and a rolled-up beach umbrella in hand, grim-faced.

"You'll be sorry," the mum warned Jem and her friends. "This isn't a festival. It's nothing but a cash grab."

One of the youngsters trailing behind the mum piped up, "That's not a pirate ship. It's a joke."

The dad shushed the boy. As the disappointed family followed the path's fork toward St. Nicholas Church and the New Inn, Jem shielded her eyes against the sun. Scanning the water, she quickly spied the so-called "real pirate ship," the *Jolly Codger*.

"Bloody hell."

"Is that—" Pauley asked, whipping off her shades to stare harder.

Micki made a helpless sound of disbelief and Rhys went into gales of laughter. When tickled, literally or figuratively, he gave himself completely to the moment, closing his eyes, throwing back his head, pressing his hands against his chest and laughing with every fiber of his being. In this case, he was so amused by the alleged pirate ship in New Grimsby Bay, he even forgot to hold onto his jacket. It dropped to the sand by his feet.

Watching Rhys laugh touched something deep inside of Jem. She could withstand his chiseled good looks; she could look away from his big, well-muscled body. But when she saw him laugh the way only Rhys could laugh, a pin slipped into her heart, moving the tumblers and threatening to pop the lock.

Better to concentrate on the bay and the so-called *Jolly Codger*. It was actually Bart the Ferryman's boat, *Merry Maid*. Bart's vessel, a thirty-foot converted fishing boat with a huge red patch in the side, was often seen around Penzance and the Isles of Scilly, providing bargain-basement rides to those who required no frills.

Merry Maid ran on diesel, so it naturally had no sails, which Jem and probably every other rational person would agree was essential to a pirate ship. To get around this, Bart had painted a Jolly Roger on a bit of plywood and affixed the sloppy product to a long pole. The result looked like a giant cocktail favor.

As for *Merry Maid*'s sides, which were dull gray apart from the patched area, Bart had draped them in long, vertical sheets of brown plastic. Even if he'd secured the sheets perfectly, the effect would have been nothing like planked wood. As it was, the sheets had come loose in transit, and fluttered like a grass skirt in a breeze.

"I can't believe people are sticking around for this," Micki said. "I talked this up to everyone in the Kernow Arms. If they took my advice, my next shift isn't going to be much fun," she added nervously.

"I don't know. Some of them are actually… smiling," Pauley said.

It was true. Although some folks were angrily clearing out at the sight of the *Jolly Codger*, they appeared to be posh tourists who were accustomed to nothing but the best. The majority of people gathered around the Old Blockhouse hardly seemed to consider the absurdity of the "real pirate ship" a deal-breaker. Spreading blankets on the grass, they were unpacking hampers, putting on sun cream, or heading down to the surf to wade. One young couple was dancing to the music, while in the shadow of the old fort a knot of giggling girls chased each other round and round.

"It's a pretty day," Pauley continued. "The water's okay for swimming, if you don't mind it brisk. And there's music."

Rhys managed to stop laughing long enough to gasp, "I didn't give a fig for this until I saw that monstrosity. Now I'm glad I came."

From a DJ set-up on *Merry Maid*'s deck, an amplified voice declared, "Pirate Radio returns with a tune I know you'll all remember." Bart's PA system didn't have much range, but as Jem looked around the field, she saw portable speakers strategically placed in the grassy zones. At least one of the flyer's promises, the pirate radio broadcast, was being fulfilled.

The song that followed, from the animated film *Peter Pan*, had some of the most recognizable—not to mention copyright protected—lyrics in the pirate universe. Kids and adults sang along happily as Jem and her friends swapped looks.

"Better hope Mickey Mouse isn't on holiday in the Scillies," Micki said.

"Bart won't stop breaking rules until he's banged up for life. He can't help himself." Pauley shrugged. "Oh, look, there's a pop-up drinks stand. Should we yo-ho-ho and a bottle of Double Drowned?" Glancing at Rhys, she added, "Plus a soda."

Retrieving his jacket, he dusted it off and shook his head, smiling. "It's been fun, ladies, but I need to get back to St. Morwenna. There's an arts and crafts fair in the Square at the end of the month. I wasn't planning to flog my sunsets there. Figured I'd be busy with my gallery show. Now I'd better see if I can whip up some originals to liven up my booth, if there's any space left for me to rent."

"You didn't get here on one of the runabouts, did you?" Pauley asked, meaning the small number of beat-up old powerboats Rhys kept on Crescent Beach as rentals. "Wearing a suit and tie, I mean."

Rhys shook his head. "I did take a runabout, but it was last night, and I was dressed like a normal bloke. I'll change clothes before I set out. Can't come home like this or everybody and their sister will want to know what's up."

"They'll still hear about it," Micki said. "I've never lived any place where news travels so fast."

"Ah, but if they don't witness it, I can claim it never happened," Rhys said breezily. With a careless wave, he turned and started back up the wide lane the way they'd come.

"Mysterious, isn't he?" Micki murmured to Jem and Pauley. "Where's he going to change clothes?"

"There are some permanent residences in the resort. Flats and townhouses," Pauley said. "He must have a friend there." Her tone was flat, and she didn't meet Jem's eyes.

I need to have a quiet word with her. Tell her I expect nothing from Rhys, and I don't care what he gets up to in his private life, Jem thought. I don't want her tiptoeing around the subject. She knew the declaration wasn't true, but she wanted it to be true. Perhaps if she said it aloud, it would be.

As Jem, Micki, and Pauley made their way to the drinks stand, which was selling not only local beers like Double Drowned but also cocktails made with Abbey Gardens gin, Jem found herself thinking about the storm.

It started around three a.m. and lasted until seven or eight. High tide probably came in around nine, she thought. It would have been extra high, what with the full moon and the storm, and so it swept Hermie's body onto the beach. The corpse smelled like decomposition was well under way. Could he have been underwater all night? Someone killed him, weighted him down and dropped him overboard, and even sank *Family Man*, all without anyone noticing or reporting it, so it must have happened overnight. During the storm, perhaps.

She wondered how the killer had escaped from the sinking vessel. A boat the size of *Family Man* would surely have an inflatable rescue craft. Or if the murderer was, like her, comfortable in the sea, they might have simply swam ashore and walked inland. Even in the profound darkness of the Scillies, a full moon would have made the castle and other natural landmarks plainly visible.

There are plenty of places on Tresco for a killer to hide. Perhaps he has a holiday let. Or worse—he lives here.

They'd inched halfway to the front of the drinks queue when Jem overheard a man behind her say quite clearly, "Well, Hermie had to know he was on borrowed time, didn't he?"

Turning her head as casually as possible, Jem saw a group of well-dressed men had joined the queue. Some were in light summer suits. Others were in crisp, logo-adorned island wear: cotton-blend polo shirts and short trousers that probably cost almost as much as the suits. All wore GET ART SMART lanyards and printed ID badges. Jem couldn't quite make out the name of the speaker, a bearded man with what appeared to be dyed gray hair and round glasses.

"It's a bit rich for you to turn on him now," another man said, chuckling. "You're the one who brought him into our midst, aren't you? Vouched for him as a broker and told us about his connection to Sotheby's?" The nastiness in his tone suggested the man with the dyed gray hair had been caught in an inaccuracy, if not an outright lie.

"Never mind all that. It's bad taste to talk about the dead this way," a different lanyard-wearing man said, pointedly fixing his gaze on Jem.

Facing forward quickly, she nudged her friend. "Pauley?" she whispered.

"What?"

"I'm getting out of line. Order my drink, will you?" Slipping aside, Jem headed toward an imaginary destination that would lead her past the men in lanyards, whom she presumed were art dealers. She tried to look purposeful, like a woman who'd received a message or realized she'd misplaced her cash.

"I accompanied Hermie to one meeting that he was already planning to attend," the man with the dyed hair said. He sounded insulted. "So he was a fabulist. So what? Nothing he did or said has anything to do with me."

As Jem passed, she saw the man's name badge. R. LEVITT, KING & CASTLE, PENZANCE.

She went around one of the tall speakers, dithered for about five seconds, and hurried back, passing the men on the other side. Whatever she'd missed in her short absence must've been significant, because the man, who she assumed was Roddy Levitt, had exited the queue. He was marching south, as if leaving the festival altogether.

"Come on, Roddy! Don't leave it like this," one of the men called at his back. If Roddy heard, he didn't turn around.

"Hermie was a fabulist? Hah. Takes one to know one," another muttered.

"Shh," said the one who'd noticed Jem looking the first time. He glared at her as she passed.

Rejoining Pauley and Micki, Jem kept her eyes front but her ears attuned to any other bits of conversation about the dead man. She heard nothing. When she and her friends received their plastic tumblers of Double Drowned, they passed the art dealers once more while leaving the queue. All waited silently, arms folded across their chest, and the man who'd caught her eavesdropping gave her one final scowl.

CHAPTER TEN

The Pirates of Zen Dance

Bart the Ferryman's counterfeit pirate ship was a bust, but otherwise, most attendees seemed to be enjoying the festival. Pirate Radio went on for a couple of hours, with local DJs taking turns at the mic and amusing the crowd with their banter and novelty songs. Then at five o'clock, Bart himself turned up dressed like Cap'n Crunch, with a huge, plumed hat and one leg wrapped below the knee in brown plastic sheeting, apparently to simulate a peg leg. It worked about as well as the sheets hanging limply off the gunwale of the *Jolly Codger*. Bart—or Black Bart, as he styled himself in character—took a lot of ribbing, not all of it friendly, from the guests, but he basked in the praise and shook off the rebukes like a mild rain.

A big fellow, well over six feet and with enough flesh on his bones for two men, Bartholomew Bottom, aka Bart the Ferryman, had a perpetually scrubby beard that served mainly to give a suggestion of a chin; otherwise, his face melted into his neck. Loud, boisterous, and prone to promising things he couldn't hope to deliver, Bart had a grin and an insincere compliment for everyone. Though Jem had known him just a short while, she'd seen him called a gobshite to his face, only to laugh it off and shamble away. She pegged him as an eternal optimist, and indeed he had to be, to cheerfully live a life of endless scrapes with police, local authorities, and creditors.

After he'd made the circuit, strutting around the beach and greenway shouting "Arrr!" and "Avast!" Bart led the costumed children in a procession around the Old Blockhouse. Grown-ups in pirate regalia were invited to fill out the small group, but when Jem turned to Micki to urge her participation, the tricorn, sash, gold hoops, and flintlock had disappeared back into her friend's dry bag.

"I was the only woman in costume," Micki whispered. "If Bart noticed, he would've declared me his pirate queen. I get enough double entendres and cheeky looks from him while I'm paid to put up with it. I won't do it for free."

"You know, you keep saying you're in a drought as far as men go," Jem said slyly. "Bart's tall. Self-employed. Certainly… *available*." Finding truthful descriptors was as hard as keeping a straight face.

"If Bart were the last man on earth, I'd be trying to mate with a dolphin. Or a cockroach," Micki said.

"What about those blokes?" Pauley asked. "Looks like the band has arrived."

Four men, all dressed in jeans and hibiscus printed shirts, were carrying instrument cases and bits of equipment down the path. They were making for an improvised bandstand at the edge of the greenway, overlooking the beach.

"Hey. I know the bald one," Micki said. "He's called Monty. He drinks at the Kernow Arms sometimes. I thought he rented golf carts in Hugh Town. Never heard him say he was in a band. Hmh." She began digging in her bag again.

"Now you're putting the pirate stuff on again?" Jem asked.

"Nope." Micki came up with her bottle of tequila. "It's time for something a bit stronger."

When Bart's costume procession ended, he joined the band, helping connect long weatherproofed cords to power generators. The radio broadcast's speakers were co-opted, and before long the four musicians were readying their instruments, the amplified tuning-up sounds signaling to the crowd that live music was next. Micki watched the process with particular interest, but Jem didn't know why. In her considered opinion, they were all pleasant-looking, ranging in age from thirty-something to perhaps fifty, but none deserved such rapt attention. Maybe Monty was actually an old flame?

Thoughts of old flames reminded her of someone who certainly qualified as a new flame. Scanning the crowd, which had swelled as the sun dipped lower on the horizon, Jem searched for a certain dark-haired man with a neat goatee and black cowboy boots. He didn't seem to be among them.

Of course not. Even if the mainland murder squad had taken total control of the case, they'd probably still want Hack to coordinate locally.

As the sound check proceeded, tables were set up, selling dinners from local restaurants. Most of it had a seaside twist: cod burgers, fried calamari baskets, crab dip and chips. Other Isles of Scilly-made goodies were on offer too—homemade jam, salads made from local veg, and boxes of fudge. By the time Monty stepped up to the mic and called, "Hello, Tresco!" Jem had spent twice what she'd intended and was completely stuffed.

"We're the Pirates of Zen Dance," he declared. The band broke into a cover of a classic Jimmy Buffett song, its lyrics known to all.

"Funny name. I mean, kind of funny," Pauley said doubtfully.

"It's an alias," Micki replied with a wheezy laugh. Always up for a good time, she seemed even livelier after two shots of tequila. "Sometimes when bands play iffy gigs, they rename themselves for the occasion. Monty's a clever one. I reckon the second he saw the *Jolly Codger*, he cooked up a nom de guerre on the spot."

"Jem! Hey!"

Someone landed on Jem's back, gripping her shoulders and wrapping skinny legs around her middle. Having spent the morning with a corpse and much of the afternoon contemplating how the murder happened, Jem could've been forgiven for screaming in terror. But during her short stint back in the Scillies, she'd grown accustomed to Kenzie DeYoung's exuberant ways of saying hello.

"Get off or I'll spew. I ate too much," Jem said, trying to pry Kenzie's fingers loose. The girl had a good grip. It was easier to attack her bare legs by tickling them.

"No fair!" Kenzie let go, dropped to the ground on one knee, shouted, "Superhero landing!" and sprang up again.

A childless couple chose that moment to go and stand somewhere else. Meanwhile, the exhausted mums and dads enjoying the music from their picnic blankets didn't even glance Kenzie's way. They were used to bellowing.

Kenzie was thirteen years old, bursting with confidence, and excited by all things edgy, dodgy, or unfit for teen consumption. Recently she'd ditched her fauxhawk for a buzz cut. With her small frame and fine features, it made her look positively elfin. Lavender hair was over, too. These days it was colored bright blue. Her mum, Lissa, didn't like it. She complained her daughter now resembled a ballpoint pen.

Jem glanced around the nearby knots of people, some standing, some sitting, a few dancing, but Lissa was nowhere in sight.

"Where's your mum?"

"At home watching telly. With her boyfriend." Kenzie made a stabbing finger-down-the-throat motion. "She heard a rumor that Bart the Ferryman was behind the Pirate Extravaganza and wouldn't come. Said it was liable to be an embarrassment."

"The boat was. Otherwise, it's not half bad."

"Except for the dead guy by the castle, right?" Kenzie's eyes danced. There was nothing she liked better than blurting out something she wasn't expected to know.

"How did you hear about that?"

"Mum phoned me."

The band had shifted into another classic, this time from Crosby, Stills, and Nash. Pauley and Micki were dancing, and the crowd seemed to be enjoying the performance. Jem wondered if the Pirates of Zen Dance wouldn't end up telling everyone their actual band name before the evening's end. To keep from spoiling other people's enjoyment of the music, she led Kenzie across the sand and closer to the surf, where they could talk without shouting.

"She phoned you? How did she hear?" Jem asked. Lissa lived on St. Morwenna. Once famous for partying all over the islands, she still occasionally went out at night, but her intensive regime of drinking in front of the TV kept her indoors most of the day.

"From Randy Andy. Who I'm now meant to call Uncle Mike. Can you believe that?"

Jem sighed. Michael Anderson, aka Uncle Mike, aka Randy Andy, was the former Isles of Scilly chief of police. After his retirement, many people had expected him to ditch Lissa, his girlfriend of a few months, and head for the mainland, where there were fresh women to chase. Lissa had a penchant for older, emotionally damaged men, but Randy Andy was more of a question mark. Jem knew he'd made noises about finding law enforcement consulting work in Penzance or Exeter.

"I guess he's kept in touch with his old contacts."

Kenzie nodded. "He has a police scanner. He still belongs to all the secret copper chat rooms. And he has PC Newt over once a week to pump him for gossip. It's pathetic. He really needs to get a life."

Of course, Jem thought. He can't leave the Scillies without the satisfaction of watching Hack, his successor, fail at his old job.

"Hang on, after she heard about the body, Lissa still let you—" Jem stopped, realized she'd glossed over a detail. "You said she called you. Did you come here alone?" Like teenage Jem, Kenzie had been known to "borrow" boats for daytrips around the islands. And just like teenage Jem, she seemed blissfully unaware of the trouble that could befall a lone teen girl.

"I'm not alone. I'm with the Sea Guides. They're over there with Mr. Mourby and Ms. Addis-Clark." Kenzie pointed to a group of about twenty teens of wildly varying ages. Like her, all were attired in T-shirts and shorts with matching windcheaters. The two adults both looked like they could do with some antacid tablets, a stiff drink, or both.

"This is the last day of our summer camp," she concluded.

"It was held on Tresco?" Jem was impressed.

"Pull the other one. We're on Bryher. *Again.* This time the club rented out part of the Hell Bay Hotel. It's been a dream getting away from Mum and so-called Uncle Mike. But we're going home tomorrow, and then I'll be staring down the barrel of Year Eight."

"You might enjoy it," Jem ventured.

Kenzie gave her a pitying look. "We both know that's unlikely. Anyway, I wanted to get your theory on the murder. I know you have one."

"I'm afraid I don't. Except that it might be a drug deal gone bad. How much did your mum tell you?"

"Oh, everything, I reckon. Poor Mr. Castleberry's throat was cut. He didn't appear to be robbed. Discovered by Ms. Jemima Jago and her two friends," Kenzie said, assuming a Colonel Blimp voice to indicate all the details had come from Randy Andy.

"Poor Mr. Castleberry?" Jem repeated. "Did you know him?"

"No, but I know his son, Leo. He's in Sea Guides with me."

"What's he like?"

"Brill. Never fake. Says what he means. We had a lot of fun in SUP. That's stand-up paddle boarding," she added helpfully, as if Jem wasn't cool enough to know the sport.

"Ms. Addis-Clark said Mrs. Castleberry was gutted, and Leo did his best to comfort her. I hope he's okay."

"I met Leo and Georgia today," Jem said. "We talked for a little while. I came away with the impression that Hermie Castleberry had a lot of enemies."

Kenzie looked intrigued. "Should I try and find out?"

"What do you mean?"

The girl folded her arms across her flat chest, all attitude again. "I *do* more or less live with the ex-chief of police, and he *does* still know everybody. Whatever he digs up, he'll brag about it to Mum. All I have to do is keep my earbuds in and pretend not to hear. Some detective. He'll never cotton on that the music's switched off."

Jem wasn't sure how to answer. It was entirely possible that the girl might ferret out an interesting nugget or two, especially if she could eavesdrop on Randy Andy talking to PC Newt. On the one hand, it seemed irresponsible to encourage Kenzie to meddle. These were adult problems; the girl ought to be concentrating on kid stuff as she enjoyed the last of the summer. On the other hand, Kenzie would probably go right ahead and do it whether Jem approved or not—and Jem was curious about what facts the girl might glean from Randy Andy.

Twilight was dissolving into dusk. Around the perimeter of the crowd, Bart and his helpers were putting out tiki torches, fitting them into pre-drilled holes in the sand. The little tongues of fire illuminated the beach and greenway, while overhead the full moon was rising and the stars were coming out.

"Okay, tell me whatever you hear," Jem told Kenzie. "But don't get yourself in trouble with Lissa. And don't mention me at all or it's burn notice, get it?"

"Got it," the girl said happily. "I—"

"Ms. DeYoung." The man Jem had glimpsed with the Sea Guides, presumably Mr. Mourby, was suddenly in front of them. Tall and wiry, he probably was about Jem's age, though his prematurely lined face made her first take him for someone much older. "I've asked you not to run off and leave the group. We've been ready to leave for ten minutes. You're making your fellow guides late for hot cocoa and stories around the campfire."

"Whoops," Kenzie muttered.

"Let's go," Mr. Mourby said, pointing in the Guides' direction.

"Wait! Remember that little boat we saw anchored near the channel? The one I said belonged to a friend? This is her," Kenzie said, indicating Jem. "Just leave me with her! She can take me home."

"Absolutely not. We can't leave anyone behind on Tresco for any reason."

"Fine. Then let me swim out to her boat as we pass it. You know what a good swimmer I am," Kenzie pleaded. "I'll wait for her on board. I don't mind."

"You're missing the point. As usual," Mr. Mourby said. He had a clipped way of speaking that put Jem in mind of a magistrate or politician. Fixing her with his cold, dark gaze, he said, "And you are?"

"Jemima Jago. St. Morwenna." She put out her hand.

Mr. Mourby ignored it. "You look a bit long in the tooth to be spending time with schoolgirls, Ms. Jago. Take care that you don't become a bad influence." With that, he hustled Kenzie back to her fellow Sea Guides.

"Where were you?" Pauley asked as Jem returned to her and Micki.

"Getting told off by a jerk of a camp counselor. Do you know anyone called Mourby?"

Pauley, who knew almost everyone, nodded. "He's an ex-Olympic swimming hopeful. Trained for years. Missed the cut by one slot. It's nothing personal, Jem. He's been taking out his frustrations on all of us for years."

Onstage, the music ceased. Stepping up to the microphone, Monty announced a short break, assuring the crowd that the Pirates of Zen Dance would soon return.

"Now's my chance to have a quick word with Monty," Micki told Jem and Pauley. "We kept making eye contact during the set. Not like that," she added when they broke in with *ooo* noises. "Musician to musician." She poured herself another shot and knocked it back.

"Careful. Too much of that and you might end up doing something you'll regret," Jem said.

"No, I'm pacing myself. Just enough liquid courage to get the job done."

As Jem watched her friend head for the makeshift bandstand, she recalled what she'd learned about Micki on the night they met. Not only did her friend play guitar, she'd mentioned singing folk songs, too.

"I wonder if she wants to join the band," Jem whispered to Pauley.

"I thought she liked bartending."

"She does," Jem said, but she wasn't sure if Micki truly enjoyed the work, or if she was merely good at it. Maybe her friend had a creative side that yearned for expression.

"Well, I don't know about you, but I need the bathroom," Pauley announced.

"Of course I do. But is there one?" Jem looked around as if Portaloos might have popped in from a better-equipped dimension. In a Bart the Ferryman production, missing facilities were just another broken promise.

"No, we'll have to head back to the resort."

Sighing, Jem agreed. In the gloom, the walk seemed longer than she remembered, and once they arrived there was a long queue ahead of them. By the time they made it back to the torch-ringed festival grounds, the band had begun to play again.

"Is that—" Jem began, surprised and delighted by what she saw. Lead singer Monty had moved aside. In his former place a metal equipment case was positioned vertically, like a stool. Settling upon it gracefully, Micki accepted the microphone. The guitarist picked out a gentle, familiar melody, and she sang,

Pray sit yourself down
With me on the ground,

On this bank where sweet primroses grow;
You shall hear the fond tale
Of the sweet nightingale,
As she sings in those valleys below;
So be not afraid
To walk in the shade,
Nor yet in those valleys below,
Nor yet in those valleys below.

"Oh my God. She's amazing," Pauley whispered.

Jem nodded. She'd had no notion Micki had such a clear, true voice. Much less the gift of phrasing and selective emphasis that turns a good performance into a great one.

After "Sweet Nightingale," Micki performed two other Cornish folk ballads: "Trelawny," also known as "The Song of the Western Men," and a traditional sea shanty, "Roll the Old Chariot Along." Jem didn't know the words to either, but the sea shanty's refrain was simple and catchy:

Oh, we'd be alright if the wind's in ourselves
Oh, we'd be alright if the wind's in ourselves
Oh, we'd be alright if the wind's in ourselves
And we'll all hang on behind.

Jem, Pauley, and most of the crowd sang it with her. After she finished "Roll the Old Chariot Along," Micki stood up and took a bow, beaming her pleasure at the applause. Pauley put two fingers in her mouth and blew out a piercing whistle. Jem shouted, "Another! Give us another!" But Micki only blew a kiss at the audience and handed the microphone back to Monty.

"Well," he said, fitting it back into its stand and grinning out at the crowd. "Before we say goodnight, we'll do one more song you can carry home in your heart. By the way, we're not really the Pirates of Zen Dance. We're called Tommy and the Knockers. We have a proper website and music for sale, if you're so inclined. Now give it up once more for tonight's special songbird, Micki Latham. If you cheer enough, perhaps it will convince her to sing with us again."

The cheering was loud and long. Micki, looking more than slightly dazed, didn't rejoin Jem and Pauley in the audience. Instead, she dashed off down the path that led to the resort. It was quite dark now, and her figure disappeared almost at once.

"We'd better follow her," Pauley said in Jem's ear, as the band kicked into more classic rock. "I have her bag and phone. Let's bring it to her so she can light her way, or else she might break a leg in the dark."

Even with the full moon shining over the sea, it was pitch black within less than a hundred yards of the tiki torches. When Micki heard footsteps and whirled to see who was following her, she sighed with relief to realize it was only Jem and Pauley.

"Sorry, ladies. You caught me running away."

"Let's get you some light," Jem said, training her mobile's torch beam at Micki's feet. "Why are you running away? You were amazing!"

"You were!" Pauley agreed. "I'm terribly envious, if I'm being honest. What's wrong?"

"I have terrible stage fright. Singing in public makes me have to wee. Bad," Micki gasped, picking up the pace. "No more talking till we find the toilets!"

CHAPTER ELEVEN

Shiver Me Timbers

Jem had never thought of her friend as inhibited in any way, so the revelation that Micki suffered from stage fright came as a surprise. In the lavatory, she locked herself in a stall and showed no inclination to come back out. Finally, Jem and Pauley took the hint and went outside to wait.

"Maybe she's having a full-blown anxiety attack in there," Pauley suggested.

"I don't know. She slings pints every night, tells off gobby fishermen twice her size, and will ask anyone about anything," Jem said. "The whole reason we're friends is because she kept poking at my shell until she broke through. But I guess taking a big risk in public takes a different kind of courage."

"Yeah. Explains why she broke out the tequila before asking to sing with the band." Pauley sighed. "If I could sing that way, I wouldn't be afraid of anything. I always wanted to have a talent like that. With that kind of talent, I could've done something with my life."

"Uh-huh. I thought you were going to try and be more positive? Keep talking that way and I'll grass to Rhys," Jem said. "He'll pack you off to the non-religious nunnery for used-up old husks. Speaking of him… does he have a girlfriend on Tresco?" She kept her voice light.

Pauley shrugged. "If he does, it isn't serious."

Jem wanted to follow up immediately with, "Why do you say that?" but demanding additional details didn't align with the aura of benign indifference she wanted to project.

Rhys had been Jem's first boyfriend. But although their sexual awakening had happened in tandem, unfolding over the summer when she was fourteen and he was sixteen, there had been no consummation. That was probably why a powerful magnetism persisted between them—the sense of a promise as yet unfulfilled. Over the last twenty years, their lives had gone in very different directions. Why shouldn't Rhys have a girlfriend? Why shouldn't Jem stop dodging Hack and see what he had to offer?

"Oh." Jem sighed, remembering. "I just realized Hack never showed up. He asked me to save a dance for him."

"I'm sure he's still working the case. Who knows, maybe the police have already solved it," Pauley said. The wind picked up, and she shivered. "I'll bet the water temp has dropped a few degrees. Micki won't be happy when we have to wade back. Do you have blankets stowed on *Bellatrix*?"

"No, but I have a paraffin heater. Once we're aboard, you two will be warm before you know it."

"There she is!" Pauley called as Micki emerged from the bathrooms. "Ready to trek back to Old Grimsby Bay?"

"I reckon. Sorry to always be dragging you from one bog to another."

"Are you daft? That's every trip for this one." Jem nodded at Pauley.

"My memoir shall be called *Pauley Gwyn: In Search of a Loo*." She hooked her arm in Micki's. "Ooh, feel that breeze. Let's walk fast to warm up. I promise not to interrogate you about your singing career until we're safely aboard ship."

✳

They made good time across country. As they passed the ruins of King Charles's Castle, a glow of artificial light became visible from the beach below. Jem and her friends paused to look over the staging area, which was lit with portable floodlights. A white plastic tarp had been spread out for evidence collection, but Jem's farsighted eyes could pick out nothing but the bits of flotsam Micki had discovered hours ago. The dive team appeared to have already left and the forensic field techs were in the process of packing up.

"Stop!" PC Robbins shone her halogen flashlight into their faces as they descended the hill.

"Hey!" Jem and the others cringed, covering their eyes.

"Oh, it's you lot." PC Robbins switched off her torch. "We didn't know when to expect you back. Hack," she called over her shoulder to a figure loading gear into the RIB. "Here's Ms. Jago and two other females!"

"Mel, you know my name," Pauley said.

"I'm Micki Latham. We've met at least twice," Micki said.

PC Robbins pretended not to hear. As scrupulously professional as PC Newt was loose-lipped, she rarely got personal on the job. At the moment, she appeared to be practicing the impenetrable blank expression that seemed to be mandatory for law enforcement.

"Hiya, ladies." Hack climbed up to meet them, trying to keep to the gorse and heather but nevertheless almost falling thanks to a particularly slippery patch of mud. If he kept on wearing those cowboy boots, the islands would keep on making him pay for it.

"Perfect timing," he declared, pretending he hadn't almost slipped. "If you'd come any sooner, we would've made you wait out of sight, over by the resort. If you'd left it any later, you would've missed me."

Jem laughed. "You're never short of confidence, are you?"

"Would have missed me setting off in the RIB, I mean," he amended, grinning. "Or did you fancy braving the cold water when you could let me run you over to your little boat, safe and dry?"

"It *is* perfect timing," Micki said, clapping her hands.

Pauley eyed the RIB doubtfully. "I'm just gonna ask. Is that thing rated to carry all of us?"

"That little jewel is rated to carry two and a half tons," Hack said proudly. "It can handle you, me, Jem, Micki *and* the equipment without springing a leak."

With PC Robbins staying behind to mind the scene, Jem and her friends donned life vests and helped Hack push the boat halfway into the surf. Holding the hem of her lacy dress above the water, Pauley climbed in first, followed by Micki, then Jem.

Giving the boat a final shove, Hack got aboard by vaulting over the gunwale like a gymnast on a pommel horse. He landed hard, giving everyone a mild splash, but they were too grateful for the ride to complain. Thumbing the ignition, he set off toward *Bellatrix*. The RIB's top speed was forty-five miles per hour, but during his short stint in the Isles of Scilly, Hack had learned to respect the sea. He proceeded to *Bellatrix* at a sedate pace.

"Where'd PC Newt get to?" Micki asked.

"Interviewing a potential witness. The station received a couple of anonymous tips after Castleberry's death was announced to the media."

"So you *aren't* Johnny No Mates, the local yokel," Jem said, meaning how Devon & Cornwall viewed Hack.

"Not completely. The mainland murder squad is in control, obviously, but they didn't object to letting us locals chase down leads," Hack said. "Especially when those leads are likely to be pranks, or calls from sickos who get off on pretending they have information. You know. Attention-seekers. Hero syndrome."

"What's hero syndrome?" Micki called over the motor's hum. Hack, seated too far away to hear, signaled for her to wait until he'd come up alongside *Bellatrix*'s aft section and cut the engine.

"Hero syndrome comes up sometimes when the police set up a tip line or make a public appeal," he explained, helping Micki board, though she was agile and could have managed it alone. "There are people who don't get enough excitement in life, or don't feel appreciated.

"They call and claim they've worked out how it happened. Or pretend they're psychic and saw a vision about the murderer's whereabouts," Hack continued, helping Pauley next. With him steadying her from behind and Micki offering a hand up top, she made it aboard *Bellatrix* in one go.

"Sometimes hero syndrome goes even farther," Hack went on. "There are firefighters who commit arson, then join the brigade to put out the fire. And coppers who commit crimes, only to turn around and 'solve' them by fitting up someone else." Taking Jem's hand, Hack lifted it as if he might kiss it. He didn't, though. He just held it, looking into her eyes and smiling his rakish smile.

"Any other hero syndrome facts?" she asked.

"I'm trying to think of some. Just to prolong the moment."

"Missed you at the Pirate Extravaganza."

"I know. Sorry. Give me a rain check on that dance?"

Before Jem could answer, Rhys's face popped into her mind: firm chin, sensuous mouth, and dark blue eyes like the depths of the sea. It wasn't a new experience. It had happened to her time and again, over the years, whenever she felt attracted to someone new. Only now, it wasn't the memory of her sixteen-year-old boyfriend. It was the image of a real person, here in the Scillies, only a phone call or boat ride away.

Hack was waiting for her. Pushing thoughts of Rhys away, she said, "You bet." It felt good to take that risk, and see the immediate delight in Hack's face.

Leaning closer, he asked, "Can I kiss you?"

A pleasant little shiver went up the back of her neck. "In front of the peanut gallery?"

He dismissed Micki and Pauley with a shake of the head. "Forget them. There's a full moon. And stars. *Stargazer*." His voice dropped low on the nickname, with a sexy growl no one had ever given it.

She nodded, and he kissed her. It was gentle, just a brush of his lips on hers, but the shiver intensified. Suddenly she wanted that dance here, now, under the moon and stars. That dance—and more.

Slipping an arm around her waist, Hack pulled her closer, parting his lips to deepen the kiss. Reluctantly, she broke away, smiling so he wouldn't be stung by her retreat.

"Rain check," he said firmly.

"I promise."

Once Jem was aboard *Bellatrix*, she found Micki and Pauley standing with their backs to her, pointedly studying the dark shape of Bryher a few hundred yards away.

"Goodbye, Hack!" she called down to him. That was her friends' cue to turn and join in, thanking him for sparing them a cold, wet walk.

"My pleasure, ladies! Take care." Gunning the RIB's engine, Hack wheeled it around in a practiced arc, making for Tresco's stony shore.

"He's come a long way with seamanship," Micki said.

"And he's every bit as fine as the first day I saw him," Pauley added. "How was the kiss?"

Jem headed for the wheelhouse. She didn't intend to answer the question, but a phrase escaped her nonetheless. "Shiver me timbers."

CHAPTER TWELVE

Prime Suspect

Jem fell into her work as she always did, grateful for another week among the Gwyn family collection. She loved many things about her job as a Special Collections Librarian, not least that the majority of it was done under little to no supervision. She answered to the Royal Institute of Cornwall, of course. She also had a direct supervisor, Mr. Atherton, a nervous bow-tie-and-sweater-vest type who often soliloquized like a character in a Victorian novel. He could be thorny at times—the last time she'd discovered a corpse, he'd had the vapors and threatened to sack her—but she'd learned to let him pitch the occasional wobbly without taking it too personally. Apart from appeasing him, Jem set her own schedule, reported in as she saw fit, and handled coordination between the various scholarly collections that might like to examine her finds.

The library at Lyonesse House was a remarkable place. The wallpaper was a French turquoise color Jem adored, its pattern hand-drawn with gilt accents. On two walls, the shelves climbed all the way to the sixteen-foot ceiling. Made from elder wood, those shelves were mismatched, added by successive Gwyns as the collection grew and grew. Libraries are always special rooms. Intended to contain and protect knowledge, most are also meant to be beautiful. To feed the eyes and the soul with graceful lines and soft, inviting silence. That wasn't the Gwyn family library. Basically, it was nothing but a giant book hoard. And it was glorious.

When Jem and Pauley were girls, the late Mrs. Gwyn had permanently locked them out—an eminently reasonable act, considering they'd been a pair of savage little monkeys that couldn't be trusted around nice things. It was deliciously ironic that Jem had grown up to be a lover of old books, papers, maps, and antiquarian ephemera in general; now that Mrs. Gwyn was gone, it fell to Jem to protect the three-hundred-and-fifty-year-old collection.

On the Thursday after Hermie Castleberry was found dead, Jem was once again reorganizing Captain Mortimer Gwyn's Civil War-era letters and documents. Every time she thought she'd definitively arranged them, another letter fell out of a book or a new diary was discovered tucked in a box of maps. The growing tranche of papers shed new light on the political climate and international dealings of the Isles of Scilly during that era. Captain Gwyn, once viewed as a staunch Royalist, now appeared to be a man who maintained an open dialogue with the Parliamentarians, too. He'd been determined to survive the Civil War with his fortune and property intact, no matter which side ultimately won.

In addition to Captain Gwyn, Jem felt she was coming to know his son, Sir Declan Gwyn. A literate and thoughtful man, his diaries turned the popular image of murderous Cornish wreckers on its head.

The idea of wrecking, or deliberately causing ships to steer into rocks so the cargo might be stolen, was a notion so firmly established in the British consciousness, even modern newspapers treated the legend as fact. It had a long pedigree; Daniel Defoe had called Scillonians "so greedy, and eager for the prey," while William Falconer's 1762 poem *The Shipwreck* had popularized the image of "grim hellhounds" luring ships to their destruction via false lights.

Sir Declan's diaries mentioned several shipwrecks, but there was nothing about missing cargo or mariners found on the beach with their throats cut. In fact, Sir Declan noted that several sailors had been rescued by the people of St. Mary's and St. Morwenna. His records were meticulous and precise. All of the saved individuals were listed by name, along with the name of the wrecked vessel and the day the rescue occurred.

Hermie's corpse was a bit like the wrecker legend, Jem thought, realizing it for the first time. *Family Man* was sunk, he was washed ashore, and his throat was cut. Is it possible he wasn't killed because of who he was, or any enemies he made, but just because someone decided to wreck the boat? And maybe steal whatever cargo was aboard?

Over the past few days, she'd thought of Hermie many times. The wire-rimmed spectacles, the missing ring finger, Roddy Levitt's comment that his former friend "had to know he was on borrowed time"—they were all tantalizing, and many times she'd stopped herself from ringing Hack and doing her best to casually pump him for information. Once she'd even caught herself on the brink of texting Kenzie, her thirteen-year-old informant, to see if she'd overheard anything juicy from Randy Andy. Talk about a bad influence. Besides, Hermie's death was really none of her business. If Mr. Atherton heard of her mixed up in another local murder, he'd go into conniptions.

It was past five o'clock, and Jem's stomach was beginning to complain. Her eyes were bleary, too. Was it possible her reading glasses were no longer strong enough? She was only thirty-three, and her distance vision was still sharper than average. Yet it seemed like another trip to the eye doctor was in her future.

I wonder if Pauley would be up for dinner in the Square. Plus a Mr. Whippy cone to end on. Now that the Ice Cream Hut's reopened, we all need to buy something daily to get it going strong again.

Pauley was quite a good cook, and more than capable of whipping up a delicious meal each and every night. But now that she was finally emerging from her depression, Jem thought it was important for her to get out and about as much as possible. Besides, St. Morwenna had a brand new business to support.

Wired Java, the coffee shop/Wi-Fi café, had given up the ghost and been replaced by Pirate's Pizza. With a name like that, everyone's first priority had been to make sure Bart the Ferryman had nothing to do with it. Fortunately, the similarity of themes was purely a coincidence, and the new owner was a recent transplant from York. Early reports were positive, but if St. Morwennians wanted Pirate's Pizza to survive longer than Wired Java, they needed to support it. Jem was perfectly willing to do her part.

A loud creak signaled the opening of the library door. Thinking Pauley had read her mind and come to declare it officially dinnertime, Jem looked up with a smile. But the person who entered was Hack.

"Oh! Hiya." Closing her book, Jem got to her feet. She had a long habit of reading cross-legged on the floor, and doubted she'd ever outgrow it. "It's half-five. Still in uniform?"

"Justice never sleeps," Hack said.

"You're like Batman. *Hack*-man," Jem said, making it sound like an action movie advert. She expected him to be amused. Instead, he took a deep breath, closed the library door, and regarded Jem warily.

"Who died?" The instant she said the words, she wanted them back. "Wait. Nobody else died, did they?"

"No. But I came to tell you there's been a break in the case. A witness came forward."

"That's great. Isn't it?" Jem's eyes narrowed. "Do *not* say you're here to arrest me, or I swear, I'll kick you in the goolies."

He chuckled weakly. "No. Not at all. Only I wanted you to hear it from me first. Rhys Tremayne has been arrested for the murder of Hermie Castleberry."

Jem stared at him.

"It only just happened." Hack cleared his throat. "I accompanied DS Conrad and his team from Devon & Cornwall to the lighthouse. Rhys agreed to sit down and answer our questions. Conrad explained the witness's allegations and the corroboration gathered over the last few days. At the end of the interview, Conrad read him the caution and placed him under arrest."

"What are the allegations?"

Hack looked unhappy. "I can't disclose the details."

"What sort of corroboration?"

He didn't answer.

"Did you find a murder weapon?"

"Jem, I'm sorry, but I absolutely cannot share anything, except what I could reasonably dictate to a reporter. This isn't my investigation, it's DS Conrad's. He determined there was sufficient evidence to arrest Rhys as the prime suspect."

"But you disagreed," she said.

"No. Had I been in charge, I would've done the same thing."

Jem began to cast about the library. First on Captain Mortimer's gargantuan mahogany desk, then under the ten-foot metal ladder, an inelegant but effective way to reach the library's uppermost shelves.

"Jem, what are you doing?"

"Looking for my bag. I need to get to St. Mary's and have Rhys tell me what the hell is going on. Unless next you're going to say I'm not allowed to visit him?"

Hack grimaced. "Come on, Jem. I'm not trying to aggravate you. I'm trying to save you the shock of watching it on telly, or hearing it gossiped about in the Square."

"Ah!" Pouncing on her handbag, Jem seized it so roughly half the contents flew out and she had to bend to retrieve them. Her pulse thudded in her ears, and her cheeks grew hot.

Slower breaths, she told herself, fighting to modulate her breathing. *I won't melt down in front of Hack. I won't.*

"Any road, Rhys isn't being held at Hugh Town Station," Hack continued. "He's in Exeter, at the HQ. Once he's processed, the

CPS will decide whether or not to charge him. It's almost certain they will. In which case, Rhys will go before a judge and either be given bail or be remanded to HM Prison Exeter to await trial."

"But this is absurd," Jem burst out, throwing her bag down on the floor and spilling its contents all over again. "Rhys went to Tresco to meet Hermie Castleberry. He was wearing a suit, for heaven's sake, which he *never* does. He waited around The Ruin for hours. He was there so long, even Stuart, the manager, felt bad for him. He had no idea Hermie was dead. I'm the one who told him."

"Rhys was close to Hermie? They were good friends?" Hack asked. He didn't sound genuinely curious. He spoke in the carefully neutral tone of a lawman who was nudging a witness toward self-incrimination.

"No. Hermie was Rhys's quote-unquote agent, as I'm sure you know, and he wasn't doing much for him. It was a crappy business relationship on the brink of blowing up. But that's not the stuff of murder!"

"Crappy business relationships end in violence every day," Hack said. "Especially if one party feels cheated. Not just of money. If they feel humiliated. If they think their hopes were cruelly raised, then dashed."

"Fine. But if Rhys was all that angry, he could've sued the bastard. Maybe he planned to sue him," Jem said. "That last meeting at The Ruin was meant to be make-or-break. You should have seen him, dressed up like the dog's dinner, which he *never* does—"

"Jem," Hack broke in, "try and think of this unemotionally."

Jem stared at him. Her cheeks grew warmer; it felt like her face was on fire.

"Consider this. Let's say Rhys was involved with Hermie's murder. The next day, he went to The Ruin right around the time anyone could reasonably expect traces of *Family Man*, or Hermie himself, to wash ashore. The place was packed. He's a good-looking man in a suit—sure to be remembered, especially by anyone who knew him and was surprised by his get-up. He told everyone he was waiting for Hermie, which created the impression he believed him to still be alive, and stayed so long the staff could be counted on to swear to his presence. Doesn't that sound like the actions of a man trying to establish an alibi?"

It took Jem a moment to reply. Then she said, "Did you just tell me to *try* and think of this unemotionally?"

Hack grimaced. "It's just an expression. One I use sometimes when people are getting out of hand. I didn't—"

"People? Or women?"

No answer.

"Really, I'm interested." Jem folded her arms across her chest. "In the whole of your life, have you ever asked a man to *try* and think unemotionally?"

He tried to wave it away. "Look. This has gone way off track. I wish I could sit down and lay out the entire case for you. But you know I can't do that. You won't be in the dark forever. Before long, you'll be able to visit Rhys. He might even make bail and come home to await trial. I know you two have, erm, sort of a lingering…" He tailed off.

Jem's pulse no longer pounded in her ears. Her breathing had dropped back to its normal rate. She was so icily furious, she felt plunged into a deep freeze.

"Hack. Let's say Rhys killed Hermie. Why would he stay on Tresco after the fact? He could've taken his runabout home to St. Morwenna and no one would've been the wiser.

"Then there's Hermie's boat. Rhys wouldn't have sunk it in the channel. He would've known how quickly it would be found and recovered. And since he does bodywork, he has connections. I'm sure he'd have heard about boatyards willing to handle stolen vessels. If Rhys had wanted to dispose of *Family Man*, he could've made it disappear forever."

Hack seemed about to interject something, but Jem plowed straight through. "Of course, we don't know why the boat sank. I mean—you might, if it's already been raised and inspected, but I don't. But pretend Rhys was on board. Pretend he killed Hermie and, for whatever reason, realized it was sinking. Rhys would never, ever have weighted down the body the way I described. The set-up was ridiculous. Borne as a result of panic, stupidity, or both. There must've been a hundred better ways to hide the body."

Hack sighed.

"What? Didn't the divers recover the chest and the ropes?"

"No. Maybe they went out with the current. Or maybe…"

"Maybe what?"

"Maybe they were never there." His voice took on that law enforcement monotone she now despised. "You didn't have proper diving equipment, Jem. Who knows what you saw."

She glared at him.

"Listen. I don't deny that compared to me, or any off-islander, Rhys is an expert on boats and local waterways. He seemed to be thinking clearly the next day, when he was trying to establish an alibi. But there's no reason to assume he was thinking clearly when he killed Hermie."

"You think he was mad with rage?"

"I think he was under the influence."

Jem's stomach dropped.

"He's been arrested for public intoxication many times," Hack continued inexorably. "I know he tells people he's sober now, but there's no indication he ever completed a formal rehab program. And he lives alone, so no one can vouch for his day-to-day sobriety."

"Do you have evidence that Rhys was drunk Friday night?"

"I can't share evidence with you," Hack burst out, revealing the depth of his frustration for the first time. More calmly, he continued, "But I can share the benefit of my experience. Last year, I worked a case where the murder was committed by a black-out drunk. The perp woke up in custody the next morning completely unaware of what he'd done. He was a reasonably intelligent man—when sober. Under the influence, he committed one of the stupidest, sloppiest crimes I've ever seen. This isn't unusual. It might not be the oldest story in law enforcement, but it's in the top five."

Jem felt as if he'd slapped her. On returning to St. Morwenna, she'd been disturbed to learn that Rhys, like his late father, had struggled with alcoholism. She'd taken a sort of pride in knowing he hadn't surrendered to it. According to Pauley, he was about seven months sober. That was the longest unbroken dry stretch of his adult life. Now Hack was presenting her with a logical scenario—an *unemotional* scenario, damn him—that not only explained the strange details of Hermie's death, but wiped away Jem's pride in Rhys's accomplishment.

Only if I choose to believe Hack, Jem thought. *And I don't have to.*

But even as part of her was ready to disregard Hack's perspective altogether, troubling details from the pirate festival nagged at her. During lunch at The Ruin, Rhys had evinced no surprise or sympathy when told of Hermie's death. He hadn't even asked for any of the gory details. As someone who knew Hermie, and had a negative business relationship with him, that seemed abnormal.

Then there's the artist's knife, Jem thought. Rhys had immediately denied it was his. He hadn't looked at it or even touched it until Pauley showed him the Piranesi logo, forcing him to admit the tool was his. Then he'd said it must have been lying around the site for weeks, a claim which instantly struck her as unlikely.

This is day six of the investigation, Jem thought. *DS Conrad and his Devon & Cornwall team must have found hard evidence if they were confident enough to make such a quick arrest. And transport Rhys not to Hugh Town Station, but to Exeter HQ.*

After a moment, Hack said, "I notice you didn't ask me if he confessed while being taken into custody."

His tone chilled her. Did he want her to beg for that detail? Even after saying over and over again that he wasn't at liberty to divulge investigatory specifics?

Jem lifted her chin. "No need."

"Why not?"

"Because I know he didn't." The statement was based on pure loyalty. Jem heard her emotions ring through it, loud and clear, but she didn't care. "Rhys didn't kill anyone. I'm sure of it."

Hack regarded her with what Jem thought was a speculative look. For a heartbeat, she wondered if he was about to reveal that Rhys had indeed confessed to murder.

I don't think it's that, she decided. *Maybe he just wanted to see how far I would go to defend Rhys.*

"Right." Hack cleared his throat. "I'd better get back to the station. One last thing. A message from Rhys."

Stomach twisting, Jem braced herself for the coup de grâce.

"He wants you to look after his dog while he's away."

She let out her breath. "Buck?"

"Yes. You'll find him tied up outside the glasshouse. You're welcome to go and get him anytime. But," Hack said sternly, holding her gaze, "the lighthouse and cottage are off-limits until the forensics investigation is complete. I know you like to snoop. Don't test me on this, Jem. If I find out you've meddled inside the police perimeter, I'll arrest you myself."

CHAPTER THIRTEEN

Finger Guns and a Faux Gangster

Within about five minutes of Hack's departure, Jem's frozen rage cracked wide open, and she began second-guessing everything she'd said. Fortunately, as she informed Pauley about Rhys's arrest, her friend reacted exactly the same way, with a mix of scorn and outrage. If Jem had been wrong to insist Rhys was innocent and the police were mistaken, well, she wasn't wrong alone. By six o'clock, the two of them set off for Tremayne Lighthouse to retrieve Rhys's little mongrel, Buck.

"I thought better of Hack," Pauley huffed. They were walking along the Byway, a paved pathway that bisected St. Morwenna from the southeastern Square to the island's most northwesterly point, Porthennis Beach. The western sky was a majestic orange, and the wind off the sea was beginning to cool.

"I know he's just doing his job," Jem said unhappily. "But his attitude made me so mad. And he cautioned me against snooping."

"If snooping was illegal, the whole of England would be banged up," Pauley said. "Why do you think everyone watches mysteries on telly? Because when we can't snoop in real life, we do it vicariously."

"I'm hoping this is all a stupid mistake," Jem said. "But how can it be, when they went ahead and transported Rhys to Exeter? They obviously expect him to be charged right away."

Jem had more to say, but the popularity of the Byway constrained her. As they walked, they passed all sorts: emmets taking in the sea view, local kids riding bikes, and mature islanders kitted out in trackies and trainers, walking for health.

Among the locals, everyone knew Pauley, the last Gwyn heiress, and most of them knew Jem. Thus, they had to keep interrupting their private conversation, forcing a smile and a polite response to every greeting. Jem didn't think their acting would win them any BAFTAs; their rapid pace and short replies left many curious glances in their wake. Tomorrow, when everyone knew that Rhys had been arrested for murder, they would look back on Jem and Pauley's behavior and dissect it down to the molecular level. As her gran had often said, "What would we talk about on St. Morwenna, if we didn't talk about one another?"

When they were halfway to the lighthouse and could finally talk again, Pauley asked, "So what's your plan?"

"For Buck?"

"For Rhys. To find out who really killed Hermie Castleberry."

"I don't know. I can't stop thinking about that artist's knife."

"He's painted sunsets all over the islands. It's a coincidence," Pauley said firmly. "I'm glad you didn't turn it in to Hack."

"I would've. It just never occurred to me that anything belonging to Rhys might actually be connected to the murder," Jem said. "As far as snooping, I reckon the best place to start is with Hermie's private life. That orange canister suggested he lived a dangerous life. I wonder if Georgia will talk to me."

"Georgia's on record as the doting wife to the perfect husband," Pauley reminded her.

"Yeah. But even if she tries her best to snow me, she still might accidentally give something away. And she's part of 'Library World'," Jem said, using her unofficial term for that vast web of librarians, assistants, volunteers, and donors that kept books and reading accessible to all.

"Maybe she can tell me more about Roddy Levitt," Jem continued. "He said Hermie had to know he was on borrowed time. You could interpret that as blaming Hermie for his own death. Putting himself in danger, anyway."

Pauley looked startled. "When did you talk to Roddy?"

"You know him?"

"By sight. He's our age but does his best to look like an old man. Where did you meet him?"

"I didn't meet him. I eavesdropped on him while we were at the festival, in the drinks queue," Jem said. "He said Hermie knew he was on borrowed time. Someone else said it was bold of Roddy to speak ill of the dead. It sounded as if Roddy introduced Hermie to his crowd, and then wanted to wash his hands of the whole thing. He called Hermie a fabulist."

"He did? Pot, meet kettle," Pauley retorted. "Roddy lives in Hugh Town, but he has a gallery in Penzance. Very prickly, very artier-than-thou. Roddy was the first gallery owner Rhys ever approached about a showing. Apparently he was a ginormous git about it."

Jem took that in. Immediately a scenario occurred to her: Roddy Levitt had killed Hermie. He'd befriended the newcomer to the Cornish art scene, vouching for him among the established brokers. Then as Hermie's habit of fleecing unknown artists became widely known, pretentious Roddy had done away with his former associate to save his own reputation. Now he was content to let Rhys, whom he already disliked for whatever reason, take the fall.

Well, isn't that neat, easy, and about as deep as a thimble? Jem thought, annoyed with herself. The truth was, she already believed Rhys was innocent. That didn't mean she could jump to conclusions or go after the first convenient scapegoat.

No wonder Hack's comment about thinking unemotionally infuriated me. It touched a nerve.

"Who was the other enemy of Hermie someone mentioned?" Jem asked, surprised to find herself drawing a blank on the name.

Apparently, the shock of Rhys's arrest and her fight with Hack had overloaded her normally reliable memory.

"That was—" Pauley broke off as two people came toward them on the Byway. The first loped along with the marionette jerkiness of a gangly teen. The second trailed by several meters, shuffling at a far less energetic pace.

With the sun behind him and his face in shadow, Jem initially took the first for Hermie's stepson, Leo. But as she and Pauley closed the distance between the two newcomers, Jem saw the gangly teen was darker than Leo, with a clear complexion and features that suggested Pacific Islander heritage. His black hair fell to his shoulders and he had a nice smile, all the more endearing for his somewhat crooked teeth.

"Hiya, Ms. Gwyn. Hiya, Ms. Gwyn's friend," he said pleasantly.

"Hiya, Simon. Jem, this is Simon Weatherby. He lives in Hugh Town. Simon, this is Jem Jago. She's a librarian working on my family's books and papers."

"I've heard of you. The super sleuth." Simon made finger guns and shot them at Jem, *pew-pew-pew*. "Cool, cool. So are you cross that the police already solved the Candlewick murder?"

Before Jem or Pauley could reply, the second figure caught up to Simon. Hanging back, he remained a step or two behind the boy, keeping his head down and avoiding Jem and Pauley's gaze as a small child might look away from unfamiliar adults. He was dressed like a teen, in surf shorts and plastic sandals. He wore his hair down to his shoulders and had cultivated a straggly mustache, or something meant to be a mustache, over his upper lip. But years of sun damage had left crinkles around his eyes and a deep line across his forehead. If Simon was still south of twenty, this other man was pushing forty.

"And who's this?" Pauley asked Simon, nodding to the man. To a casual observer, she would no doubt sound polite, but Jem recognized the suspicion in her tone. Although impatient to reach their destination, she suspected this disreputable-looking man was the reason Pauley had stopped to engage Simon instead of hurrying past.

"Him? That's Noah," Simon said, as casually as if someone had asked after a stray dog.

"Noah?" Pauley repeated the name so pointedly, its owner finally looked up. His smile was instant, like a flagman's sign spinning from STOP to GO.

"Hello, Noah. I'm Pauley Gwyn." She put out her hand, forcing the man to give it an unconvincing shake. "I've known Simon since he was born. But I don't know you. What brings you to the Scillies?"

He laughed, a little heh-heh-heh as artificial as his smile. "I live here. On Bryher."

"Really? Where?" Pauley didn't even try to sound as if she was casually inquiring. Rather, she flicked her eyes from Noah to Simon, as if transparently considering all the reasons a grown man might follow a youngster across St. Morwenna.

"Oh, don't be like that, Mrs. Gwyn," Simon said. "Noah's very cool. Couch surfer extraordinaire. He's been kipping with my friend Barney ever since his landlord illegally evicted him."

"Illegally evicted him?" Jem repeated. The quick invocation of a sob story made her instantly suspicious. "I hope you reported that to the authorities. I can put you in touch with Sergeant Hackman at Hugh Town Station."

"Illegal but sort of a gray area," Noah hedged. "He said we were squatting. But Article Twenty-Five of the Universal Declaration of Human Rights says adequate housing is a human right."

"Which makes it the law," Simon agreed wisely. "Anyway, Noah's cool. Too bad you didn't get to solve the murder," he added, smiling at Jem as if discussing the weather.

"What do you mean?" Jem asked.

"We just came from Crescent Beach." Simon jerked a thumb over his shoulder.

"We watched as the police entered Tremayne Cottage," Noah added. "We could see everything from below. They were in there for half an hour, and then they brought out Rhys Tremayne in cuffs."

"The girls didn't like that," Simon said. "They were all, uh-oh, he's too pretty to go to prison!"

Noah emitted that heh-heh-heh again, like a toady laughing for his boss's weak pun. Whatever his relationship to the boy, it seemed that young Simon currently had the upper hand.

Impatient to move on and irritated by Simon and Noah's evident unconcern for Rhys, Jem gave Pauley the side-eye, trying to signal it was time to go. But Pauley wasn't out of questions yet.

"Simon, you turned up at exactly the right moment. I was just about to tell Jem about Jimmy Franks. Do you still work for him at Franks All Marine?"

"Bullseye." Simon brought out the finger guns again. "The pay's no good, but hey, that's all right, cause the work sucks!"

Pauley smiled tolerantly. "I suppose you work there, too, Noah?"

"Work?" Noah blinked at her. "No. Corporate world's not my style."

"Anyway, Simon, maybe you can help me out," Pauley said in a confidential tone that made the boy lean forward.

"It's about Hermie Castleberry's boat. The one that sank, *Family Man*. Someone told me Jimmy Franks sold Hermie that boat. And Hermie was way behind on his payments. Is that right?"

Simon winced. "Oh, no can do, Ms. Gwyn. Mr. Franks says what happens at All Marine stays at All Marine. If he catches me gossiping, I'll be sleeping with the fishes."

In her mind's eye, Jem had a flash of the weighted ice chest on the seabed; the way those empty wingtips had swayed at the ends of their rope tethers, like the tentacles of some well-shod jellyfish. Hermie really had slept with the fishes, at least for a while.

Noah nudged Simon. "Last water taxi to HT departs in ten minutes."

"Yeah, we'd best be off," Simon said. "Bye, Ms. Gwyn! Bye, super sleuth!" He blew them away with another volley of finger guns. Noah mumbled something that sounded like "Sayonara" and trudged after his friend, picking up his feet with apparent effort. Either he really wanted to make that water taxi, or he was ready to get away from Jem and Pauley. Soon they disappeared around the corner, heading for the Square and St. Morwenna's little quay.

"I do *not* like that man," Pauley said.

"Did you get a whiff of him?" Jem asked. It didn't take a sleuth, super or otherwise, to recognize that particular herbal smell.

"Yes. It's not hard to guess what he sells to kids like Simon. And now he's couch surfing in the Scillies. I plan on speaking to Hack," Pauley said. "After I forgive him, that is."

As they resumed their walk toward the lighthouse, Jem told Pauley, "That was clever of you. Now I remember what Leo said. That Jimmy Franks had been calling their home a lot, leaving messages for Hermie. And Hermie told Stuart he was hurting financially because of the new boat. It was a good guess that Hermie bought the boat from All Marine."

"I suppose. Didn't get us anywhere, though," Pauley said. "And maybe I shouldn't have put Simon on the spot like that. Jimmy Franks is one of those people we all have to deal with, living the island life. Nobody gives us better prices. But he's an arse, full stop. One of those leering, gobby, full-of-himself guys who thinks he's sex on a stick. Talks like an American gangster."

"You're kidding."

"Nope. I reckon he watched *Goodfellas* one too many times. Woke up believing he's a made man from New Jersey."

"What's he look like? Robert DeNiro?"

Pauley giggled. "More like Mr. Bean. Without his winning personality."

"You're having me on."

"I'm not. Maybe you can dream up a reason to go to All Marine and talk to him," Pauley said. "I know you don't usually get seasick, but pick up some Avomine pills just in case. Jimmy fancies himself a ladies' man. It'll turn your stomach."

CHAPTER FOURTEEN

Buck the Wonder Dog

Rhys Tremayne's cottage sat on St. Morwenna's highest point, overlooking Crescent Beach to the northwest and the island's deep green heart to the southeast. The lighthouse had been designed for a solitary keeper, and would have been enough for a single man of modest needs. The nearby cottage, a two-story affair that was white stucco with a gray-tiled roof, had been built for the larger families of the pre-Second World War period. With its charming chimney pots, rough-stone fence, and neat white accents, it would've been ideal for an upscale rental. Jem marveled at Rhys's determination to keep his family home. He'd worked two jobs ever since leaving school, paid for the upkeep, and even saved enough to reactivate the lighthouse. At least until Hermie Castleberry swooped in and plucked those hard-earned savings away, like a buzzard seizing a bit of carrion.

As foretold, Rhys's cottage was taped off, the crime scene tape adding an air of foreboding to the ordinarily beautiful landscape. A team of forensic scientists, all of them in head-to-toe whites with matching shoe covers, gloves, and face-shielding hoods, went in and out the front door like ants on a hill.

The scene was guarded by none other than PC Newt, who looked positively mutinous. Jem and Pauley found him sitting at the edge of the perimeter. He'd taken a large, empty clay pot, turned it upside down, and plopped himself down on it. Now he sat with his arms folded and his legs sticking straight out in front of him, like a sulky boy in time out. At the sight of Pauley, however, he brightened.

"Oh! Hey!" He jumped to his feet. "Lovely to see you out and about. I've been worried about you, indoors all summer." Seeming to remember her recent bereavement, he managed to dial back the grin, though his eyes still shone with happiness. "How are you, er, feeling today?"

"Not great, Newt," Pauley snapped. "Finding out a friend's been arrested for murder will do that to you."

"Oh. Of course. Yes. Sorry. You're right," PC Newt said sheepishly. "Don't worry. If he's innocent, and I'm sure he is, it will all come right in the end." After a glance over his shoulder to ensure none of the mainland forensics scientists were in earshot, he added, "They all think they're so smart. Need taking down a peg, if you ask me."

Jem was tempted to remark sarcastically on the notorious stupidity of crime lab professionals, what with their foolish propensity for cataloging, testing, and analyzing vital evidence, etc. Then she realized that PC Newt was probably speaking of Devon & Cornwall in general. Like Hack, he probably felt ignored and perhaps even infantilized by the mainlanders. They'd parachuted into the Scillies with their own detectives, support staff, and best practices, leaving the IoS PD with little to do but sit about on clay pots and sulk. Indiscreet under the best of circumstances, an aggrieved Newt was quite likely to reveal something helpful. Jem just had to encourage him to unburden himself.

"We're here to collect Buck," she said, giving the officer her friendliest smile. "Pauley and I will take him back to Lyonesse House and care for him until Rhys comes home."

"Oh, sure. Poor little mite. Already pining for his master. Follow me." PC Newt led them up the narrow gravel path toward the glasshouse. As they passed, the wind kicked up and the weathervane atop the glasshouse creaked into life, sending St. George and the dragon whirling into combat once again.

The weathervane was cunningly devised. It placed the mounted St. George with his lance on one axis, and the dragon rampant, tail lashing, fire pluming, on the opposite axis. When the breeze stirred them, the saint and his nemesis swung toward one another, always dancing, never closing. It was Jem's favorite feature of the Tremayne compound, and there was something particularly poignant about it today, silhouetted against the pink-orange clouds of sunset.

Is it a sign for me and Rhys? That it will always be round and round, just a lot of near misses, and we'll never get back to what we once had?

It was the first time she'd admitted to herself that she might actually want something more than friendship from Rhys. But were these feelings real? When she was around Hack, she felt one way. When she was around Rhys, old emotions resurfaced, threatening everything new.

Jem wondered if she'd been disconnected from her romantic desires for so long, she no longer could recognize them. For twenty years she'd avoided any man who reminded her of Rhys, keeping her relationships with books deep, and with men shallow. Pauley clearly feared she'd missed her best chances in life while looking after her parents. Had Jem missed any chance at real love while fiercely guarding her heart?

Never mind that. Buck needs me, she thought, hurrying toward the little dog.

She'd never seen him tied up before. Attached to a tree with a length of rope tied to his collar, he lay with his chin atop his paws, looking every bit as disconsolate as PC Newt on his big clay pot. A white mutt with brown patches and the occasional black spot, Buck had bright button eyes and a highly inquisitive nature. Catching sight of Jem and Pauley, he leapt up, barking indignantly. It was clear that he was reporting a very severe incident of dog abuse, and he wanted Jem and Pauley, friends who were always good for a pat on the head or a scritch behind the ears, to take swift action.

"Okay, little man, stop bouncing. Pulling is just going to hurt your neck." Kneeling beside Buck, Jem untied the rope and released the dog. Barking triumphantly, Buck jumped on Jem, almost knocking her over. His pink tongue shot out, and her entire face was subjected to a comprehensive licking. It was a good thing she rarely wore make-up during the day, or Buck's greeting would've resulted in a melted clown face.

"Ah, now, that's what I call sweet," PC Newt told Pauley. "I really am sorry about Rhys, you know. They've got the wrong man, as far as I'm concerned. Rush job. Total rush job."

Jem tried to relocate Buck back to the ground, or at least to shield her mouth from his tongue so she could probe PC Newt further. But the little dog wouldn't have his joy curtailed. Fortunately, Pauley kept PC Newt talking.

"I know he's innocent, full stop. But *why* did they arrest him?"

"Because of the witnesses. And because of the money," PC Newt said.

"What witnesses?"

PC Newt sighed. "One saw Rhys threaten Hermie's life a couple of weeks ago. Another saw Rhys aboard Hermie's boat last Friday. And another saw Rhys on the beach near Hermie's body."

"But *who* are these witnesses? Are they islanders or emmets? What are their names?"

PC Newt looked like it caused him real physical pain to hold anything back. "I can't tell you."

Jem, who'd been listening closely, finally succeeded in disentangling herself from Buck. Rising, she decided to try a different tack on PC Newt.

"About the money. I reckon the teller at Hugh Town Bank thought it was odd for Rhys to deposit so much in euros."

"Yeah," PC Newt said. "He told DS Conrad he found the cash on the beach, and only took what Hermie owed him. He counted it out and left the rest in the canister along with the cocaine. But it—wait. Did I tell you that?"

"Sorry, Newt. I guessed," Jem said gently. "So let me get this straight. Rhys is accused of killing Hermie, stealing his money, sinking the boat, and then going to The Ruin to create an alibi?"

"That's Hack's scenario," PC Newt said. "DS Conrad thinks it's more of a wrecker crime. Hermie got into difficulty because of the storm and the boat sank. He was swept ashore, barely alive. That morning, Rhys carried his easel down to Candlewick Castle to paint and found Hermie. It was too good an opportunity to get revenge and get back the money he thought he was entitled to, so he killed him."

Jem and Pauley exchanged glances. "That's even more ridiculous than Hack's scenario. Why would DS Conrad think that?"

"Because Rhys admitted to it. Going down to the castle to paint, and coming upon the canister full of drugs and money, and Hermie, too." PC Newt looked confused. "I said that, didn't I? Though I probably shouldn't have."

"He admitted it?" Pauley said, stunned.

"Well, not that he killed Hermie," PC Newt replied with the air of someone rapidly tying himself up in knots. "He said Hermie's throat was already cut. But the witness—the other witness—disputes that."

Jem wanted to throw her hands up and demand that PC Newt start all over. Pauley looked ready to actually seize him by the neck and shake him until he agreed to walk them through it again, preferably using a whiteboard and clear diagrams. Sensing their combined frustration, Newt looked alarmed and backed away.

"I've said too much. Yes. Too much. Officially," he added, wagging a finger at them, "I'm not permitted to discuss the details of the case with anyone. Let's just forget this unofficial little chat ever happened."

"We'd never trouble you by asking," Pauley said sweetly. "But we're Rhys's oldest friends. We have to be on his side."

"We're on your side, too," Jem added. "We won't grass on you to Hack or DS Conrad."

"Good." He spared another glance over his shoulder at the white-suited ants marching in and out of the scene. Buck, now roaming on the grass, also seemed momentarily captivated by their movements. Then he put his wet black nose to the ground and started sniffing. Maybe he was trying to pick up his master's trail.

"Forget the witnesses and the other stuff you can't talk about. Just clear up this one detail for me," Jem said. "When Rhys left the pirate festival, he said he was going to change clothes, and take a runabout back to St. Morwenna. He must've stayed overnight with someone. Who was it?"

PC Newt winced. He loved to hobnob and gossip, and he especially enjoyed being the center of attention. But once he realized he was explicitly failing in his duty, he always straightened up and tried to fly right.

"I'm sorry, Ms. Jago. I promised Hack to keep a lid on it. DS Conrad's an absolute monster. Not at all pleasant. But Sergeant Hackman's a good man. I like working for him, and I wouldn't want to lose his confidence."

"Just a name. Please," Jem whispered, while beside her, Pauley threw in a pleading look.

"Sharon MacAfee," PC Newt muttered. "She lives on Tresco in-season. Works at the Abbey Gardens. But you didn't hear it from me."

"Thanks, Newt," Jem said warmly.

"Newt, you're the best," Pauley said, surprising him with a hug. Before he could fully revel in the moment, she released him, calling after Buck, "Where are you going?"

The little dog paid her no heed. Still following his nose, he headed toward a weedy stretch of land between the glasshouse and the lighthouse. It wasn't taped off, probably because there was almost nothing there, apart from a moss-covered stone bench under a gray sallow tree. Propped against the bench was an old shovel.

Eyes on Buck, Jem tried to make sense of everything she knew about Rhys's arrest.

I wonder if that witness owns the wire-rimmed specs I found in the rubble. If only there was a way for me to figure out who it is, and whether or not their word can be trusted.

"Would you look at this?" Pauley called.

Shaken out of her reverie, Jem focused on Buck, whom she'd been watching but not seeing. Under the stone bench, he was digging a hole with the manic determination of a small dog with a big hunch. His tail lashed, his paws worked, and his white-furred legs were getting dirty fast.

"Look at him go! Wonder dog!" PC Newt called, laughing.

"Pick that little rascal up," Jem told Pauley. "Otherwise we'll have to give him a bath the moment we get him home."

Pauley scooped up Buck, who barked in protest, little paws still scraping the air. As she soothed him, her gaze fell upon the shallow hole he'd made, and her smile disappeared.

"Guys. Erm. Come have a look," Pauley said uncertainly, her voice quivering.

With a prickle of foreboding, Jem walked uphill to view Buck's discovery. Propped against the mossy bench, the shovel looked like something out of a time capsule, its wooden handle stained with hard use, its metal scoop pitted with rust. Someone had recently dug a hole; Buck, having sniffed out the disturbed area, had gone looking for buried treasure. Not *too* deeply buried; the soil overlooking Crescent Beach was sandy and loose, with only spotty ground cover holding it together. And the person who'd dug the hole had only delved about a foot.

"What is it?" Pauley asked Jem.

"Don't touch it," PC Newt cried, hurrying over. Peering into the hole, he opened his mouth to pronounce what they were looking at, then closed it again, uncertain.

Jem dropped to one knee. Inside the hole was a pair of gloves. They appeared to be made of fine-grain chainmail, like something belonging to a medieval knight. Each glove was composed of what looked like tiny interwoven steel rings.

"I think they're meant for chefs," Jem said. "To protect their hands from a cut by a sharp knife. Oh, and there's—"

"Don't touch it!" Newt cried.

Jem, who had no intention of using her fingers, snagged a nearby twig and gently flipped one glove aside. Beneath it was a steel kitchen knife. Its long, narrow blade curved to a sharp point.

"A boning knife," Pauley said.

Jem nodded. Her eyes were back on the top glove. Inside its interlocking rings, the palm and fingers were soaked with something that appeared to be dried blood.

CHAPTER FIFTEEN

Sleuthing 101

The next morning, which was Friday, Jem had originally planned to re-enter the world of Sir Declan Gwyn and his wonderfully detailed diaries. There was so much information on the Isles of Scilly in the eighteenth century, an enterprising scholar could easily distill it all into a book. Perhaps even a popular history—the kind of book that interested the general reading public, rather than only academics. It had occurred to Jem that she might be just the person to undertake such a task… when she wasn't brooding over a murder, of course.

Today, murder brooding won out. Gritting her teeth, she undertook the mandatory weekly phone chat with her boss, Mr. Atherton, who was as not-charming as ever, then suffered through a Zoom meeting with two colleagues from London. They were experts in ecclesiastical books from the medieval period, and desired digitally scanned copies of the Gwyn family's oldest Bibles. Ordinarily, a deep dive with fellow Special Collections Librarians was a pleasure, and Jem enjoyed communion with her literary soulmates. But after everything that had happened—the shock of Rhys's arrest, her fight with Hack, the information PC Newt had shared, and the discovery of what might be the murder weapon, as well as a pair of bloody gloves—Jem couldn't keep her mind focused on bosses or Bibles. She wanted answers.

The discovery of the shallowly buried gloves had been an infuriating setback, but what was done was done. Even if Buck hadn't dug them up, Jem had no doubt the forensic team would've eventually widened their survey of the property and noticed the mound of disturbed earth. Whomever had planted the evidence—and Jem was absolutely certain it had been planted—had taken care to leave the shovel propped up by the spot, no doubt to tip off the detectives in case they weren't on top of their game.

Rhys knows every inch of St. Morwenna. If he used those gloves and that knife to kill Hermie, he could've cached them where no one would ever find them. He could've flung them into the sea. It would do more harm than good ringing Hack and telling him this is an obvious fit-up. He'll just say Rhys must have been drunk when he did it.

She didn't like feeling at odds with Hack. He was sexy, funny, and that single kiss they'd shared had been electric. But with Rhys's future at stake, she refused to linger on her own happiness. Clearing Rhys's name had to come first.

By half-eleven, the essentials of Jem's workday were checked off. Now she could spend the rest of the day, and the entire weekend that followed, chasing down leads to her heart's content. She just had to figure out where to start.

She found Pauley inside her usual hub, the kitchen in Lyonesse House's small wing. Sir Mortimer Gwyn had built the original house when he settled on St. Morwenna, then added the larger wing, including the library, as his fortunes rose. His descendants had tacked on the smaller wing, originally meant for servants. Their descendants had modernized it during that ugliest of all decorating eras, the 1970s.

An unhappy vision in avocado and orange, with a lino floor and crudely drawn daisies on the wallpaper, Pauley's kitchen nevertheless had its virtues. It got good light. The landline was there, and the Wi-Fi was strongest there. The back door lead directly to the garden, where she ate half her meals, and her electric kettle occupied the countertop, ever ready for tea.

Today, Pauley sat at the dining nook, laptop in front of her, reading something with interest. Her eyes barely flicked up as Jem dropped heavily into the chair across from her.

"Taking a break?"

"Not a break. I'm done with books. Time to focus on Hermie and Rhys." She sighed, refusing to rehash her worries aloud. She and Pauley had done just that the previous night, and it had resulted in nothing but lost sleep and a gnawing sense of frustration. "What are you doing?"

"Checking the credentials of Rhys's attorney. She's from Legal Aid, but she seems all right. No red flags."

Jem sat up straight. "You've heard from him?"

"Not directly. He can't ring anyone just yet. But I got a message through the island grapevine," Pauley said. "One of the employees at the Exeter Police HQ is a transplanted Scillonian. Rhys asked him to get a message to Carenza at Hugh Town Station. Carenza passed it to Newt, and Newt passed it to me."

"Bless him. He's so good-natured, and he doesn't mind sticking his neck out for a friend. You really have to stop being so abrupt with him."

"Cruel to be kind," Pauley said. "I like Newt. I appreciate him. But I'm not going out on a pity date with him or anyone else. If I butter him up, he'll take it as a sign that we're meant to be, and never stop pestering me."

Jem couldn't argue with that. "So Rhys can't afford a solicitor?"

"No. I reckon Hermie cleaned him out. Rhys's message didn't go into that," Pauley said. "Just that he's fine, he's not worried, and his attorney expects to get him released on bail."

"He's been officially charged with murder then?"

"Yes," Pauley answered softly.

"Well I'm glad he's in good spirits," Jem said. "But why didn't you come and tell me straightaway?"

"I cracked the door of the library, but you were in a virtual meeting. Since it wasn't earth-shattering, I didn't fancy breaking in like the Kool-Aid Man." Pauley tapped the keyboard, brought up a different website, and turned the laptop so Jem could see. It was a public Facebook group called the Isles of Scilly Noticeboard.

"Did you join?" Pauley said.

"Yeah, but I'm always too busy to check it. Are people talking about the murder?"

"Not here. This is more of a tourist-friendly, hashtag Team Scilly kind of place," Pauley said. "But this morning's post about Vera Vet caught my eye."

Jem had heard of Vera Baker, aka "Vera Vet," the Scillies' one and only resident veterinarian. A petite, middle-aged lady with white hair perpetually held in place with matching barrettes, she was well known throughout the islands and parts of the Cornish coast.

"Beautiful bird in distress," Jem murmured, reading the headline. Two pictures accompanied the post. One was a quick, blurry shot of a large brown raptor wrapped in a blanket. The second was of a more quiescent bird in an animal hospital cage, the sort of secure place where patients recovered after treatment or surgery. This creature, which Jem now recognized as a buzzard, was either a satisfied client of Vera Vet, or it was stoned out of its mind on some very good bird drugs.

"What happened to it?" Jem asked.

"I don't know. Do you reckon it's one of the birds that picked over Hermie?" Pauley asked. "I thought scavengers could eat literally anything. Is it possible that Hermie made him sick?"

"You mean, like poison?" Jem asked, her mind whirring. "I suppose it's possible. Until there's an autopsy, we're working on the assumption that Hermie died on the boat when his throat was cut. I don't know why poison would be in the mix, but I suppose that's why the post-mortem checks for everything, rather than assuming what seems obvious."

"Hack isn't going to tell us what the autopsy says," Pauley grimaced, apparently still irritated by their friend's insistence on doing his job in accordance with the law.

"Do you know Vera?"

"Sure. Not well. She's friendly, but crazy busy," Pauley said. "I don't think she ever takes a day off. When she isn't in surgery at her Hugh Town office, she's zipping between the islands to make house calls."

Jem took that in. "I'd love to quiz her about the sick buzzard. Too bad there isn't a poorly pet we could borrow."

"But there is!" Pauley sat up straight. "Let's take Buck to see Vera. We can say he seems awfully depressed without Rhys. Then while we're in the office, we'll just casually inquire as to the health of the bird. Since her office posted about it on social media, she's invited questions, hasn't she?"

Jem beamed at her friend. "Look at you! I think that just might work. How'd you come up with that?"

"Oh, well, it's Sleuthing 101, isn't it?" Pauley said with the smoothness of someone who'd been waiting to deploy such a remark. "Figure out who has information and shoehorn yourself into their orbit."

Jem chuckled. "Perfect. Did you say she's in Hugh Town? That means we could kill two birds"—she paused slyly so her friend could appreciate what she'd done there—"with one stone. Roddy Levitt and Jimmy Franks live there, too. Why don't we invent a reason to ask one or both of them about Rhys?"

"Jimmy's probably at All Marine, as always. But I'm not sure Roddy will be home. We might have to take *Bellatrix* to Penzance to visit his gallery. I've already cyber-snooped on the website," Pauley said. Keys clicking, she pulled up the URL. "Here it is.

King & Castle Art Gallery. *Castle*," Pauley repeated, counting on her fingers, "The body was found near Candlewick Castle. There was a castle on the victim's polo shirt. Now we have a suspect who put the word castle in the name of his business."

"I know the word castle keeps coming up, but surely that's just a coincidence, right?" Jem said.

Pauley wagged a finger at her. "In novels, the great detectives always say they don't believe in coincidences."

"Of course they say that. They're in novels. Random coincidences will be edited out," Jem said. "That's why truth is stranger than fiction. Fiction has to make sense. Not to mention conclude at a reasonable length."

Pauley refused to let herself be bowled over by what Jem considered an airtight argument. "I still consider Roddy a suspect, even if it's only because his gallery's called King & Castle. As far as I'm concerned, I trust no one until we clear Rhys."

Using the laptop, Jem found and read the "About" section on Roddy Levitt's web page. "Apparently the name is a carry-over. He turned an old pub into a gallery. Still—it is a coincidence and we don't have many other credible leads at this point." The moment she said it, a new possibility popped into her head. "I don't suppose anyone posted on the noticeboard about losing a pair of wire-rimmed specs?"

Taking possession of the laptop again, Pauley returned to Facebook and checked. There were a few lost and found posts, including a dropped hearing aid, but nothing about spectacles.

"It's a good idea, though," Pauley said. "There are lots of private chat rooms and old school bulletin boards I can check, or ask a friend on another island to look at. If the specs belong to a witness who saw the real killer, it would exonerate Rhys."

"Or if the glasses belong to the real killer, their presence on the beach would tie him to the murder."

"Or her. Don't be sexist. Little girls can grow up to be brutal killers, too."

"Of course. How silly of me. The specs would tie *him or her* to the murder."

The house phone, an old slimline with an eight foot curly cord, trilled. Pauley popped up to answer it.

"What? Oh, yes, of course. Are you quite all right?" she asked. "Only I can't… sorry… perhaps if you blow your nose…"

Putting her hand over the mouthpiece, Pauley whispered to Jem, "It's Georgia. Calling for you. She's in a state."

When Jem put the receiver to her ear, Georgia was in the process of blowing her nose. After a few loud sniffs, she asked, "Is that Jem Jago?"

"Yes, it's me. I'm terribly sorry you're so upset. What can I do for you?"

"Help me!" Georgia all but screamed. "Please, help me!"

CHAPTER SIXTEEN

Finger Bones and a Platinum Monstrosity

Jem found it impossible to get much sense out of Georgia over the phone, so she insisted they meet up in Hugh Town. It fitted into the plans she and Pauley had already agreed upon, and made her feel like she was helping the grieving widow in some way.

"She's really latched onto you," Pauley said. "I wonder why?"

Jem shrugged. Obviously, Georgia would have done better to consult Hack, or DS Conrad of Devon & Cornwall, or a licensed psychotherapist.

"Maybe it's that good old 'Library World' connection," she said. "If I were just any islander who solved a murder case, Georgia might be afraid to ask. But people who gravitate toward library work are used to reaching out to each other. Doesn't matter where you stand in the ecosystem," she added, meaning whether one worked as a volunteer, page, assistant, librarian, or manager. "Preserving knowledge is a monumental task that goes back centuries. It's always been a team effort, and it always will be."

Because they planned to drop in on Vera Vet while in Hugh Town, it was necessary to take Buck along. Because dropping in on Roddy Levitt at his Penzance gallery was also on the table, Jem decided it would be far more practical, not to mention economical, to make the trip on *Bellatrix*. All they had to do was suit up, snap Buck's lead onto his red leather collar, and follow the Byway down to St. Morwenna Quay, where Jem's boat was moored not far from shore.

"I wonder if we should try and fit Buck into a dry bag," Jem said.

"Don't be ridiculous. He's a tough little doggie. Born to swim, aren't you, my lad?" Pauley inquired of Buck, who wagged his tail fiercely in reply.

"Hold onto him. We can wade at first, but we'll probably have to swim the last few feet," Jem said, glancing around the quay for any passing fisherman or pleasure boater who might give two gals and a mutt a lift out to *Bellatrix*.

"We'll be fine. When Buck doesn't want to do something, he bolts. And when he can't bolt, he whines. Look at him," Pauley said, smiling fondly at the dog. "I'll bet he thinks Rhys is across the water and waiting for him on board."

"If only," Jem said unthinkingly. Realizing how it sounded, she added, "For Buck's sake. We really won't be stretching the truth too much with Vera Vet. I just hope he manages to look at least slightly downcast while being examined."

True to Pauley's prediction, Buck was an enthusiastic, fearless swimmer, his paws churning rapidly in the clear, gentle water. To Jem, it felt summery-warm, though she knew most emmets wouldn't dare put more than a toe in. In no time, she and Pauley were aboard *Bellatrix*, and Buck was roaming happily across the deck, sniffing at gear and barking at seagulls.

"You're meant to be a depressed doggie," Jem said, slipping on her orange life vest. "This is frolicking. Outright, conspicuous frolicking."

"We're meeting poor Georgia before we go see Vera," Pauley reminded her. "She'll bring him down, if anything will."

*

At a quarter to noon, they found Georgia Castleberry waiting for them outside Vera's office, a squat yellow building with an adobe-tiled roof. As with most Hugh Town businesses, there was only a fig leaf of a parking lot, large enough for perhaps two cars. Today there were three rented golf carts lodged in the space. Judging from a peek inside the waiting room, in which every chair was occupied and plastic pet carriers of various sizes took up most of the floor, the office was having a busy day.

"I'll go inside and have a chat with the receptionist," Pauley said. "You two might as well wait under the shade of that awning. There's no room inside, unless you want to squat on someone's cat carrier."

"Don't forget about Buck," Jem said, attempting to hand off the leash. The little dog was still wet from his second dip in the water, and was still shaking himself at random intervals, always managing to spray Jem's cover-up sundress in the process.

"Keep him out here. I saw an Alsatian crouched in one corner. Buck can't see a big dog without trying to take him on," Pauley said. "Vera Vet isn't likely to do us a favor and squeeze us in if we create pandemonium among her other patients."

As Pauley went inside, Jem turned to Georgia. The other woman looked less frantic than she'd sounded, but she still looked so miserable, Jem's heart went out to her. Dressed in a shapeless maxi dress that hung off her like a limp sail, her collarbones stuck out and her cheekbones protruded. She'd aged ten years in less than a week.

"I understand you want my help. And I'll give it to you, gladly," she told Georgia. "But are you sure you're up for this right now? You look like you could do with a hot meal first."

"I can't eat," Georgia said bleakly. "Haven't set foot in the kitchen to cook a meal. Leo brings me takeout. I can barely keep it down, but I do my best for his sake."

"All right, then. Now try again, calmly, to tell me what made you so upset."

"I'm just so frustrated. I'm beginning to think no one in these islands is up to the job," she said, taking a deep breath as if to prevent the words from tumbling out of her all at once. "Sergeant Hackman returns my calls, but he won't tell me anything. DS Conrad's secretary puts me off whenever I ring his office. I know there's been an arrest, but all they'll tell me is his name. Rhys Tremayne. Isn't that your friend? The artist who was eating lunch with you at The Ruin?"

Jem nodded. "I might as well tell you, I'm certain he's not guilty. It seems like he had a history with your late husband. A dispute over whether or not Hermie was acting in good faith as Rhys's agent. But nothing anyone would kill over. And Rhys isn't a killer. I'd stake my life on that."

Georgia held her gaze for a moment, then nodded. "That's what other people are saying. That it must be a mistake. Do you think it's possible the whole thing is a mistake?"

"What do you mean?"

"I mean, something's been fishy from the start. I wasn't allowed to see Hermie's body. There's all this nonsense about a boat purchase he hid from me. Now a local man that everyone likes has been arrested, maybe just to shut me up so I stop asking questions." Eyes widening hopefully, Georgia said, "What if Hermie isn't dead? Suppose he was lost at sea, and he's still out there, waiting for rescue? Suppose the body they found was someone else, and this is all a case of mistaken identity and incompetence!"

Jem glanced around hastily to make sure no passersby were listening in. Georgia sounded hysterically happy, like someone about to slingshot round the bend.

"Let's stay calm," Jem said, putting on her most soothing librarian voice. "I don't think the police are deliberately stiff-arming you. They can be maddeningly tight-lipped when they have a case to make. Believe me, I know," she added, softening a little toward Hack. "Have they assigned you a liaison officer?"

"Yes, she turns up daily and she's as helpful as a potted plant," Georgia snapped, veering back to anger again. "This morning, I told her my theory that Hermie was still alive. You know what she did?"

The vet office's door banged open, and an Alsatian on a lead emerged, followed by an elderly couple.

"She gave me a shrink's business card," Georgia continued. "A shrink! The nerve!"

The Alsatian took Georgia's rant in stride, but the elderly couple peered fearfully at her as they passed. It was clear they thought a referral to a psychologist was a cracking good idea.

"Yes, well, I can see how that might be insulting," Jem said, still in soothing mode.

"Don't try to manage me," Georgia flared. "I'm not crazy. I'm being gaslit, I know it. People ringing the landline and hanging up. Insurance companies telling me my claim can't be discussed until it's escalated up the line. Hermie told me he had a pension from his years at Sotheby's but it seems to have gone up in smoke!"

Buck, who'd been growling softly at the Alsatian's departing form, shifted his liquid black eyes to Georgia instead. A soft whine escaped him. He, too, apparently found her sudden mood shifts unnerving.

"It's all right, boy," Jem said, leaning down to give his head a scratch. "Did you say ringing and hanging up?" she asked Georgia, choosing to seize on the simplest complaint. "How long has this been going on?"

"Since yesterday," Georgia said. "The first time, a woman said, 'Is that Mrs. Castleberry?' I said yes, and the line went dead. After that, they stay on the line, but refuse to speak. It's maddening."

The vet office's door banged open again. This time, a man with a cat-sized carrier exited, speaking gently to the unseen animal behind the door's metal grille.

His soothing tone is better than mine, Jem thought.

"No joy," Pauley announced, joining Jem and Georgia under the awning's rectangle of shade. "We came too late. Vera Vet and her assistant are breaking for lunch any minute. When they come back, they expect it will take the rest of the afternoon to clear their appointments."

"I don't understand why we're here anyway," Georgia said. "I thought it was just a meeting point, not an actual destination."

Her voice had shot up again, and a woman across the lane appeared to be taking an avid interest. She held a watering can over the top of some roses, but Jem didn't see anything coming from the spout.

"Let's talk behind the office," she said, leading them to the other side of the building, where the back door was marked EMPLOYEES ONLY and a wheelie bin stank to high heaven. With a rapturous bark, Buck surged for the bin, only to be jerked back by his lead. He gave Jem a mutinous stare. Whatever he smelled decomposing in that bin, he desperately wanted to taste, or perhaps roll in.

"Will you take him?" Jem asked, handing the lead to Pauley. She'd only just succeeded in explaining to Georgia about the buzzard in distress, and their theory that it might relate to Hermie's murder, when the back door opened and Vera Vet came out, trailed by her assistant. Both wore white lab coats with green piping. Vera had accessorized with matching green barrettes that stood out against her snow-white hair.

A compact middle-aged woman with a plain face and a normally sunny smile, Vera looked a bit harried, as if she really needed this break. The sight of three women and a dog lurking behind her office made her sag momentarily. Her assistant, a very short man with a high forehead and stern features, said, "Surgery is closed for lunch!" He stepped protectively in front of Vera, as if to shield her from further demands on her time.

"Just a moment," Vera said, peering at Georgia. "Don't I know you? Didn't I see you on the news?"

Georgia nodded.

"You're the Castleberry widow, aren't you? I have something for you. Luke," she said, addressing her assistant, "you can go ahead if you'd like. I won't be a moment."

She re-entered the office through the back door. Luke, who seemed dismayed that Vera would cut into her meal time, declined to head to lunch without his boss. Instead, he waited with Jem, Pauley, Georgia, and Buck until Vera Vet reappeared, an ordinary envelope in her hand.

"I don't suppose any of you saw the post online about a buzzard?"

"We did," Jem said.

"Was the bird poisoned?" Pauley asked eagerly.

Vera Vet looked surprised. Luke stared at Pauley like she'd grown a third eye.

"It was just a thought," Pauley muttered.

"Mrs. Castleberry, I hope I'm not speaking out of turn when I say, your late husband's, erm, body attracted a bit of attention on the shore," Vera said. "It's only natural for scavengers to take an interest. Literally the circle of life. Forgive me if I'm upsetting you."

"You're not." Georgia lifted her chin defiantly. "Just tell me."

"Well. A cottager on Tresco found a buzzard in distress and brought it to me," Vera continued. "It had, erm, bitten off more than it could chew. There was something hard wedged in its gullet. This isn't uncommon with scavenger birds, especially when there's a lot of competition. When they discover a big, meaty carcass, they tear off huge pieces and—"

Luke coughed urgently.

"Never mind. The point is, many birds are also attracted to shiny objects. This particular buzzard," Vera said, smiling fondly as if she and the bird had become best mates, "allowed both instincts to get the better of him. He swallowed Mr. Castleberry's ring finger, got it halfway down, and almost choked to death on it."

Georgia looked horrified. Afraid she might faint, Jem put a steadying arm around the widow's shoulders.

"At any rate, I removed the offending objects and the bird will be just fine," Vera Vet announced. "I intend to call the Hugh Town Police Station so they can send over someone to recover the finger bones for the burial. But I thought you might like the ring, as a remembrance."

At last, the proffered envelope no longer seemed mysterious. Georgia reached for it like a drowning woman toward a rope. Tearing it open, she dropped its contents into her palm and stared. It was a man's platinum band, 9 mm thick, with decorative grooves. Jem thought it looked as handsome and stylish as the Rolex she remembered on Hermie's dead wrist.

Georgia let out an incoherent cry. Screaming, "You're an idiot!" at Vera Vet, she hurled the wedding band at the startled woman. "That monstrosity isn't Hermie's ring!"

CHAPTER SEVENTEEN

Pompous Young Windbag

"I'm sorry. I'm so sorry," Georgia said for the tenth time.

"I know," Jem murmured. She was in the front room of Georgia's cottage, the one she'd shared with Hermie. Leo wasn't home, which was just as well. Since her meltdown at the vet's office, Georgia couldn't stop vacillating between rage and contrition. Pauley and Buck were outside, playing fetch in the front garden. Every so often, Pauley would look into the front window, catching Jem's eye and giving her a meaningful glance. If they wanted to make the trip to Roddy Levitt's Penzance gallery, they needed to set off soon.

"I'll send the vet some flowers," Georgia added. "I know I was ghastly. But for her to tell me that awful story about scavengers—to put those terrible images in my head—and then pull out the wrong ring? It was outrageous. I'm being gaslit, I tell you. I know I am."

"I know it feels that way," Jem said. "But remember, I found the body. Hermie was missing the ring finger of his left hand. It's a reasonable supposition. And I suppose the forensics lab can DNA match the finger bones to be absolutely sure."

Georgia stared at Jem. "You never said anything about a missing finger."

"Well. No. When I met you that day at The Ruin, you were in agony," Jem said. "I told you as little as possible. The truth is, I had a very good look at the body."

"Including his face?"

Jem nodded.

"Then look at this." Rising, Georgia scooped a framed picture off the credenza and stuck it under Jem's nose. "Here's my Hermie. You found a totally different person, didn't you? No resemblance at all, am I right?"

It took only a glance to see that the man in the picture was indeed the same man Jem had found dead on the beach. Hermie was even dressed identically, in a white polo shirt, cargo shorts, black knee-length socks, and black wingtips. He was more attractive than he'd been in death, of course, but clearly the same person.

"I'm sorry, Georgia," Jem said gently. "Unless Hermie had a twin or a doppelganger, that's the man I found."

"But this isn't his ring. That must prove that this whole investigation is wrong—off—just pure rubbish," Georgia cried, tossing the photo into the nearest wall. The sound of glass shattering seemed to give Georgia pause. For a moment, she sat frozen. Then she laughed like a woman on the brink of losing her mind.

"That's my life, isn't it? Splintered into a million pieces. I told you, the insurance company says Hermie's policy is under review. The bank says it's doing an investigation and they won't get back to me before next week. And I thought we owned our cottage free and clear, but I had a letter today saying the lease is up next month. I need someone to make sense of this. Jem, help me. Give me something to do besides sit here and wait for the other shoe to drop."

Jem had been looking forward to leaving Georgia at home and returning to *Bellatrix* with Pauley and Buck. Putting that hopeful anticipation out of her mind, she forced herself to say, "We want to talk to a gallery owner on the mainland. Why don't you come with us to Penzance?"

*

Jem found a berth for *Bellatrix* at Newlyn Harbor, not too far from the gallery. Buck seemed sleepy after his many adventures, so they left him on the boat, curled up on the deck. Disembarking on the promenade, they strolled past fish markets, restaurants, a marine supply shop, and the Strand antique shop, a place Jem hoped to visit on some happier day. King & Castle Art Gallery was located on an intersection, and just as the website had promised, was open to the public that day.

A squat stone building with a peaked roof, it looked more like a renovated Protestant church than an old pub. However, it turned out they'd approached from the back door, which was locked, with a sign asking visitors to go around to the front. From that angle, King & Castle did resemble a converted pub. The swinging wooden sign depicted a Leonardo da Vinci-type artist admiring his finished canvas, and the aged wooden barrel near the door proclaimed, ART ON TAP.

"I don't suppose you've thought up any brilliant opening gambits," Pauley muttered in Jem's ear.

"Nope. I reckon I'll just tell him the truth."

"Which is?"

"I overheard him say Hermie was on borrowed time, and I'd like to know what he meant by that."

Georgia, the only one of the three who'd ever been to Roddy Levitt's gallery before, had been striding a little ahead of them, shoulders back and fists clenched, like a woman determined to beat the truth out of someone. Now she stopped and turned to look at Jem and Pauley.

"What? Why are you whispering?"

"Sorry. We don't mean to be rude," Jem said quickly. "Only we've never been properly introduced to Roddy. We're trying to figure out the best way to ask him what we need to know."

"Never mind about that," Georgia said. "He was Hermie's first friend in the Cornish art scene. I expect when I tell him what I've been through, he'll be as frustrated and furious as I am."

The gallery's interior was stark white. Most of the light appeared to be natural, provided by skylights. Jem looked around at various pieces, a few of them sculptures, the rest huge abstract canvases, and wondered if she lacked the gene to appreciate such things. Were these all meant to be individual works of genius? Were there buyers for such things?

I hope I like Rhys's better, Jem thought. *Then again, if I ever get around to writing that book about Sir Declan and his diary, I doubt Rhys will ever crack it.*

"Roddy's office will be in the rear," Georgia said. "Pauley, you might want to wait out here. Roddy can be a little… finicky. When too many people come upon him at once, he gets flustered."

Pauley folded her arms across her chest. "He can't handle three people?"

"He can't handle an acquaintance and two strangers. Not without an appointment," Georgia said. "If he's in a good mood, I'll coax him out to meet you. If not—well, you're better off out here, with the art."

"Oh, I'm loving it," Pauley said doubtfully.

Georgia led Jem to the back of the gallery, where they found Roddy Levitt looking just as he had at the pirate festival—bearded with gray-streaked hair and thick glasses, twice as large and heavy as they needed to be. The sort of specs that declared the wearer to be an artiste, and those who failed to recognize him as such would be sorry. Jem wondered if he actually needed glasses, or if they were just for show.

Roddy's office, little more than a broom closet, was too small for anyone but him to occupy. His massive desk and round inflatable balance ball took up all the space. Visitors like Jem and Georgia, unable to enter and sit, were forced to hover outside in the hall, like supplicants lurking in hope of a favor.

"Georgia Castleberry," Roddy said, so slowly he seemed to imbue the name with some extra syllables. "I'm terribly sorry for your loss. Who's this fresh-faced young creature with you?"

Jem tried to look pleasantly neutral. Up close, his gray hair looked completely phony. If she was a "fresh-faced young creature" at thirty-three, Roddy was a pompous young windbag of perhaps thirty-five.

"This is Jem Jago. She's a Special Collections Librarian working on St. Morwenna," Georgia said. "She solved a mystery not long ago and I'm hoping she can help me."

Roddy leaned back on his stability ball in a way that suggested the conversation was already testing his patience. "Bully for her. Why did you bring her here?"

Georgia put on a smile so forced and pained, Jem hoped it made Roddy feel at least a little ashamed of himself. "The police are telling me Hermie's dead. That he was murdered on the beach near Candlewick Castle. But how can that be? He was a lovely man. The perfect man. You worked with him. You know what a good person he was, surely, even if you quarreled from time to time."

Roddy pursed his lips and stuck his nose in the air as if something odiferous had assailed his nostrils. "Georgia. I don't want to speak ill of the dead. But Hermie was, at best, a dilettante. More money than taste. He embarrassed me among the serious artists and collectors more often than I can say."

Georgia bristled. It was the first time Jem had seen her show any emotion other than misery or grief.

"He was well-respected. He helped emerging artists get started. I met one just the other day."

"Who? Rhys Tremayne?" Roddy gave a short bark of laughter. "You know they arrested him, don't you? And I wouldn't be surprised if Tremayne really is the killer. He's another no-talent determined to force himself upon the world. Hermie had an uncanny knack for sniffing out weak artists with money to burn. Word is, he drained Tremayne dry and sold his scribbles to a fleabag hotel."

It was Jem's turn to bristle, but she reminded herself not to unload on Roddy until she at least took a stab at learning something useful.

"Besides Rhys, can you think of anyone else who might have wanted Hermie dead?" Jem asked.

"Well, if I'm being honest… this poor lady I see before me," Roddy said. The more he enjoyed himself, the more pretentious and supercilious his tone became.

"Me? How can you say that?" Georgia cried.

"Hermie had a wandering eye. He was seen at least twice in the company of a very lovely woman who wasn't you," Roddy said. "I'm sorry to tell you," he added happily, "but honesty is the best policy. That's what I told the police when I tipped then off about Rhys confronting Hermie."

Georgia openly seethed, but Jem noticed she didn't deny Roddy's statement.

"What do you mean?" Jem asked.

He blinked at her sharpness. "Excuse me, Ms. Librarian. Are you empowered to barge into a man's place of business and interrogate him?"

"I'm sorry," Jem said, wishing with all her might that his beard would burst into flames. "Only, I'm a longtime friend of Rhys. It's impossible for me to think he could have killed someone. Even if they'd cheated him out of a lot of money. Could you, erm, please tell me what you saw?"

Roddy studied her for a long moment, as if trying to decide which would amuse him more—to speak, or to refuse to speak. Then he said, "It's nothing earth-shattering. On Friday night, I was on my yar little vessel when I saw Hermie aboard his vulgar yacht, making ready to cast off. Then Rhys Tremayne stormed up the gangplank, looking very much like a stevedore, and confronted Hermie on deck."

"What was said?" Georgia asked.

Roddy waved a hand. "You swindled me. You never got me a showing. You toyed with my creative ambitions and my tender feelings are hurt."

Jem began to wish the man's hair would catch fire along with his beard. "Sounds like you had fun eavesdropping."

"Oh, I did. Hermie was on borrowed time in the art community. I didn't think someone would kill him, but I knew he'd soon be driven off, never to be seen again," Roddy said. "As for Rhys, I hope the whole story comes out in excruciating detail. I want the no-talents to read it and recognize themselves. That would be a silver lining indeed."

"Roddy, I never thought you were a man of great character, but I thought you were better than this," Georgia said stiffly. "I don't believe a word you said about Hermie. Goodbye."

She turned on her heel and marched back into the gallery, no doubt to reassure Pauley that she'd missed absolutely nothing. But Jem couldn't flounce out of King & Castle without asking this deeply unpleasant man one more question.

"What, precisely, is wrong with Rhys's art?" She said each word distinctly, in the tone of a challenge.

"Young lady." Roddy stood up. "I was educated at the Roseland Academy. Afterward, I studied at the Ruskin School of Art at Oxford. I am what some would call a gifted sculptor and painter. But in a world that demands genius, I fall short. Therefore, I chose the only honorable route. I now facilitate those who are capable of greatness, and help them achieve what I could not.

"Rhys Tremayne was educated, if you can call it that, at St. Mary's School. He had an amateur tutor him for one summer.

After that, he began to prostitute his alleged art, as all such people do, by painting for the lowest common denominator and selling those paintings for a few pounds each. Then, in his unforgivable hubris, he woke up one morning and decided he could make a contribution to the serious art world. Ergo, he decided he was better than me, and equal to the fine artists I represent." Roddy's cheeks were pink, and he was breathing hard. If he hadn't already spoken these words aloud to someone else, Jem suspected he'd recited them silently to himself, many times.

"Any barnyard animal can draw a paintbrush across a canvas," Roddy said. "But the chicken who makes pictures is not the equal of Jean-Michel Basquiat. People like Rhys Tremayne cannot make art. Full stop," he concluded, and slammed his office door in Jem's face.

CHAPTER EIGHTEEN

Free Rhys

On Saturday morning, Jem decided to break out the big guns: her brand new, virgin journal and best gel ink pen.

There was a magic to writing by hand in journals that was so acute, it felt like a guilty pleasure. Dictating into her phone's notebook or typing up a computer document were faster, easier, infinitely correctable, spell-checked, and shareable in myriad ways. But when Jem opened a new, carefully-chosen journal—this particular one had a purple cover with pink thread accents—and wrote in it by hand, she felt her brain engage very differently than it did with a laptop or phone. The act of writing mysteriously seemed to lend additional weight.

In the journal, Jem wrote,

Georgia—seems genuinely distraught. Gutted to lose Hermie.

Roddy Levitt—thinks he's the smartest guy in the room. The reasons he gave for disliking Hermie seemed believable. But someone so quick to anger might be capable of serious violence.

Jimmy Franks—owed money by Hermie. Broken friendship. Pauley doesn't like him. Why sink a boat he could legally repossess?

Stuart at The Ruin—disliked Hermie. Seems interested in Pauley. The fact that I'm writing about him means I'm grasping at straws.

She stopped, chewing on the end of her pen as she read over what she'd written. Whenever her lists turned somewhat meta, it was time to pause and reassess.

Gloves
Boning knife
Ice chest
Sunken boat
Artist's knife
Word castle keeps coming up
Why is this so hard?

She decided to go check on Pauley, who'd started her day by checking IoS chat rooms for any mention of missing wire-framed spectacles. When that search didn't pan out, she went through her contacts list, calling friends on St. Mary's, Bryher, St. Martin's, and Tresco and asking them to check the local bulletin boards for any appeal regarding lost specs. No one had anything helpful to report, though virtually all of them supported Rhys and were pleased to do anything that might help his defense.

"Kind of warms my heart to hear people speak so well of Rhys," Pauley told Jem. "I thought this would be a chance for anyone who didn't like him to pile on. But instead they're rallying around him. It's making Hack a lot less popular, though. And he already had some ground to make up."

Jem blew out a sigh. "The faster we clear this up, the faster everything will be set to rights again. We saw the body. I saw *Family Man* at the bottom of the channel. We followed up on Roddy Levitt and he's still a big question mark, as far as I'm concerned…"

"And we may have a witness, or the killer, tied to the specs, but no one's asking about them," Pauley said. "Which makes me wonder if they don't actually belong to the killer."

"I think we need more people with their ears to the ground," Jem said. "Fancy a walk to the Square?"

As if drawn by the word "walk," Buck hurried into the kitchen, a knotted length of rope in his mouth. Pauley had made it for him, since she didn't own any store bought dog toys. Buck seemed to enjoy fetching it, savaging it, and even tossing it on the floor and barking at it. Every time a door opened, the sound of his doggie nails echoed through the house as he broke into a trot, eager to see if his master was back at last.

"Hiya, Bucky boy." Pauley gently wrested the knotted rope from his mouth, then tossed it into the hall for him to fetch. "Where's Micki? Is she working at the Kernow Arms tonight?"

"Yes, it's her Saturday night on."

"It's not even noon yet. Ring *Gwin & Gweli* and see if she spent the night with Clarence again. Maybe they can meet us in the Square for an early lunch before she's off to Hugh Town for her shift. I think it's time we asked them to help us poke around for Rhys."

"What about Buck? Should we take him with us?"

"I don't think so," Jem said. "There's sure to be a lot of foot traffic around the new pizza place. I'm not sure how Buck would do in a crowd without Rhys there to comfort him. Let's leave him here, in the small wing, with his toy and the telly on."

Buck regarded them sadly, his black button eyes shifting from Pauley to Jem and back again. Then he lay down, put his head on his paws, and let out a low, mournful whine.

*

In the Square, it was another beautiful August day, sunny and bright and packed with emmets, which was great for St. Morwenna's bottom line. The reopened Ice Cream Hut was doing a brisk business with Kenzie's mum, Lissa DeYoung, taking a shift behind the counter.

The hut's owner, Bettie Quick, was getting on in years, and her health no longer permitted her to serve the public. She'd made no firm decision about who to hire as the Ice Cream Hut's permanent staff, and was taking on different locals on a trial basis. From what Jem observed, Lissa was a natural, chatting up a storm as she passed out Mr. Whippys and frozen novelties with great aplomb. But jobs on St. Morwenna were scarce, and the competition was fierce. Bettie wouldn't have to make her final choice for weeks, even months.

Micki and Clarence weren't in sight, so Jem and Pauley headed for Pirate's Pizza, which was also enjoying a busy afternoon. Like Wired Java before it, it offered on-site Wi-Fi, but anyone lingering inside was required to make a purchase. The result was a cluster of young people around the building's perimeter, angling for a bit of free juice to show them their messages or get them on the web. Scanning the group, Jem soon located Kenzie's shorn blue head bent over her mobile, eyes trained on whatever digital revelation she momentarily couldn't live without. Her presence was a lucky coincidence—it would give Jem a chance to inquire about anything interesting Randy Andy might have unwittingly revealed.

"Kenzie!" Jem called, steering Pauley along with her. "What's the verdict on this year's Sea Guides summer camp?"

Pocketing her phone, Kenzie sauntered over with a world-weary smile. "Well, we've seen it all before, haven't we? The last two days were a joke. Mr. Mourby is the worst," she added with an eye-roll. "He was missing in action for the whole of Friday night. Apparently he thought making us watch some creaking old diving film about Jacques Padstow counted as a fun activity. And Ms. Addis-Clark—"

"Cousteau," Pauley interrupted. "Jacques Cousteau."

"Pretty sure it's Padstow. Anyway, Ms. Addis-Clark did the exact same syllabus as last year, which is what I call phoning it in. And this year all the catered food was health-conscious, which was bloody awful. I told Mum that next year, I'm not going. My time is valuable."

Jem nodded along with Kenzie's narrative, careful not to smirk. No matter her mood, the kid always made her laugh.

"Anyway, never mind that, what about you? What are you doing to free Rhys?" she cried, bouncing on her toes in frustration. "He's being persecuted. We should be setting a trap for the real killer."

That statement drew looks from several people, even among the previously cyber-hypnotized.

"Keep your voice down," Pauley whispered harshly. "Come over here, close to the quay."

St. Morwenna's Quay had no boats tied up at the moment, although the dissipating wake of a powerboat suggested that someone had just departed. Jem and Pauley sat on a bench overlooking the sea while Kenzie, too energized to sit, went through a series of stretches. At the limber age of thirteen, she made them look effortless, but Jem suspected the moves would send most adults to the casualty ward.

"You said you'd keep an eye on Randy Andy," Jem said. "What's happened with that?"

"Oh. That was a bust," Kenzie said, fleetingly meeting her eyes. "He's always been jealous of Rhys, because Rhys asked Mum to marry him a thousand years ago. It's not like they did get married," she groaned, as if referencing something that had happened in an earlier century, instead of an event that had occurred a few months before she was born. Kenzie treated Rhys like an uncle, but the true relationship was more complicated, and for all her world-weary attitude, the thirteen-year-old remained blissfully unaware.

"Anyway, he was so happy to hear Rhys was arrested, all he did was ring up his mates and laugh with them over the phone. He was such a jerk, Mum shouted at him," Kenzie said, eyes wide. "She never stands up for herself. He walked out! I was doing the Snoopy dance. But he'll be back," she added, deflating. "No matter what, he always comes back."

Jem nodded, trying not to look as disappointed as she felt. Asking a child to gather information should probably always be a no-go, anyway.

"Mum thought it was all a mistake and he'd already be released by now," Kenzie continued. "But Leo said DS Conrad spoke to his mum and promised her they had the right man. She's been half doolally since Mr. Castleberry died."

"We know," Jem said. "When did you see Leo?"

"I didn't see him, I rang him up," Kenzie said. "He said the police have witnesses. One saw Rhys arguing with Mr. Castleberry near some rubbish bins. Another saw Rhys come aboard *Family Man*—"

"Hack told me about the first one. The second one is Roddy Levitt. We talked to him yesterday," Jem cut in, eager for fresh information. "But is there another one?"

"Yeah. They claim they saw Rhys at Candlewick Castle on Saturday morning. Mr. Castleberry was supposedly half-drowned and crawling along the shore. The witness says Rhys bent over him, and when he walked away, Mr. Castleberry was still and never moved again."

"There's a witness who says they saw Rhys cut his throat?" Pauley burst out, incensed.

"Yeah. *Mental*," Kenzie cried, bouncing again with indignation.

"Wait," Jem broke in. "Pauley, I know you didn't mean to, but I think you're putting an idea in Kenzie's head. Kenzie," she said, putting both hands on the teen's narrow shoulders to keep her still. "Did anyone say anything about a cut throat?"

Kenzie seemed to mull it over. "I don't know. I don't think so. Randy Andy just said the witnesses had Rhys bang to rights. But he *would* say that, wouldn't he? And Leo knew more but he didn't, like, read me a transcript. He just said the witness saw Rhys bend over a moving body and walk away from a still one."

"They probably didn't want to get into the specifics," Pauley said. "It means the same thing."

"No, it doesn't," Jem said.

"If the witness was so shocked and frightened that he dropped his specs, maybe he didn't stick around to verify how Hermie died."

"We can't assume the specs belong to a witness. They could be the killer's. Or they could've been dropped by someone else and mean nothing at all," Jem said. "I think this sounds like someone watching from afar."

Pauley and Kenzie looked at one another. "You mean like from a roof at the Sea Garden Cottages resort?"

"I mean from Bryher. With binoculars."

"Oh," Pauley muttered. "Yeah. The channel isn't that wide, is it?"

"Kenzie, could you give Leo another ring? See if you can feel out whether or not the witness who's accusing Rhys of murder is a local? Someone with an ax to grind? Or maybe someone unreliable, who might have misunderstood who or what they saw?"

"That's a good idea," Pauley said. "Though I don't think anyone can argue that they mistook someone else for Rhys. He stands out."

"Ringing Leo's a no-go," Kenzie said. "I got a little cross with him, and he told me to piss off. Maybe it's not really a surprise. His stepdad is dead and Rhys has been arrested. This puts us on opposite sides."

At that moment, her mobile chimed. Her face lit up as she saw the alert. "Ten likes! At this rate, my post is going viral for sure."

"Post about what?" Pauley asked suspiciously.

"Nothing," Kenzie replied in a way that would've reassured absolutely no one.

"Give me that." Pauley held out her hand for the mobile. "Don't just pass me it. Unlock it first."

Sighing, Kenzie obeyed. Pauley scrolled, tutted, and tutted some more.

"What is it?" Jem asked, shading her eyes against the noonday sun to get a look.

Kenzie had been making GIFs and posting them across social media. She'd done vulgar ones, glittery ones, psychedelic ones, and rainbow unicorn ones. All were emblazoned with two words: FREE RHYS. Many went further, accusing the police of incompetence, malice, or rank stupidity.

"This isn't helpful. Delete the lot," Pauley commanded, handing the phone back.

"But it's all true! Besides, what else can I do, but protest and put pressure on the police?"

Pauley's eyes sparkled, but she managed to keep a stern expression. "You could take a chance and call Leo again. Make friends, and then see if he knows anything else. Or you could ring up Randy Andy and see what he's willing to reveal while gloating."

"Hah!" Kenzie laughed. "Never. As for Leo... I don't know. I used to think he was so cool. He's never a jerk about it, but he does his own thing. When Ms. Addis-Clark made us watch the same PowerPoint presentation we saw last year, he read a book down low, where she couldn't see. And when Mr. Mourby put on Jacques Padstow and left us to do God knows what, Leo slipped out of the hotel ballroom and swam in the heated pool. I thought I was daft for sitting there, listening to this geezer go on and on, when I could've slipped out, too. But now I reckon he's the daft one, not to work out that Rhys *must* be innocent."

This must be how I sounded to Hack, Jem thought, though she appreciated the girl's unwavering loyalty. *Like a naïve child, so caught up in my personal feelings, I couldn't look at the case from an objective point of view.*

"I wouldn't worry about Leo's opinion. He has every right to be emotional. We're the ones who need to stay rational," Jem said. "I think the autopsy will show that Hermie died late Friday or early

Saturday, and washed ashore after being underwater for a time. That will discredit the witness who placed Rhys next to Hermie on the beach.

"The next thing we need to do is help Rhys establish an alibi from sunset Friday to high tide on Saturday morning. He was on Tresco to visit someone called Sharon MacAfee. Have you heard Rhys mention that name?"

Kenzie nodded.

"What can you tell us about her?"

"I don't know. She lives on Tresco. She's blonde. And she works in the Abbey Gardens."

"Jem. Don't forget, we promised not to get anyone in trouble," Pauley murmured, meaning PC Newt, who'd supplied Sharon's name the previous day.

"Trouble? What do you mean? I heard it through the grapevine," Jem said innocently. To Kenzie, she continued, "I take it Sharon is Rhys's girlfriend?"

Kenzie shrugged.

"Do you like her?"

"Define like."

"All right, I think we've browbeat this witness as much as we can in one session," Pauley said lightly. "And look, here comes our lunch dates," she added, indicating Micki and Clarence, who were walking down Quay Road in the direction of Pirate's Pizza.

"Sharon MacAfee's number seems to be ex-directory. Do you have it?" Jem asked Kenzie.

"Yeah." For some reason, the girl didn't seem to want to discuss Sharon, but she clearly wasn't willing to lie to Jem to wiggle out of answering the question.

"Great. We're off to lunch. Text that number to me, okay?"

"Okay. But you didn't get it from me. I'm providing this as an unnamed source," Kenzie warned. "Deep background."

"Understood. And, Kenzie—until this situation is resolved, don't go off alone."

"Lock your doors and windows, too," Pauley added. "Lissa may forget, but I know you'll remember."

"I can take care of myself," Kenzie said, back to her world-weary attitude. "Wrong person fingered, real killer at large. Been there, done that, got the commemorative plate. See you around."

As Jem and Pauley started uphill toward Micki and Clarence, Pauley muttered, "Just had to go Nancy Drew in pursuit of that particular phone number, huh?"

"All for the cause," Jem said. "Free Rhys."

CHAPTER NINETEEN

Romeo Breeches and a Florentine Fop

Pirate's Pizza wasn't half bad. The food was fresh, and while by-the-slice prices were high, the whole pie rates were reasonable. In honor of the grand opening, each patron received a complimentary cannoli for dessert.

"Complimentary," Clarence Latham muttered. "I don't know how complimentary a little twist of pastry is when we paid twice the usual price for a fountain drink."

"It all works out," Micki said, grabbing herself a slice. For a second, the cheese refused to release the next slice over, super-attenuating itself in an attempt to hold on. Then the bonds snapped, sending most of the cheese rebounding onto Micki's slice, while its former neighbor was left half-naked.

"That one's yours, too," Jem said, tearing off the half-naked one and adding it to Micki's plate. That left her with a normal slice that looked and smelled delicious.

"But it's all crust." Micki turned to her cousin. "You want it?"

Clarence, a sixtyish man with dark skin, close-cropped gray hair, and deep crinkles around his eyes, snatched it as if she were foolish for asking. "You'd better believe it. This meal was an investment. Letting any part of it go to waste would be a crime."

"Business still slow at the B&B?" Pauley asked sympathetically.

"I'm lucky if I let a room a week. Even then, it's usually just for the weekend," he said. "My business model assumed one room constantly in service during the off-season, and three rooms constantly in service during the peak. If things don't turn around by next spring, the cottage will be back on the market."

"Maybe you need a business partner," Pauley suggested.

He laughed. "You know anyone? Everybody I meet in the islands is already working three jobs. They don't have cash to invest."

Pauley seemed to take that in. "I suppose the extra space gives you room to have Micki over, right? That must be nice."

"It's better than nice. I think she ought to move in with me."

"I'm tempted. In one sense, I would save money," Micki said, referring to the rent on her tiny flat in Hugh Town, a place she sometimes described as a shoebox with love beads. "But I'd have to pay for a water taxi twice a day, wouldn't I?"

"They offer weekly rates," Clarence said. "And there's always the chance Bart will resurface."

Micki answered with her trademark wheezy laugh. "I heard Bart's still in trouble over the Pirate Extravaganza."

"Trouble how?" Jem asked.

"You name it. False advertising. Inadequate planning—"

"Multiple broken ordinances," Clarence cut in, as if quoting from an official meeting agenda. "I have a friend on the council. They may call a meeting."

"Bart will escape the consequences," Pauley predicted. "He always wriggles off the hook."

"Maybe, but he's likely to owe fines. That's probably why he hasn't been seen around the islands lately," Clarence said.

"Anyway, getting back to the B&B," Micki said. "You know how much I enjoy staying with you, Clar. But that room is meant for a paying guest. We should be drumming up business, not resigning ourselves to failure so early in the game."

"What about a sideline business?" Jem suggested. "The day I met Micki, she said something about psychic consultations. Just for fun—tarot cards, palmistry, and all that. Of course, that was before we discovered she can sing like an angel."

"That she can," Clarence said, smiling broadly at his cousin. "Of course, this particular angel has a massive case of stage fright. I'm proud of her for overcoming it at the festival. Wish I'd been there to see it. But I'm not going to schedule her for anything, even an informal do to raise interest in *Gwin & Gweli*, until I'm sure she's ready to commit to live singing performances."

Micki fiddled with her pizza.

"By that I mean, specific dates and times," Clarence continued, emphasizing *dates* and *times* in his powerful bass voice.

"I blew off some dates, all right?" Micki burst out, looking from Pauley to Jem. "Left Clar in the lurch at his old job. I didn't know it would be so hard to follow through! I don't think of myself as a fearful person. I can talk to anyone. I can climb on a bar top and shout down drunks. I *like* being the center of attention. But when it comes to singing, it's different.

"I can do it privately," she continued. "One or two people, no problem. But when I try to do it publicly, especially for strangers, a feeling of doom comes over me. My heart races. It's like I'm poorly, or I might even be dying. The thought of stepping on stage becomes as scary as walking a tightrope between two skyscrapers. Unless I have a few stiff drinks first, I can't do it, and even then, it's not a sure thing."

"So I experienced a string of tequila-related no-shows," Clarence said. "And got the sack as a result, since I vouched for her."

"I was too ashamed to face him, after," Micki said. "I dodged him for an entire summer."

"Still don't know how you managed that. Must've taken on a whole new identity." Clarence chuckled, clearly more amused by the memory than irritated. "In the Latham family, we have a saying—you can run, but you can't hide. Because there's too many of us to hide from! But Micki disappeared so completely, I thought she'd left the country."

"I went to stay with an old boyfriend in Wolverhampton. In the Black Country," Micki admitted. "Quite the culture shock for a Cornish lass like myself. In the end I couldn't stand city life. The noise. The smells."

"Fitting punishment," Clarence said. "When she came back, she explained everything, and I must say, I get it. I really do. I don't suffer from anxiety myself, but sometimes I have low spirits. So low that on certain days, I have to force myself just to get out of bed in the morning. When our head does us in, it's as real as appendicitis. And sometimes just as deadly. But," he added more severely, "skipping the dates without so much as a text was a dirty trick, my love. I won't put myself in that position again until you play some gigs on the regular and prove to me that you can do it."

"Your performance at the festival was brill," Jem said, smiling encouragingly at Micki. "Any chance of a repeat?"

"Monty, the lead singer from Tommy and the Knockers, has been in touch." Micki sounded both excited and apprehensive. "I wanted to do it. But I had to say no to the first gig he offered because it was such short notice, and I was already down for a shift at the pub. The next gig is a week from Sunday. I want to say yes. But what if I lose my nerve? I don't know. So… we'll see, won't we?" On that uncertain note, she nibbled her pizza.

It seemed time to change the subject, so Jem filled in Clarence and Micki on what they'd learned about Hermie's murder and Rhys's arrest.

"Roddy Levitt sounds shady as hell," Clarence said.

"I don't mean to be cruel, but Georgia sounds a bit unhinged, too," Micki said. "You don't suppose she's putting it on, do you? Running around crying and saying Hermie's not really dead so no one will suspect her?"

Jem considered the idea. "Do you think Georgia could've cut her husband's throat right down to the bone?"

"No," Pauley said.

"No." Micki sighed, as if sorry to see her theory torched so quickly.

"I say, when a married man dies by violence, look hard at the wife," Clarence declared. "Even if she didn't do it herself, she might have hired someone to do it for her. But as I've never said two words to the poor woman, I reckon it wouldn't be fair to accuse her. Whereas Roddy Levitt sounds like someone who could kill a rival if he had a good enough reason."

"I wonder about Mr. Mourby," Pauley said.

Jem, Micki, and Clarence looked at her, nonplussed.

"The Sea Guides teacher? The one who called me a bad influence?" Jem asked.

"Yeah. Didn't you hear what Kenzie said? He put on an old diving documentary film and left the kids for hours. On Friday night. Potentially during the time of the murder," Pauley said.

Everyone sat silently, turning over the notion in their minds. It was a good catch by Pauley. But was it too farfetched to take seriously?

"Well, Mourby happens to be one of our thespians at the Empire," Clarence said. "We never really talk, but I'll sidle up to him. Anything for Captain Kernow." That was the nickname he'd given Rhys in the days before they'd been introduced.

"That theater group keeps him busy. His phone rang all last night," Micki said. "He's already an integral part of the Tidal Pool Players. Can't go a day without talking someone off the proverbial ledge. What was the calamity last night?"

"Missing wardrobe items," Clarence announced with the air of someone who relished a good drama. "At first, there was a good faith search effort among the thespians. Now it's devolved to everyone accusing everyone else. Including benighted non-thespians, such as myself."

"He's desperate to be in the ensemble," Micki said. "You can hear the raw jealousy every time he says 'thespian.'"

"Jealousy has nothing to do with it," Clarence said. "As for the missing wardrobe items, I predicted it. I said, this free-for-all of loaning anything to anybody has got to end. The costume inventory exists only in the minds of the people who've been around the longest. There's not even a sign-out sheet. In the last meeting, I laid all this out."

"Did anyone listen?" Pauley asked.

"Of course not. And some of those costumes are rather valuable—if not in cash, in the time and effort it would take to replace them. You could probably pick up a pair of wire specs in any secondhand shop, but the missing velvet breeches and silk hose are part of a Florentine set meant for Shakespearian dramas. If they don't turn up, they'll cost a couple of hundred quid to replace."

"Wire specs?" Jem asked.

"What wire specs?" Pauley said at almost the same moment.

Clarence raised his eyebrows. "You know. The sort worn by Santa Claus or Scrooge. This was a vintage pair with weak lenses, which is perfect, because it doesn't blur the actor's vision too much."

"Guess what? I think we found them at the crime scene," Jem said. "Lying in the rubble close to where Hermie Castleberry's body washed up."

"That's right," Micki cried. "The specs that made Hack tell you off."

"I'd let that man tell me off anytime," Clarence said. Currently between relationships, he made no bones about his loneliness, often commenting on attractive men and their respective merits. He sounded quite forceful, but Jem was beginning to suspect he was all talk and no nerve. All the bluster that came out when chatting with the girls turned into meek silence when he found himself in the actual presence of a heartthrob. On the day Jem had finally introduced him to Rhys, Clarence had hardly managed to choke out a hello.

"So the Tidal Pool Players are missing a pair of vintage wire-framed specs and some velvet Romeo breeches. What color?"

"Midnight blue."

"And some silk hose. White?"

"White," Clarence affirmed. "No idea where we'll find such sumptuous fabric to make new breeches. As for the hose, they may get replaced with off-the-rack tights from Asda."

"We've been thinking the specs either belonged to an eyewitness or the murderer," Pauley said. "But this makes it sound like the specs, breeches, and hose were taken at the same time. Do the actors—thespians," she corrected herself, smiling at Clarence, "borrow the costumes for outside performances?"

"They're not supposed to," Clarence said.

"Not sure why anyone would wear bits of costume to a murder," Micki said. "As disguises go, it seems counterproductive to turn up looking like a Florentine fop."

"Maybe the murderer was in costume, but the murder was spur-of-the-moment," Pauley suggested. "Maybe the specs were dropped in the struggle, and the missing trousers and hose are too bloodstained to return to the stage wardrobe." Pauley paused to eat the last bite of her complimentary cannoli. "I mean… it's ridiculous, but that's the best I can do."

"It's not about Romeo breeches, but I have a bit of scuttlebutt from the pub," Micki volunteered suddenly. "Some of the fishermen remembered seeing *Family Man* when she belonged to a second-homer on Tresco. In those days, it was called *White Tiger*. Then the bloke sold it to Jimmy Franks and it took him a year to offload it onto Hermie."

"I wonder how we could find out if Hermie was defaulting on the payments," Pauley said. "And if so, for how long?"

"You think Franks All Marine financed the sale? Not a bank?" Clarence asked.

"Jimmy does deals with people," Pauley said. "He prides himself on it. His whole 'I take care of you, you take care of me. One hand washes another' act," she said, dropping briefly into a passable Hollywood mafia accent. "But most people think it's really about creative bookkeeping to get around Inland Revenue."

"Are you sure you won't swallow your dislike long enough to introduce me?" Jem asked her.

"Nope. I can't stand the man, and the feeling is mutual. But there might be a better way," Pauley said, warming to whatever idea had suddenly come to her. "When Jimmy was a young man, he started out at the Ice Cream Hut. That was before he discovered his inner Al Pacino, but from what I've heard, he was still a handful. The only person he ever respected—the only one who could make him behave—was Bettie Quick."

Jem was intrigued. "I was planning to drop by her house sometime soon, anyway. Maybe if I steer the conversation toward Jimmy Franks, she'll be willing to tell me about him."

Pauley giggled. "Maybe? You know Bettie. She's always up for a good gossip."

CHAPTER TWENTY

"I Wasn't Always a Beach Ball with Legs"

Bettie Quick lived in the Square, in a terraced townhouse built in the 1950s. It was a claustrophobic two-story affair, narrower than modern tastes would approve, with the typical layout: front room for company and gathering around the telly, a kitchen in the back, and a steep staircase in the hall leading up to three bedrooms. As a child, Jem had been frequently dragged over to the Quick residence to sit and read her Lloyd Alexander or Susan Cooper books while Gran and Bettie knitted, or baked treats to sell on festival weekends, or played cribbage with friends around the kitchen table. She remembered the house as dark and smoky, with nicotine-stained ceilings that Gran had contributed to as much as Bettie. But a lot had changed in the years Jem was away.

Since Bettie's diagnosis of chronic pulmonary obstructive disease, she'd given up the cigarettes for good. Then she'd had the painters in, doing the whole place over in robin's egg blue with crisp white wainscoting. The dull, smoky carpets had been pulled up and laminate oak-look floorboards had been laid down, the perfect choice for an island home. Nicotine's baleful ghost had been exorcised.

Bettie, a widow of many years, had recently cleared out much of the junk accumulated over her married life and started afresh with her passion—owls. Nowadays, the only thing Jem recognized about the front room was the electric fire, a remarkably old specimen that had come with the house. Owls peeped out at Jem from everywhere. Ceramic owls, stuffed owls, rustic carved owls recognizable only by shape. Killer beaks, round heads, and wide perceptive eyes were everywhere.

Jem thought she understood the attraction for Bettie. Shrunken in frame but expanded in girth, Bettie's quite spherical middle was balanced on bandy legs. Her face was round; her sparse hair, which was dyed a deep, dark, improbable brown, floated around her head like feathers. Her large, rather protuberant eyes saw everything. And if you found yourself on the wrong side of her, that rosebud mouth would tear you to shreds.

"Is that you, Jem?" Bettie called from the sofa when Jem knocked. Once her front door had been unlocked night and day. Visitors would simply shout their name or "Hello the house!" as they wandered in. But Bettie, who'd lived on St. Morwenna all her life, hadn't got over the shock of a recent murder on their tranquil little island. She probably never would, which meant the door would never stand unlocked again.

"It's me," Jem called back. "Don't get up. I have my key."

Bettie's COPD had taken a turn for the worse, stranding her at home until this latest crisis passed. Jem was in the habit of visiting the old lady once or twice a week, bringing her a takeaway from the Square's restaurants and reporting on her progress with the Gwyn family collection. Bettie liked to talk about the old days, too, when she and Gran were in their prime. Jem was perhaps Bettie's last link to Gran, who'd died too young and without the chance to say goodbye.

In the front room, Jem found Bettie comfortably sunk into her sofa, an owl-shaped pillow in her lap, watching a chat show. All her essentials were within easy reach—rollator, inhaler, daily pill organizer, *Take A Break* magazine, and the TV remote. Sometimes she could go without supplemental oxygen, but today the canister sat on her left in its wheeled cart, the thin plastic cannulae fitted beneath her nostrils. Jem noted that Bettie had taken the trouble to dress, if only in a tracksuit, and dabbed some bold pink blush on her cheeks. That was a good sign, as far as how the illness was treating her today.

"Tea?" Jem asked, setting down her bag.

"Please. Do the chamomile. Extra honey." Bettie picked up the remote, giving the TV's volume a huge boost. "Now you can hear it in the kitchen. They're about to reveal why the groom ran away and left the bride alone at the altar on her wedding day."

"I can't imagine any excuse will fly," Jem said, heading into the kitchen to put the kettle on. Discussing the minutiae of daytime telly was something she'd done with Gran. It was pleasant to fall back into the habit with Bettie, who clearly reveled in the misdeeds and controversial topics presented by the host and chewed over by the studio audience.

When Jem returned with the teapot and some digestive biscuits, Bettie pushed aside her meds and magazines to make room on the coffee table. Setting down the tray with a gentle clatter, Jem poured out two cups, stirred in extra honey, and stuck a biscuit on Bettie's saucer.

"Thanks, love. I wasn't trying to skip a meal. I was working up to venturing into the kitchen, I promise," Bettie said, snapping off the chat show so they could talk without distraction. "The new inhaler preparation is working. Next week, I'll be able to walk down to the hut and inspect things for myself."

She sounded diffident, and Jem didn't think it was because she feared overexerting herself. Bettie had deeper reasons to avoid going down to the hut. Back in June, she'd even flirted with the idea of knocking it down and letting the business die. But the Ice Cream Hut, often billed as "everyone's favorite Scilly tradition," truly was a piece of St. Morwenna's history, and no one was keen to give it up. So rather than pull the plug, which surely would have resulted in some new entrepreneur taking on the sacred Mr. Whippy mantle, Bettie had decided to reopen.

"I saw Lissa serving behind the counter today," Jem said. "She was doing well. All the customers looked happy."

"Aye, she's wonderful at everything she does. For a week," Bettie said, sipping tea. "Then something more interesting comes along—a man, usually. Nothing in Lissa's life matters like the man of the moment. If I take her on, I'll have to sack her inside a month."

"Surely it's not that bad," Jem said. Like Gran, Bettie tended to overemphasize others' shortcomings, and it took a bit of negotiation to inspire a second, more generous assessment.

"She's much improved over how she was," Bettie allowed. "But the fact remains, if our former police chief came to her tomorrow and said, 'Let's run away to Dubai, just you and me, and be together forever,' this is what would happen. Lissa would sit Kenzie down, explain that Mummy's in love, and sorry, everyone, it's time for the little girl to fly solo."

"You don't really believe that."

"Oh, but I do. Pray it never happens," Bettie said mordantly. "Or that if some man's destined to make Lissa an offer she can't refuse, it doesn't happen until Kenzie's of age."

The phrase about making an offer gave Jem the opening she'd been hoping for. "Speaking of godfathers, someone told me the oddest thing about Jimmy Franks. Apparently he likes to speak and behave like an American gangster?"

Bettie gave one of her croaking laughs. It sounded painful, but she looked genuinely amused. "Poor Jimmy. I remember the day he started that. It was the summer he worked at the hut. He'd been a pipsqueak as a boy, and even though he was all grown up, he still felt small."

Smiling fondly, Bettie continued, "It's not easy to be eighteen years old, no special skills, no family name or money, trying to make your mark. One day he started telling customers 'Fuggedaboutit' and 'Badda-bing, badda-boom.' They thought it was hilarious. He thought he was impressing them. So he's only taken on more and more affectations over the years."

"Well, in a way, I guess it worked," Jem said, sipping her tea. "Franks All Marine has been around for a long time and seems pretty successful." She'd been surprised to realize that while on St. Mary's to shop or visit Micki, she'd glimpsed Franks All Marine many times, but never registered it. The compound was situated between the Kernow Arms and the Empire Theater. It was made up of a boatyard, scrap pile, repair shop, and show room. Jimmy Franks maintained at least twenty regular employees, plus freelancers like Rhys, who took on extra work in the high season.

"Oh, yes, he's done well for himself, our Jimmy. He was a handful when we took him on, always starting fights he couldn't finish and chatting up girls instead of working. My Owen," Bettie added, meaning her late husband the crab fisherman, "regretted hiring him. In those days he might be gone three weeks at a time, out to sea and incommunicado. But I said I'd take Jimmy in hand, and I did." Bettie smiled again, her large eyes boring into Jem with a meaning that was impossible to mistake.

"Bettie." Jem was as pleasantly shocked as if it were her own gran confessing an illicit love affair. "Are you telling me something happened between you and Jimmy?"

"How could he resist me? I wasn't always a beach ball with legs."

Clapping a hand over her mouth, Jem stifled her laughter as Bettie broke into more croaks of mirth. After a twenty-year absence, Jem's first glimpse of Bettie had been a shock. Watching the old lady struggle down the steep lane to the Ice Cream Hut, all Jem had been able to think of was an inflatable ball wobbling toward the water. But of course she'd never said so aloud to anyone.

"What? You think I don't have a mirror?" Bettie said. "But I was pretty in my day. In a red dress and stockings, I could knock any man for six. See that leather album on the mantelpiece? Fetch it down for me and I'll prove it."

With the photo album in her hands, Bettie thumbed through the plastic sleeves until she found a photo of herself taken at around age thirty. This must have been in the late eighties, judging by her mass of permed hair, cowl neck sweater, acid wash jeans, and tall black boots.

"Bettie, you were a knockout," Jem said truthfully.

"Yes, well, I still had a bit of it left when Jimmy came along." Flipping more pages, Bettie indicated another picture of herself posing by the Ice Cream Hut. Her hair was straight and shorter, and though she looked far more serious and mature, she filled out her red dress perfectly. Even her pumps were sexy, with peek-a-boo toes.

"I used to have a few pics of Jimmy, but my Owen chucked them in the bin. I think he knew what went on between us." Bettie returned to her tea. "Don't feel sorry for him. He had a girlfriend or two in his time. We made it work for twenty-five years, but it was never perfect. Nothing in this world is, I reckon."

"Do you still see Jimmy from time to time?"

That predatory stare fixed on Jem. "Why? Do you think he murdered the man by the castle?"

"You're on to me." Jem nibbled at a digestive biscuit. "Am I that obvious?"

"Well, when I heard Rhys was arrested, I thought you might have something to say about that. You kids always were inseparable. If you thought he was guilty, you'd be gutted. Since you're clearly not gutted, I figure you must be on the case. Again," she added with a smile. "Why Jimmy?"

"He's one of the few leads I have. After we stumbled upon Hermie Castleberry's corpse, we had lunch at The Ruin. A man who worked there turned out to be Hermie's brother-in-law. There was no love lost between them. He told me that Hermie was in financial difficulties because of a posh sport fishing boat that Jimmy Franks sold to him. And I had the impression he'd been ringing the Castleberries quite a lot, trying to get his money."

"What good would it do to kill the man and sink the boat? Jimmy would've been better off to sue Hermie," Bettie said reasonably.

"I said the same thing. But I can't just make assumptions and then give up. I have to follow up every lead until I come across something that's sure to help Rhys." Jem polished off the biscuit's other half. After lunch at Pirate's Pizza, she wasn't truly hungry. But in this mood, she could eat her way through a whole packet just to feel like she was accomplishing something.

"If you're going to nose around Jimmy, don't forget about Georgia," Bettie said.

Jem blinked. "You know Mrs. Castleberry?"

"In passing." Bettie waved a hand with the air of one whose acquaintance is vast. "When she first came to the Scillies with her boy, she tried lots of jobs. Now she's in that snug little cottage and volunteers at the library. But for at least six months, she worked at All Marine."

"Doing what?"

"Doing what, indeed." Bettie winked. "Whenever I go to St. Mary's, if it's convenient, I pop in to see Jimmy. Not because there's still a spark," she added, as if Jem might accuse her of plying her feminine wiles. "Just to catch up. He's a successful, confident man and I played a part in that. I like to go admire my handiwork, don't I? But as I was saying, at All Marine, Georgia wore all sorts of hats. Once she was in the billing office. Another time, she was in the showroom. Wherever Jimmy was, Georgia wasn't far away."

"Now, I never caught them in the clinch, as it were," Bettie continued, eyes glittering. "But I must say, she gave him such an adoring stare. And Lord knows he played Mr. Big to her swooning secretary. Strutted around in his best suits, jeweled pinkie rings on both hands. And all the gestures," she added, bunching her fingers against her thumb and waving it in a vaguely intimidating manner. "Whenever he does that, I hear guitars strumming and accordions piping."

"Jimmy and Georgia," Jem repeated, turning it over in her mind. Hermie's gruesome death and the destruction of the boat did seem more like a crime of rage or passion than the reaction of a businessman who needed to recoup his losses. "Did it end badly?"

Bettie nodded. "Because of Georgia's ex. She doesn't speak much about him, but apparently he's a brute. That's why she and her boy moved way out to the ends of the earth. She said it was either the Scillies or America, and she hated to leave England altogether."

"What did the ex do?"

"Beat on Jimmy," Bettie said. "Hugh Town buzzed about it for weeks. Poor Jimmy had a black eye and a swollen nose. Our former chief of police claimed he looked into it, but I doubt he looked anywhere except up some bird's skirt."

Jem sat back in her chair, taking it in. Georgia Castleberry had gone from a malevolent ex to the prosperous Jimmy Franks. After the relationship went kaput, she'd met and married the even more prosperous Hermie Castleberry. They'd apparently been quite happy. Teenage stepchildren could be tricky, but at The Ruin, Leo had agreed when Georgia said Hermie treated Leo "like his own." But the marriage only lasted a year. Then Hermie the husband had died by violence, while Jimmy the boyfriend had gotten off with a beating.

There's so much swirling around to muddy the waters, Jem thought. *If there weren't three witnesses, the police wouldn't be laser-focused on Rhys. But witnesses can lie, or be mistaken. And obviously someone is out to make sure Rhys takes the fall, since they planted the bloody gloves and knife on his property.*

In her mind's eye she saw the cut-resistant chef's gloves Buck had uncovered between Tremayne Lighthouse and Rhys's cottage. Looking them up online, she'd learned they weren't actually metal, as she'd first imagined, but a blend of materials, including fiberglass. They were affordable and widely available, which meant that tracing those particular gloves would be a needle in a haystack proposition. Anyone who believed in kitchen safety might own a pair.

"You're miles away," Bettie said, breaking into Jem's reverie.

"Oh. Right. Sorry." Jem smiled. "You've given me a lot to think about. I just wish I had a reason to go to Hugh Town tomorrow and talk to Jimmy Franks. I'll even pretend to enjoy the mafioso routine if it gets him to tell me about Hermie. Or Georgia's violent ex."

"Nothing so easy," Bettie said. "I'll give him a ring. Tell him you'd like to come by at his earliest convenience to discuss selling your boat."

"*Bellatrix*?"

"Oh, don't look like that. You don't have to actually go through with it. Just pretend the boat's not all it's cracked up to be and you'd like to trade up. Jimmy always turns on the charm to a pretty woman with ready money to spend. And when he turns on the charm, he talks."

"You'll ring him now? You don't mind?"

"Mind? If I help you solve a mystery, I'll have bragging rights for the rest of my life," Bettie said. "Fetch me another cup of tea, love, and hand me that phone."

CHAPTER TWENTY-ONE

Downton Abbey Dresses and a Smoker's Cough

When Jem returned to the Square, it was past three o'clock. Micki had already departed for her job on St. Mary's, and Clarence had gone back to *Gwin & Gweli*, where he always had some small repair or improvement in progress. Pauley, seated on a bench near Pirate's Pizza, was holding up a doggie treat for Buck, who'd learned to sit up and beg.

"Wow, that's impressive. Good job, Buck," Jem said, applauding as the treat disappeared into the little dog's mouth. "And well done you," she told Pauley. "He's finally learned a trick. Rhys will be green with envy with he gets back. Why did you go back to the house to get him? Were you tortured by the memory of him whining with his little face on his paws?"

"Nothing like," Pauley said, smiling. "I was in the Co-op browsing the veg when Milo said, 'Hey, Pauley, I don't mean to be a pain, but there's no pets allowed inside.' I turned around to ask him why on earth he was telling me that, and that's when I saw this fellow"—she gave Buck's ears an affectionate pull—"standing next to the melons looking pleased as punch."

"But we locked up the house before we left."

"I know. Rhys always says Buck's like Houdini. I thought he was just being careless and blaming it on the pup. But look at him. That's a very cheeky stare," Pauley said, tucking the rest of the doggie treats safely inside her bag. "So I told Milo thanks very much, bought these canine nibbles, and carried Buck out here to work on his tricks."

"You don't think he got out through a window?" Jem asked, alarmed. In the past, there had been serious problems with the sturdiness of Lyonesse House's windows.

"No. The glazier promised me the new ones would last twenty years, minimum. Of course, I didn't ask him if a little bloody-minded dog might break out."

"There isn't a cat flap I overlooked?"

"No."

"Buck." Jem squatted down beside him. "When we get home, I expect you to lead us to your escape hatch."

Buck's black button eyes shone serenely. The little dog liked her, but he clearly had no intention of turning over his hole card.

As Jem, Pauley, and Buck walked back to Lyonesse House, Jem explained about her upcoming appointment at Franks All Marine.

"Jimmy's out for the weekend, so Bettie couldn't get me in before half-ten the following Tuesday," Jem said. "I hate to delay—heaven knows what it's like for Rhys in jail—but that was the best she could do."

"It might be for the best," Pauley said. "It'll probably be easier to pump Jimmy for information on a weekday, when he's less likely to be swamped, than on one of the last Saturdays in the high season."

"I didn't think of it like that. In the meantime, Kenzie texted me Sharon MacAfee's number," Jem said. "I'll call her and see what she has to say. If she's Rhys's girlfriend, surely she'll be able to help establish an alibi."

"Don't you think Hack or the detective in charge would've talked to her already?" Pauley asked.

"Probably. But I think they're hanging everything on the witnesses, and the idea that Hermie died on Saturday morning. Just because no one believes me about Hermie being tied down under water doesn't mean proof isn't forthcoming. The chest and ropes might wash up. The autopsy might show that Hermie died hours earlier. If either or both of those things happen, the witnesses won't seem so reliable. If Sharon can vouch for Rhys's whereabouts Friday night, that will prove he's not the killer."

Jem then filled Pauley in on the rest of Bettie's gossip about Georgia: her previous employment at Franks All Marine, her apparent romance with Jimmy, and how her brutish ex had scared the faux gangster away.

"That sounds interesting. And you know I love Bettie," Pauley said doubtfully. "But was she absolutely sure about this? Sometimes she leaps to conclusions. Big ones."

"Like what?"

Pauley snorted. "Like about you, not so long ago."

"That was an emotional time. What else?"

"Well, last March she heard I got a call from St. Mary's Hospice in the middle of the night, telling me to come as fast as I could. So while I was gone, she told everyone that Mum had died and they should offer condolences. When I got back to St. Morwenna, I had to tell every single person on the island that Mum was still very much alive."

Jem took that in. "All right. Well, strictly speaking, she didn't say that Georgia and Jimmy were an item, just that they seemed like one. As for the ex…" Jem thought back, trying to recall exactly how the old woman had phrased her information. "She must have got at least some of it straight from Georgia, because she said when Georgia fled, she chose between the Isles of Scilly or America. And because she didn't want to leave England, she came here."

"Yeah, well, I'll ask around. I hear things, too, you know," Pauley said with a grin. "Guess what? After Micki left, I chatted with Clarence and we came up with an idea about how to solve his mystery—the missing Romeo breeches and hose."

Jem snorted. "Our cause is Free Rhys, not replenish the costume closet."

"Oh, it's just for a lark. Might even earn me some money. Did I mention I still have a ton of vintage stuff from my grandparents?" Pauley asked. "My great-grandparents, even. It's all packed in crates in the large wing, waiting for the day I decide what to do with it. There are real furs, which is gross, but it's not like we can resurrect the minks that died a hundred years ago. Might as well reuse them, and they'd be great for costumes. There are also some gorgeous, but tiny, *Downton Abbey* style dresses I couldn't get one leg into, and I don't have the heart to cut up."

Jem, who repeatedly caught herself imagining her forthcoming phone call with Sharon MacAfee, didn't follow. "So, selling your family's old clothes will bring back the Romeo breeches... how?"

"The wardrobe is bait. I'll write up a placard and Clarence will post it on the message center inside the theater. If someone ruined the breeches with Hermie's blood or anything else, they might be looking to replace them. I'll put on the card that I have Shakespearian outfits and Florentine outfits. That should do the trick."

"And when he or she comes to see the collection, you'll tell them...?"

"That they were sold. But at least I will have flushed out the guilty party. And maybe if I talk to this person just right, I'll get them to confess about the Romeo breeches. And the wire specs, too."

Jem pulled a face. "You're pretty confident about your powers of persuasion. I have a decent cover story for talking to Jimmy Franks, and I'm still worried he'll stonewall me. You're just assuming you can win over some actor—some *thespian*, as Clarence likes to say—and get him to bare his soul to you?"

"Listen, if you can run around pulling silly stunts, so can I. The wire specs were found awfully close to Hermie's body. They still might link back to him."

"If you really want to free Rhys, why don't you come with me to Franks All Marine? Give me moral support while I deal with Jimmy?"

"No, thank you," Pauley said. "The man is both underhanded and handsy. Under-handsy, as I call it, and I don't need that. I'll stay home with Buck and get the vintage wardrobe smoothed and aired. If you need backup, take Micki. He might be so smitten by the two of you together, he'll be respectful. For once."

*

Back inside Lyonesse House, Jem and Pauley did what felt like a comprehensive survey of each and every room, but still couldn't determine how Buck had escaped. The new windows in the small wing were secure; the doors were closed and locked. Unless Buck had done a reverse Santa up a chimney and then taken a flying leap off the roof, there seemed to be no explanation for how he'd got out.

"All right. It will have to remain a mystery for now," Pauley said. "Buck and I are off to do yoga. Come along. You're making great progress," she said, and the little dog trotted after her into the small wing, leaving Jem alone. It was time to call Sharon MacAfee.

Although Jem had set up residence in one of Lyonesse House's guest rooms, she went into the library to make her call. During her weeks of work on the Gwyn family collection, she'd begun to think of the room as her exclusive province. Even with half the shelves bare and all the most fragile books already transferred to the Courtney Library in Penzance, the room still possessed a residue of its old magic. Jem suspected that magic would never leave it, and it made her want to refill those gaping shelves with a brand new collection. But of course she did—she wouldn't have been much of a librarian if she didn't.

Since it was late afternoon, Jem expected Sharon MacAfee to still be at work. To her surprise, the woman not only answered, but picked up on the first ring.

"This is Sharon. What's up?"

The blunt greeting startled Jem. She'd expected a lilting voice, one that conjured up the image of a woman with bikini curves and bouncy blonde hair. Sharon sounded no-nonsense and raspy, like she was already on her second pack of the day.

"Hello, Sharon. My name's Jem. I wonder if you have a moment to talk about something very important to me."

"Sure. What's eating you, lovely?"

Surprised by Sharon's earthy willingness to chat, it took Jem a moment to formulate her question. "It's about last Friday. The night before Hermie Castleberry was discovered dead on the beach. I understand my friend Rhys Tremayne visited you on Tresco?"

A pause. "How did you get this number?"

"From one of Rhys's other friends. As I'm sure you know, he's been arrested for something he didn't do, and we're all terribly concerned."

"I've already talked to the police. If that's all—"

"Please don't hang up. I'm so sorry, I know I'm intruding," Jem said, amazed at how rapidly Sharon had pivoted from wide open to tight as a drum. "But the police won't discuss the evidence they have on Rhys, and we haven't been allowed to speak with him.

"They seem to think that on Saturday morning, he went out to Candlewick Castle and found Hermie washed up, still alive. A witness claims to have seen Rhys near Hermie that morning, with the implication that Rhys killed him then and there.

"But I'm the person who found the body," Jem continued, a little unnerved by Sharon's steady silence. Not many people had the trick of simply listening without interjecting or making a sound. "He'd been dead for hours. Also, I dove into the channel and saw the shipwreck before the police arrived. I'm sure Hermie was weighted down underwater. Even though the evidence got washed away before the dive team saw it, I think the autopsy will prove me right about time of death. If we can establish Rhys's whereabouts during Friday night, plus when Hermie actually died and when he was put in the channel, the police might drop the charges."

Jem waited. For a moment, she thought the other woman had hung up on her. Then Sharon broke into a smoker's cough so harsh, Jem had to jerk her ear away from the phone.

"Are you, erm, quite all right?"

"Yeah. Need to kick the habit. It's on my to-do list," Sharon rasped. If she had any other comments about Jem's rationale for calling, she kept them to herself.

"So, without meaning to be too personal or invade your privacy, could you tell me about last Friday night? When Rhys arrived, for example, and how the, erm, night went?" That last bit came out slightly wrong, but rather than dither and correct herself, Jem let the inelegant question stand.

Sharon coughed again, but this time it sounded manufactured. "I'm afraid not, Ms. Jago."

"I don't think I gave you my surname. I take it you've heard of me?" Jem asked warily.

"Oh, I know all about you," Sharon said, in a significant tone Jem found more unsettling. Then, seeming to backpedal, Sharon said, "Not personally, of course. Just that you came back to the islands and solved a mystery. And now it looks like you're crashing your way into this investigation. Just have to be the hero, don't you?"

That reminded Jem of what Hack had told her about hero syndrome—how people sometimes enjoyed being helpful to investigators so much, they actually committed crimes in order to solve them. At the time, she'd believed he was just sharing a police anecdote. Had he actually been hinting that if she kept on digging, she risked going down the same road?

"I'm one of Rhys's oldest friends," Jem said levelly, refusing to rise to Sharon's bait. "When it comes to clearing his name, I'll gladly be the hero, villain, or anything in-between. Please, Sharon, whatever you can tell me will be greatly appreciated."

Sharon sighed. "All right. This is what I said to the police. Rhys turned up on Tresco around nine o'clock. I'd just come in from work—there's always extra garden chores in summer," she said, reminding Jem that she worked in the famous Abbey Gardens, arguably the Isles of Scilly's number one attraction.

"We were together for an hour. Then I went off to do my thing while he set up an easel on my deck and painted. When I went to bed, it was around one a.m., and he was still up."

Jem stifled a sigh. That covered Rhys for part of the night, but not all of it. The gale had blown in around three a.m., leaving two hours unaccounted. And that was assuming Sharon was being completely candid. If she had an attachment to Rhys—if he frequently met her on Fridays and spent the night—she might lie or obfuscate in an effort to make him seem innocent.

"Could he have left your place during the night and returned without you noticing?"

"Anything's possible."

That surprised Jem. "Wouldn't it wake you up?"

"I'm a heavy sleeper. And he has his key."

Once again, Jem choked back her reaction. She'd been imagining a friends-with-benefits situation, the sort of thing that was (1) none of her business and (2) easier to accept than a resplendent love story for the ages. But if Rhys possessed a key to Sharon's place, that implied something serious.

"How did he seem the next morning?"

Sharon laughed. It quickly turned into another long, hacking cough. "You mean, was he guilty and nervous and whatnot? I was wiped out from the extra hours at the garden and slept past ten o'clock. When I came out for coffee, he seemed normal. Then he got the phone call."

Jem waited. Sharon seemed to enjoy these abrupt conversational stops, as if to emphasize her reluctance to reveal anything. Trying not to sound as exasperated as she felt, Jem asked, "What phone call?"

"I don't know. He didn't say. His mobile rang, he answered, listened, and the next thing I knew, he was packing up his art stuff. Said he had to dress for a lunch meeting with his agent. I said, I thought you fired your agent. He said, it's on again. Then he left for The Ruin, and I left for a run on the beach. The end."

That account tallied with part of what Jem already believed. Rhys had gone out to Candlewick Castle that morning to paint the storm-washed coast. When the tide went out, Hermie's body must have been revealed. So, too, had the orange dry canister full of drugs and cash. After choosing to recoup his losses rather than ring the police, he'd returned to Sharon's, perhaps to eat breakfast and say goodbye. Now came another puzzle piece: an upsetting phone call. Whoever had called, they'd said something that disturbed Rhys enough to make him try and establish an alibi by appearing in public nattily dressed and seemingly expecting Hermie to turn up alive.

"Thanks, Sharon. I appreciate your help," Jem said, forcing herself to make nice in case she needed Sharon's assistance again. Besides, if she was speaking to Rhys's close friend—make that girlfriend—she had a duty to be friendly, didn't she?

"Don't worry about Rhys. Everything happens for a reason. It's all part of the plan," Sharon signed off with mystifying serenity. "Take care, Jem."

CHAPTER TWENTY-TWO

Peace Offering

Sunday went rather pleasantly, considering Rhys still hadn't been permitted to make or receive phone calls, and the interview with Jimmy Franks was still two days away. Kenzie checked in to say Leo was ghosting her. When Jem rang Georgia to ask how the widow was doing—and also to find out if she had any other complaints about how the police were handling the murder investigation—Georgia sounded too dazed to converse properly.

"I'm trying a new medication," she mumbled. "Doesn't help. But makes me sleepy." With that, she'd disconnected, leaving Jem to pity her once more. A good sleuth surely considered everyone a suspect, but it was hard to see anything in Georgia but misery and grief.

Jem tried to make up for her missing day in the library, but it was difficult to concentrate on her work, even her pet project of Sir Declan Gwyn's diary.

Sharon's mention of the phone call was tantalizing. If only there was some way for an ordinary citizen to check into such things. Jem hoped Rhys's lawyer had the wit to go over his phone records so the caller could be traced.

I wonder if the witness who says they saw Rhys standing over Hermie is the same person who called him, she thought. *And who is this person? A local, surely. Someone who recognized Rhys and knew exactly how to get in touch with him. Of course, even mainlanders*

*who hop over to the islands on weekends would. His runabout boat
rentals are listed on every bulletin board.*

By midafternoon, Jem and Pauley gave up on work and took
Buck for a walk on Crescent Beach. The turquoise waters were
dazzlingly clear, the rollers gentle as they spread foam on the
gleaming shore. Buck often ran to the limit of his lead, harassing
gulls and inspecting shells, apparently in hopes of finding a crab.
Ever protective of her alabaster goth skin, Pauley applied extra
sun cream to her face, since it was too windy for a hat. Jem didn't
mind. The breeze was so pleasant, she let down her hair, allowing
it to stream around her as they followed the little dog, trainers off
and toes digging deep in the sand.

By the time they got back to their shoes, Micki and Clarence
had turned up. He seemed to be in a fine mood, resplendent in a
bright red hibiscus shirt, but Micki looked slightly apprehensive.
Since that was unusual for her, Jem assumed it had something to
do with her singing career.

"What's up? Still dodging Monty's band with excuses about
your bartending schedule?"

"Yes," Clarence laughed. "But not for much longer. Tell her,
love."

"I've decided to give up my flat," Micki announced. "I'm going
to be Clarence's permanent boarder."

"Good for you!" Pauley said, squatting to give Buck a belly rub.
"That will save you a ton."

"Oh, I'll pay a fair rate," Micki said. "He wanted to let me have
the room for nothing but expenses, but I said no. We're helping
each other out. I'll get a break on my rent, and he'll have enough
guaranteed income to keep *Gwin & Gweli* in business over the
autumn and winter."

"Hallelujah," Clarence agreed. "I'm over the moon. Mind
you, if I don't get a decent slate of paying guests by spring, I'll be

bankrupt. Not the way I envisioned my retirement in the islands, I can tell you. Still, it's a problem for another day." Catching his cousin around the waist and squeezing her tight, he added, "And now that you'll be living with me, my dear, I'm sure I can help you adjust your schedule so you make those dates with Monty and the band."

Micki looked slightly green, but nodded nonetheless.

Around seven o'clock, Jem, Pauley, and Buck returned to Lyonesse House. Micki and Clarence declined their invitation to dinner—they were fond of dancing, and wanted to check out a Hugh Town club. Inside the kitchen, Pauley filled up Buck's bowl and dug into her recipe books for a favorite summer dish, red chili and ricotta pasta. Jem, who felt encrusted with salt and sand, headed off to take a shower. After she toweled off and halfway blow-dried her hair—with hair as long as Jem's, fully blow-drying it would create split ends—she put it up in a ponytail, slipped on a sundress, and walked barefoot into the kitchen. There she found Pauley, Buck, and Hack, who gave her a hopeful smile. He was dressed in his civilian clothes, which meant the visit was unofficial.

"Sorry to drop by uninvited," he said. The cocky shine in his eyes suggested that he nevertheless expected her to say it was fine.

When Jem's stubborn streak kept her from uttering those words, Pauley stepped in. "Dinner is served. I made too much, as usual, and Jem and I hate leftovers. I do hope you'll stay and help us finish the pot, Hack."

"My pleasure." He was still looking at Jem. "Is that all right with you?"

"Of course." She had no appetite for continuing the fight. Besides, seeing Hack always gave her a premonitory tingle, as if something exciting was just around the corner.

"Come on, little man," Pauley said, picking up Buck and carrying him into her bedroom.

"He can stay. I like dogs," Hack said.

"You wouldn't after he spent the whole meal begging," Pauley said, shutting the door. Buck barked in protest, and she answered, "Play with your rope toy!"

Hack sat down at the kitchen table.

"Ever tried Holy Vale?" Jem asked, pulling a bottle from the rack.

"Is that whiskey?"

"Wine. In this case, Pinot noir. It's local," Jem said. Working a corkscrew into the top, she opened it with a pop as Pauley dished up the pasta.

"This smells amazing," Hack said appreciatively as a plate was set before him.

"Give this a sniff and a taste first," Jem said, handing him a glass. To no one's surprise, it met his approval. The Scillies offered many good things, and one of them was red wine.

Dinner passed pleasantly, in part because no one mentioned Hermie's murder or Rhys's arrest. When they were done, Pauley rose to gather the dishes, asking, "Anyone up for coffee?"

"No, thanks. Stuffed," Jem said.

"I need to be up early tomorrow," Hack said.

"Fair enough. Now, don't think of washing-up. House rules are to save it for later," Pauley announced, pulling the bogus rule out of thin air. "Besides, there's a program about to come on telly that I always watch, so I'm off. Good to see you, Hack." And with that completely fraudulent exit, Pauley disappeared, leaving Jem and Hack alone.

For a moment, they stared at each other over their empty wineglasses. Then Hack said, "I come bearing a peace offering."

"Really?" Jem sat up straight, assuming it had to be about Hermie and Rhys. "It's the autopsy, isn't it? It must've proved me right about time of death."

Hack flashed an apologetic smile. "I'm sorry. I absolutely can't discuss any privileged details from Devon & Cornwall's investigation. This is a different sort of peace offering." Going to the peg where his windcheater hung, he withdrew something from its inner pocket.

Back at the table, he placed the item, a paperback book, in front of Jem. It was an old gothic, battered and perhaps forty years old, with a lurid cover depicting what looked like vampires rising from the gnarled roots of an ancient tree. The title, *Haunted Cornwall*, made her smile.

"Noticed it in the window of a charity shop," Hack said. "That's up your street, isn't it? Old books about the West Country?"

She didn't have the heart to correct him. How would he understand the work of a Special Collections Librarian when she'd spent the last few weeks avoiding him?

"Old books about the West Country it is," she said gamely. "Oh, look, this one includes a story by Daphne du Maurier. Do you like her?"

Hack shrugged. "Would you think less of me if I told you I haven't read a work of fiction since leaving school?"

"You're kidding."

Hack gave the three-finger salute of a scout. "Swear. I read all sorts of things—histories, popular science, sport, even gardening, though I lost my allotment when I relocated from Exeter, obviously. But fiction…?" He shook his head. "I prefer to stick with what's real."

"I suppose that tracks, Mr. Policeman."

"While your friend Rhys is a voracious reader, I imagine."

Jem blinked. "What?"

"Just something I heard on Tresco. While doing the scut work adjacent to the real investigation," Hack said amiably, as if he bore the mainland police no ill will. "We were charged with fact-checking certain statements. Did Rhys take one of his runabouts to Tresco? Check. Did anyone see him at the flat of Ms. Sharon MacAfee around nine o'clock Friday night? Check. According to a neighbor, he and about eight other people meet there every couple of weeks for their book club."

"Book club?"

"Yes. Apparently, they're quite serious about it. Everyone comes with a book in hand. Someone brings nibbles," Hack said. "And if Ms. MacAfee runs late, one of the other members is empowered to unlock the door to her flat and start the meeting without her. According to the neighbor across the way, a lady who notices all the comings and goings, the person who opens up is frequently Rhys."

Jem, who prided herself on her powers of deduction, wasn't following. She felt like the more Hack explained, the stupider she became.

"The neighbor said she'd been told it was a book club. But since the members always seem to arrive carrying the same book, she inferred that it might be a Twelve Step meeting."

"Oh. Oh!" Jem grinned at Hack, suddenly cottoning on. "That explains so much. I called Sharon MacAfee today, just to see if she knew anything helpful. She answered the phone like she was used to fielding calls from strangers at all hours. And while she told me Rhys was with her for an hour, she refused to give any other details."

"I should tell you off for that. Pretend I did." Taking out his phone, Hack fiddled with his web browser until he succeeded in bringing up an Alcoholics Anonymous chapter page. "See?"

Jem looked. One of the meeting locations was an address on Tresco. The contact was listed as Sharon M.

"So you no longer think inebriation was a factor?" Jem asked with only the faintest note of triumph.

"It seems less likely," Hack allowed. "Especially if, hypothetically speaking, the autopsy does suggest Castleberry was submerged in the water for quite some time. Or if sometime this morning, as I like to imagine it—this is pure imagination, mind you—an ice chest like you described was recovered on the coast of Bryher. With the ropes still on it, looped and knotted on the ends, as you said." He fixed her with a meaningful gaze. "These are my personal imaginings. I'm trusting you not to reveal them to anyone."

"Sorry. Miles away. Didn't hear a word," Jem said happily. "That knocks out one of the three witnesses, eh?"

Hack blinked at her.

"You know, the one who said Hermie was still alive on the beach until Rhys came close, and then Hermie was a corpse."

Hack still didn't answer.

"What? Was I supposed to phrase all that as a fantasy or a dream sequence?"

Finally, he laughed, shaking his head. "No. It's just… you astonish me. I don't know how you heard about the witness, and I don't want to know. But you're right. The man from Bryher recanted when I asked him today. Said he'd indulged in some strong brew Friday night, and while he definitely saw Rhys on the beach and close to the body, the rest might be wrong."

"What's he like, this man?" Jem asked. "Solid citizen? Trustworthy?"

"Not even close. More of a burnout. Ran afoul of the law by squatting on the mainland. Not the sort of person I'd ever put in front of a jury," Hack said.

Jem suddenly remembered Simon's friend from the Byway, who'd dressed like a teen, had a lined face like a fisherman, and smelled like a 70s head shop. "You don't mean Noah the couch-surfer, do you?"

"How do you do it?" Hack shook his head again. "I shouldn't tell you, obviously, but yes. Noah Atwell. No fixed address. No occupation. Likes to talk about human rights and the evils of corporations."

"I only met him briefly, but I thought he was bad news," Jem said. "I wonder why he lied about Rhys. Do you think it was hero syndrome?"

Hack shrugged. "I've been a policeman for almost twenty years. It's a myth that people only lie for rational reasons. The phrase 'Why would I lie?' is utterly pointless. People lie for every reason under the sun."

"Do you think Noah is the person who called Rhys before he left Sharon's?"

Hack made a noise that could have been admiration, aggravation, or a mixture of both. "I'm not even going to ask. Maybe you're psychic. Anyway, the answer is, I don't know yet. After discrediting his story, I thought he might be, so I pulled the records for calls to Rhys's mobile. All I managed to establish was the call lasted twenty-eight seconds, and was made from a cheap burner phone that's only been used a handful of times. The personal data was falsified. Unless we stumble across it in the course of doing a search, that avenue is hopeless."

"Falsified how? Did it link back to Mr. I. P. Freely or something?"

"No, to a real person. Mr. Seth Mourby of Hugh Town."

"Huh," Jem said.

"Do you know him?"

"We've met. How can you be sure it's falsified?"

"His first name and surname were correct, but the middle name was wrong," Hack said. "His address was right, but his date of birth was way off. Moreover, the purchase was made three weeks ago, when Mr. Mourby was in Plymouth preparing for a Sea Guides retreat. Seems like a clear case of someone using his identity to cover their purchase."

"You know that Sea Guide retreat actually took place during the time of the murder, right?" Jem asked. "It was happening on Bryher. Friday and Saturday were the final days."

Hack nodded. "This case is full of little dangling threads. The dry canister full of cocaine and cash. Those antique glasses you found near the body. The artist's knife you found on the gun deck and chose to give to Rhys instead of me."

Jem, who'd nearly forgotten that transgression, looked at him apologetically. "That wasn't a case of deliberately defying you. I forgot about it, what with diving for the wreck, finding the canister, and all that. Pauley recognized the brand as Piranesi, which is Rhys's, so we gave it back to him. It didn't occur to us at the time that he would be under suspicion for murder."

"Pauley told me as much while you were in the shower. I think she wanted to make sure there was no lingering distrust between us. All three of us, I mean."

"I'm glad she did," Jem said. "But about the phone call. The one that may or may not have been from Noah. Can't you ask Rhys what was said? Why it made him want to try and stage an alibi?"

"I could," Hack said. "Of course, that would infuriate DS Conrad, who would consider it trespassing on his patch. And if Rhys has any sort of competent counsel, they'll instruct him not to answer. It might not come out until the pre-trial discovery phase. Let's hope we can find a more compelling prime suspect for Conrad before Rhys's case goes that far."

"I may have one," Jem admitted. "Now that we're exchanging imaginings and fantasies, can I tell you about it without kicking off another row?"

"I've already abandoned my principles for some pasta and wine. Talk on."

Jem explained about her visit to Bettie Quick. Mention of Hermie Castleberry's deteriorated relationship with Jimmy Franks didn't surprise Hack. However, Georgia's past employment at Franks All Marine, as well as her alleged romance with Jimmy and its violent end, obviously came as news.

"Let me get this straight. Georgia Castleberry has a dangerous ex who attacked Jimmy and may have killed her husband? That's interesting," Hack said thoughtfully. "I wonder if he's the master-mind type who would try to set up another man to take the fall."

"You mean the knife and gloves planted near the lighthouse," Jem said. "I've been thinking about them. I wonder if the knife is actually the murder weapon, or if the bloodstains are even a match for Hermie."

"When it comes to crucial DNA evidence, I can't tell you," Hack said, nodding his head "Yes" slowly and unmistakably.

"But it was such an obvious plant. I can't believe a jury would be fooled."

He shrugged. "If Rhys ends up in the dock, CPS will find a way to make the gloves and knife work. Get an expert witness to claim recovering alcoholics are statistically incapable of flinging objects in the sea or something."

"You could find an expert witness to say that?"

"You can find an expert witness to say quite literally anything." Hack sighed. "Which is why I for one think it's best to avoiding arresting the wrong person. Once it goes to trial, the truth can get muddled, fast. About Georgia's dangerous ex. Do you know if he's the boy's father? Leo, I mean."

Jem, who'd only just been patting herself on the back for her thoroughness, realized she hadn't considered that angle. "Let me text my source and find out."

Leo's surname is Dupree.

Why? Kenzie replied.

Still working on Free Rhys.

Do you know his biological dad's full name?

Sorry. No. Kenzie sent back.

Jem relayed this information to Hack, who seemed to turn over the possibilities in his head. "I can run the name through the databases, to see if Georgia married someone called Dupree, and if he's had run-ins with the law. But…"

"But what?"

"If it comes to the attention of DS Conrad somehow, I'll be walking around with half an arse for the rest of my life." Taking out his smartphone, he added, "This may take a while. Lots of security hoops to jump through."

In truth, it took only twenty minutes for Hack to confirm that Georgia Castleberry, then Georgia Morrison, had married Conor Dupree eighteen years prior. They'd divorced seven years ago, and Georgia had left her home city, Norwich, for the Isles of Scilly.

"Conor Dupree is an ex-convict," Hack said. "Nineteen years ago, he served six months for grievous bodily harm. After he got out, he married Georgia, but if she expected to change him, she didn't get far. He was arrested seven times thereafter."

"For attempted murder?"

"No. For criminal damage, possession of offensive weapons, and drugs."

"Is he in prison?" Jem asked, hoping the answer was no.

"Not at the moment. But the drugs charge is a slender reed we can cling to, since it links back to the coke stashed in the dry canister," Hack said. "I'll spend tomorrow discreetly checking into his last known whereabouts. If we can place him in Hugh Town on the day Jimmy Franks was attacked, that's good. If we can place him anywhere in the Scillies or the Cornish coast around last Friday, even better."

"All right," Jem said. If she'd been talking this over with Pauley, she would've pulled out her pretty velvet-covered notebook and gel pen, but she didn't care to do that in front of Hack.

"Rhys had a good reason to be on Tresco," she began. "Going to the castle to paint is perfectly in character. Taking a big kitchen knife and anti-cut gloves just in case he found a half-dead enemy lying on the beach—ridiculous. Cutting Hermie's throat, transporting the murder weapon and gloves back to St. Morwenna and burying them where they were sure to be found—even more ridiculous.

"Taking Hermie's cash was stupid, and illegal, but it doesn't go along with murder," she continued. "Especially when Noah the couch-surfer has recanted and Roddy Levitt literally told me he just enjoys making trouble. So what if Rhys followed Hermie aboard *Family Man* to tell him off? That's not enough to hold or charge anyone. The only thing left against Rhys is the witness who supposedly overheard Rhys threaten Hermie, right?"

Hack nodded.

"Of course, you made it very clear that it would be unethical for you to tell m—"

"Oh, for heaven's sake," Hack broke in. "A kid who does odd jobs at Franks All Marine witnessed a verbal altercation between Rhys and Castleberry. It happened in the back lot, where the waste bins are kept. The boy told Newt he was breaking down cardboard boxes and saw Castleberry standing a little apart from the building, making a call. Rhys was seen coming upon Castleberry in a rage, shouting and waving his arms. He reportedly said something to the effect of, 'I'll have you,' and 'You're a dead man,' several times."

Jem laughed. "That doesn't sound like him at all. When Rhys is angry—really angry—he doesn't make threats. He acts. That story sounds like something taken out of a crime drama. Did the witness overhear why Rhys was angry?"

Hack shook his head. "He claimed he kept well back, sort of hidden behind the rubbish, so he wouldn't be seen."

"And how did Hermie react to his life being threatened?"

"According to the witness, he seemed so frightened by Rhys, he fled. End of confrontation. No one else saw it or had anything to add because it conveniently happened at the end of the day, beside the bins."

"It's absolute rubbish. Would I be completely mad to ask you for the kid's name?"

"Simon Weatherby. Age twenty. Lifelong resident of St. Mary's. Still lives with his mum. Never been in trouble."

"Simon," Jem repeated. "Does he tend to—?" She did the finger guns routine, complete with *pew-pew-pew* sounds.

Hack grinned. "That's a positive I.D."

"I met him just after you told me Rhys was arrested. Pauley and I were going down the Byway, on the way to fetch Buck, when we ran into Simon and his friend Noah. Simon's the one who called Noah a couch-surfer extraordinaire."

Hack sat up straight, his amiable expression vanishing.

"Simon told us that he and Noah had been on Crescent Beach, watching Rhys's arrest on the clifftop. Neither showed any sympathy for Rhys. They were cracking jokes to impress the girls."

"Simon and Noah together?" Hack repeated.

"Is that important?"

"It could be a conspiracy. I have no choice but to look into it, Conrad or no Conrad. Usually witnesses, especially younger ones like Simon, feel torn over getting involved. Particularly if they're offering supporting testimony, as opposed to direct knowledge of the crime. They feel like supplying details makes them a grass. For Mr. Weatherby and Mr. Atwell to go to St. Morwenna and watch the fruits of their labor is very troubling."

"Do you think they're working for the real killer?" Jem asked.

"Maybe. There's also a chance that Conor Dupree is our man. If so, he might even still be here, hiding somewhere in the Isles of Scilly. Mrs. Castleberry went a long way to escape him, but possibly not far enough." He stood up. "I'd better head back to the station and see what more I can find out. I hope Conrad takes the news that his case is falling apart better than I think he will."

"Did you know him from before? When you worked in Exeter?" Jem asked. Now seemed as good a time to dare the question as any.

"Yes. We weren't exactly one another's biggest fans. Now, Jem." Hack regarded her seriously. "Promise me you won't do anything to try and find the real killer yourself. You saw Castleberry's body. The person responsible is highly dangerous and probably remorseless. The burner phone, the elaborate effort to fit up Rhys—those all indicate an antisocial personality at work, as opposed to murder committed in the heat of the moment."

"I might ask a few questions," Jem said, unable to admit she'd made an appointment to see Jimmy Franks in less than forty-eight hours. Hack would only force her to break it, and the nexus of activity around Franks All Marine fascinated her. Georgia had worked there; she may or may not have dated Jimmy; her dead husband and Jimmy had a strained friendship. Now the seemingly impartial eyewitness who assigned motive to Rhys was actually employed by Jimmy Franks. Conor Dupree was an enticing shiny object, especially in light of his many arrests—and come to think of it, he had a Franks All Marine connection, too.

"No actual meddling," Hack warned, pointing his finger at her. "No mystery novel stuff, putting on disguises or eavesdropping from inside wardrobes."

Rising, Jem crossed the kitchen to see him out. "I'll be working in the library and being a good citizen. You'll see."

Hack put his head to one side. "You worry me most when you try to be sweet. So are we okay? Friends?"

"Of course."

"Good." Hack moved closer, looking steadily into her eyes. "Because I don't want to blindside you, since I'm sure you never saw this coming, but I want us to be more than friends."

She smiled. "You didn't think that first kiss got the message across?"

"I'm old school. I like to be sure."

He leaned in, and Jem lifted her face for his kiss. This time it was deeper, more passionate, followed by another shivery zing up her spine.

"Friends is a good place to start," she said warmly, holding his gaze.

"Still saving that dance for me?"

Jem nodded.

"Good. Now I'll go do what I can to help your big blond ex so you can put him out of your mind forever." Winking, Hack pulled his windcheater off its peg, slipped it on, and left.

Jem was putting the kettle on for some pre-bedtime herbal tea when Pauley returned, peeking around the door as if something indescribably racy might be happening on the kitchen table. "Is the peace officer with a peace offering gone?"

"He is."

"Good." Pauley rubbed her hands together. "Tell me everything."

CHAPTER TWENTY-THREE

The Capo Dei Capi

Jem arrived on St. Mary's around ten a.m. Tuesday morning. After mooring *Bellatrix* in the vicinity of Porthcressa Beach, she made her way into Hugh Town and toward Franks All Marine, which was visible from the bay.

Jimmy Franks had done very well for himself since his humble beginnings as a part-time employee of the Ice Cream Hut. His business was so large it had spilled out of its original digs and was now a compound that included a boatyard, machine shop, retail shop, and new boat showroom. Jem could only hope that masquerading as an unsatisfied boat owner wouldn't turn her into one. She adored *Bellatrix*, and she could afford *Bellatrix*, which was a winning combination. The prospect of *oohing* and *aahing* over sleek new fiberglass numbers with various bells and whistles made her uncomfortable. Even the idea seemed disloyal to her little fishing boat and its classic wood-paneled sides.

With time to spare, she walked a little ways up the lane to check out the Empire Theater, home of the Tidal Pool Players. It was an old brick building with a long history of entertaining the islands in various ways. First built for music hall variety shows, it was remodeled into a picture house in the early fifties, then closed and reopened as a community playhouse in the late eighties. Scillonians loved their dramas, whether on telly, at the cinema, or sat in a folding chair in front of a stage. There was a certain magic about live theater.

With set design finished, the players were now in rehearsals for their latest offering, the comedy about fractured fairy tales. Opening night was only four days away. Unless Rhys was free before Saturday at nine o'clock, someone else would have to play the Pransome Hence. It was a shame, because she'd been looking forward to seeing it. If he'd truly gone from the sheep who wouldn't baa to an actor capable of performing under the hot lights, she wanted to be there.

The double entryway was closed, the door handles bolstered with a padlock and chain, but when Jem walked across the grass to the building's east side, she discovered a side entrance that was unlocked.

Inside, the lobby was empty and the box office was unattended. Emboldened, Jem took the opportunity to peek through the open auditorium doors. The scene being rehearsed seemed to revolve around a traditional children's character, Puss in Boots.

As Jem watched, she recognized some of the people on stage. Clarence, who'd apparently joined the ensemble at last, was playing the king, using an old La-Z-Boy as a throne. Nancy, a waitress at a Hugh Town restaurant called the Piper's Hole, portrayed some kind of sword-bearing adventurer. She looked a great deal more animated acting on stage than she ever did slinging hash at the Piper's Hole. Although none of the actors were in full costume, and the man dressed as Puss in Boots wore only a pair of felted cat's ears, it still took Jem a moment to put a name to the face.

Seth Mourby, Jem thought. *He was on Bryher when the murder was committed. He even disappeared for so long on Friday night, Kenzie complained about it. And the burner phone used to call Rhys was bought with his information—minus a few key details. Was he cunning enough to submit his less accessible data incorrectly, so the police would consider him, then quickly rule him out?*

One of the actors flubbed a line. The assistant in the wings peeked out, feeding him a prompt, and noticed Jem standing alone in the doorway. Hastily, she turned and exited the auditorium. She hadn't come to the Empire Theater intending to disrupt the actors. She just wanted a look at Pauley's placard.

The theater's message board was displayed prominently near the bar, also currently bare and deserted. Pauley's card describing vintage clothing for sale was pinned up dead center. In her typical presentation-is-everything fashion, Pauley had beautifully hand-lettered the placard, dusting its edges with glitter. The attention to detail seemed to have paid off. Several tear-off strips with her phone number had been taken. Maybe the mystery of the purloined Romeo pants would be solved, after all.

The door to the stairs opened, and Leo Dupree stuck his head out.

"Oh. Hello again," he said politely.

"Hello," Jem said. Leo looked a bit different than he had at The Ruin. His curly brown hair was pulled back in a topknot, or man bun. He was dressed in his Sea Guides kit, which she found surprising. Usually even the keenest members refused to be seen in their uniforms outside of official events. Kenzie, for example, would've died rather than go shopping in the Co-op wearing it. For the early to mid-teenage bracket, signaling a parent-approved affiliation just wasn't cool. Either Leo's mates were unusually tolerant, or he didn't have many.

Across his face, a rash of new spots stood out against the old. He had good bones, and might grow to be a handsome man, but he needed to get his cystic acne under control. Leo, who was slightly taller than Jem, was big for a sixteen-year-old. He towered over his mum, his broad shoulders filling out the doorway.

"Are you here to rehearse?" Jem asked.

"I was. Mum is making me quit. She says it's unseemly for me to appear in a comedy when we're in mourning." He shrugged. "I thought 'the show must go on' was the cardinal rule around here.

Almost the only rule. But she spoke to the director and he said Mum's right. It wouldn't be seemly."

"Leo!" A woman's muffled voice came from the stairwell. "Why did you close the door?"

Rolling his eyes, Leo opened it. Georgia emerged from the stairs with a cardboard box in her arms. It was filled to the brim with all sorts of items; Jem spied a folded T-shirt, books, and a cricket bat.

"You should have held that door for me. Courtesy, Leo. It matters."

"Sorry," the boy mumbled.

"Hello, Jem," Georgia said. "Did you ring me the other day? The doctor gave me something to help me feel calmer. All it did was turn me into a zombie. I ended up flushing the pills down the loo."

Jem nodded, uncertain how to reply. It was so hard to think of something kind or helpful to say. Everything that occurred to her—her current obsession with freeing Rhys and finding Hermie's real killer—was completely inappropriate to say to a grieving widow.

"Is there anything I can do for you and Leo?"

Georgia, who probably heard that question fifty times a day, shook her head. "No, thank you. Talking to Roddy took the wind out of my sails. I'm beginning to think I'll never learn the truth about what happened. That there's no point trying to make sense of it. People keep telling me I won't always feel this way, and I'm trying to believe them."

"Watching me in the play would be a distraction." Leo offered this absurdity with what seemed like absolute sincerity, as if Georgia might not realize that what she really needed was amateur theater.

Georgia sighed, briefly closed her eyes, and said in a tight little voice, "Leo, the discussion is over. We're going home." Shifting the cardboard box, she added, "I don't know why you keep so many of your things here. The other actors need space, too."

"There's plenty of room in the trap. That's the area under the trap door," he told Jem, clearly proud of his theater terminology. "It would be so cool to use it in front of an audience, but this troupe is nothing but a bunch of cowards. If a play calls for it, they write it out. That's why I took over the trap. I use it for storage."

Judging by Georgia's expression, she could've cheerfully lived the rest of her life without hearing her son ever discuss theater minutiae again.

"My point is, you may have been inconveniencing the other actors by taking up so much space," she said, still in that tight voice. "You shouldn't just assume you can do whatever occurs to you. It's important to remember the feelings of others."

"Okay, Mum." Leo regarded Jem curiously. "It must be weird for you. Knowing the murderer all your life, I mean. I said that to Kenzie, and she went mental."

"We don't believe Rhys is a murderer," Jem said firmly. "I think the police will soon realize they've got it wrong, the charges will be dropped, and someone else will be arrested."

Mouthing the word "Sorry" at Jem, Georgia prodded Leo with a corner of the box. "You should offer to carry this for me. Come on. It's your stuff, and it's heavy. Be gallant."

Sighing dramatically, Leo accepted his overloaded box of possessions, and mother and son exited the Empire Theater. Feeling somehow discomfited by the brief conversation, Jem followed them out.

As she walked the short distance back to the Franks All Marine compound, she noticed a stone fence encircling the back lot that was low enough for her to vault without much effort. On the other side was a second fence, this time of chain link, which had to be climbed. On a hunch, Jem made the effort, hoping devoutly that no one was watching, since her usual summer uniform of sandals and sundress wasn't made for dignified climbing.

Sure enough, when she hopped down on the other side of the second fence, she was standing in the unattractive, somewhat stinky zone behind Franks All Marine. The smell came from huge metal rubbish bins. To gain access, the binman would have to be let in through a tall, padlocked gate on the other side of the building.

This is where Simon Weatherby claimed he saw Rhys threaten Hermie, Jem thought. *Even if I found his story believable, this doesn't seem like a convenient spot for an older man like Hermie to access. And the smell would automatically drive most people to go somewhere else.*

After clambering back over the fences, Jem walked to the front of the compound, smoothed her hair, checked her reflection in the showroom door's polished glass, and looked around for Micki. Her friend often seemed to live according to her own internal clock, which was at least a quarter-hour behind everyone else's.

Jem tried to wait patiently, but she checked the time on her mobile every few minutes. When she saw she was ten minutes late for her appointment with Jimmy, she gave up on Micki and started to go inside. That was when Micki appeared, half-running down the lane in towering high-heeled sandals.

"Sorry! Sorry!" she yelped, literally holding onto her straw hat as she made it to the door, panting from exertion.

"You look amazing," Jem said truthfully.

"Ah, thanks, lovely, I know," Micki said, straightening up so Jem could take her in properly. Her normal clouds of curly hair were swept up in a bun, showing off her long, elegant neck. Her heeled sandals, backless dress, and straw hat were all precisely the same color, a medium tan. On Jem, it would've looked monotonous, even drab. On Micki's rich dark skin, the effect was striking and sophisticated.

"I've never seen you in heels so high," Jem said. "With the hat, you're taller than I am."

"Psychological warfare. You'll see," Micki said with a smile. Linking her arm in Jem's, she gave the signal, and they strolled into Franks All Marine.

A quick look around revealed why the presence of Georgia had stood out to Bettie Quick. Jimmy Franks's staff appeared to be entirely male. In the far corner, none other than Simon Weatherby stood propped against a broom, looking sulky and miles away. When the bell over the door tinkled, he looked up, saw Jem and Micki and goggled at them, as indeed most of the staff was doing. Jem gave him a finger gun with a silent *pew-pew-pew*. He returned the gesture without enthusiasm.

Looks like he's having a bad day, Jem thought. *I'll bet Hack subjected him to a second interview and forced him to admit he lied. Why would the kid even do it? Did his boss, Jimmy, twist his arm?*

"Ladies, ladies, ladies!" A trim little Cornishman emerged from his grand glass-enclosed office. JAMES FRANKS, PROPRIETOR, was painted in big letters on the door. Jimmy wore a charcoal suit with subtle pinstripes, a slim black tie held in place with a gold clip, and a red carnation in his buttonhole. He was about forty, with jet-black hair slicked back from his forehead. His hands, which bore a bejeweled ring on each pinky, moved constantly as he talked.

"Is that Miss Jemima Jago? Late of Penzance, come back to the Isles of Scilly?" He wagged a finger. "Bettie Quick told me about you. A regular goombah, our Bettie. One of the family."

Jem smiled at Jimmy, amused by his manner of speaking, which was West Country peppered with Hollywood mafia affectations. That he liked the ladies was evident from the way his gaze shamelessly crawled over her. It lingered over her torso as if he could make her clothes evaporate through sheer force of will.

"And you! A vision," Jimmy declared, beaming at Micki. In heels, she towered over him, putting her chest at his eye level. Apparently that was what she'd meant by psychological warfare. He seemed momentarily overwhelmed, like a famished man teleported to a formal banquet, unable to choose between twelve-layer trifle or Peking duck.

"I'm Micki," she replied silkily. Arm still linked with Jem's, she pulled her closer and added, "I'm Jemmie's plus-one in life."

"Oh. *Oh*," he said, evidently thunderstruck. Whatever his over-heated brain was doing with the implications of Micki's remark, it seemed to be gumming up the works. When it came to disarming difficult men, this clearly wasn't Micki's first at bat.

"Well, if you're looking to trade in an old boat and acquire a new one, I'm the final word," Jimmy declared, bouncing on the balls of his feet the way little men sometimes did to emphasize a point. "The *capo dei capi*—boss of bosses," he added with a wink.

"Don't you love the Italians?" Micki asked Jem.

"You know it. Can we look at your sport fishing boats?" Jem asked.

"Are you kidding? Fuggedaboutit. You can look at absolutely anything you want," Jimmy said, throwing in a finger-purse motion for good measure. "Follow me, girls, and I'll make all your ocean dreams come true."

*

Jimmy did his best to prove his *Cosa Nostra* bonafides with anecdotes designed to make him seem ruthless to his competitors, yet generous and paternal to his customers.

"My boats are the best. Look at that sporty red yacht. Is that a killer or is that a killer? My competition, they're all Mickey Mouse operations. Who else but Jimmy has an in-house finance scheme? Strictly low vig, my hand to God."

The mention of boat payments pleased Jem. It gave her an opening to ask about Hermie Castleberry.

"Did you know I was the first person to see the *Family Man* wrecked?" Jem asked. She threw in a giggle to make it seem as if she'd done so through some silly female misadventure, like falling off a Sea-Doo. "It still looked beautiful, even on the bottom of the channel. I wonder why it sank."

"Ah. Well. First of all, that was my sale, and would have been mine to repossess, had Hermie lived. Daft bugger couldn't settle his debts," Jimmy said, dark eyes shining with malice. "I reckon he got a taste for the wild life, and it turned around and bit him, didn't it?"

"He probably got into coke and loose women," Micki said wisely, with a wink to indicate that she bore no judgment.

Jimmy theatrically looked left and right, as if wise guys from some competing family might be lurking inside his own showroom. "You have a good nose for the ways of men," he said. "Hermie had a nose, too, if you know what I mean. I asked him once, why do you mess around with that stuff? Why not relax with a nice Chianti, a good cigar, and leave it at that. But Hermie liked to say he was burning the candle at three ends. That was his phrase—not two, but three. Like I'm not up with the sun and awake till the wee hours every night myself."

Beckoning Jimmy closer, Jem whispered, "I know the police found drugs and money."

"Of course they did, sweetheart. Hermie never went anywhere without his party favors. But when it came to making things right with me, he cried poor."

"I'm still wondering why *Family Man* sank," Micki said, helpfully returning to the question Jimmy seemed to have forgotten. "Can the police work it out, do you think?"

"Of course they can! They raised it and brought it to an expert. Me," Jimmy said proudly, jerking double thumbs toward his chest. "The hose burst in the bilge pump. Plus the bung was missing. That'll sink you."

"Sabotage," Jem said, forgetting to giggle or phrase it as a question.

Jimmy cocked an eyebrow at her. "Say, little lady, you know your boats, don't you?"

"A bit. Maybe it's because I saw the wreck, but I keep coming back to Hermie Castleberry's murder, trying to work it out," Jem said. "I've heard rumors about Georgia Castleberry's ex. Conor Dupree?"

Jem would've continued, but the change in Jimmy's face told her she'd hit the bullseye. And fortunately, Jimmy wasn't content to simply look shocked and offended by the mention of Conor Dupree's name.

"That ruddy bastard! He came into my place, the business that I built from the ground up, and threatened my life," Jimmy burst out. "Came upon me from behind dressed like a ninja with a balaclava pulled down over his face. Never gave me a chance to get my fists up. No, just sucker punched me, blacked my eye and broke my nose. Me! Jimmy Franks," he continued disbelievingly. The mafioso pretensions were gone. Recalling the attack had transformed Jimmy back into an indignant Englishman.

"How terrible," Jem murmured.

"It *was* terrible. A right royal disgrace, it was. No sooner does he lay me out then he says, 'I'm Conor Dupree. Stay away from Georgia or next time, you're dead.'"

"What did you do?" Micki asked.

"What could I do? Screamed at him from the floor that he'd better run. The minute I could stand, I was ringing 999. But I reckon he didn't hear. He was already running away."

"When did it happen? What time of day, I mean," Jem asked. She had an image of a man dressed like a ninja fleeing out of Franks All Marine into touristy Hugh Town, where plenty of passersby were sure to notice, and possibly intervene to stop him.

"After closing. I'd sent everybody home and sat down to take a look at the books," Jimmy said. Mention of this nightly ritual prompted him to get back in character. "Trust your people but verify, *capisce?* The boss makes spot-checks to keep his soldiers in line."

"But if it was after hours, how did Conor get in?" Jem persisted. Despite his irritating habits and affectations, Jimmy struck her as a credible witness. But his story was odd to say the least.

"Oh, well, I blame Georgia. She must've left a door unlocked. After I got patched up at St. Mary's," he said, meaning the hospital, "I told Georgia it was over. Take a long walk off a short pier, you get me? I'm a respectable businessman." He drew himself up, hooking his fingers into his lapels. "I can't go out with a woman who used to be married to a maniac."

Jem thought she now understood some of the crushing self-abnegation Georgia had revealed over lunch at The Ruin. Her first husband, father of her child, was a violent criminal; her rebound man, Jimmy Franks, had rejected her as tainted by association. Whatever Hermie's flaws were—like a fondness for the powdered white stuff and a habit of grifting off young artists like Rhys—he'd apparently treated her and Leo well. Perhaps his desire to provide for his new family explained not only the name of his boat, but his remark about "burning the candle at three ends."

"How did the police react when you reported what happened?" Jem asked.

Jimmy waved a hand magnanimously, like a holy man absolving a sin. "I didn't rat him out. Men should settle things between men. Besides, Georgia begged me not to involve the police. On her knees, she begged me, crying her eyes out. I can never say no to a woman."

"But you must've tipped off Hermie," Micki said. "If you two used to be friendly, you surely told him about Conor Dupree."

"I did. Eventually," Jimmy said without much conviction, as if "eventually" meant he'd left it very late indeed. "When he first came around the Scillies, Hermie had a run-down yacht that looked like someone's idea of a joke. I couldn't believe Georgia went from me to him. Then again, poor thing. Guess she was desperate.

"Anyway, I made it my business to get to know him. Always check the lay of the land," Jimmy said. "Turned out he wasn't so bad. We had a few laughs down at the local. Went fishing and whatnot. Then I sold him the sport fishing boat and right off the bat, he started missing payments. Next thing I know, he's got cement shoes. Metaphorically." With the air of someone very much in the know, he added, "That copper from the mainland mentioned he actually died on the beach."

He doesn't know Hermie was first weighted down underwater, Jem thought. *"Cement shoes" is just a phrase to him.*

"Boss!" a man called frantically from the showroom's side door, which led into the retail shop. "Boss, come quick!"

"What is it? What's happened?"

"It's Simon. We've rung for an ambulance. Someone's keeping pressure on the wound, but..." The man broke off, as if struggling to keep from breaking down. "It's awful, boss. Just awful."

Jimmy went headlong toward the door, short legs pumping, shoes clacking. Jem and Micki glanced at one another, made a snap decision, and followed on his heels. Jem expected Jimmy to look over his shoulder and order them to stay back, but he seemed too focused on the emergency to register their presence.

The employee who'd alerted Jimmy led him, Jem, and Micki through the retail shop, where the man behind the counter stood white-faced, and into the stockroom. Between tall metal shelves loaded with boat components and accessories, Simon Weatherby lay on his back in a puddle of blood.

"Simon!" Jimmy cried. "What happened?"

"We don't know, boss," said the employee who'd led them. His hands trembled violently. He looked on the verge of being sick.

On the floor beside Simon's motionless body, the man pressing a blood-soaked cloth to his throat said, "I heard a yell. Almost a scream. I thought perhaps Simon was horsing around again, tossing things about. But when I came in, I saw someone holding him by the throat."

The man paused, momentarily overcome with emotion. Then he continued, "I gave a shout, and the man let go. Thank God, he let go and ran away. I saw the knife in his hand as he went. It was black. Black. But his hands were silver." The man, clearly in mild shock, seemed unable to make sense of this. "I wanted to go after him, but I couldn't. Blood was spraying out of Simon like I've never seen. All I could think to do was take hold of the boy and keep pressure on the wound."

Jimmy gaped at the blood on the floor. He appeared too stunned to speak.

"What did he look like? The knifeman?" Jem demanded.

"Black clothes. One of those mask-hat things over his face," said the employee, switching hands as he kept up firm pressure on Simon's throat.

"Did you see which way he went?" Micki asked. "Where's the nearest door? The nearest window?"

The shocked employee beside Simon shook his head helplessly.

"Look at this. I can't believe it. Whacked!" Jimmy exploded, tearing at his hair. "This is insane. Look at this. *Look how they massacred my boy!*"

CHAPTER TWENTY-FOUR

A Water Postie and One Happy Pooch

"Poor kid. I keep seeing him lying there," Micki said. They were saying goodbye on the quay before Jem boarded *Bellatrix*.

"Are you sure you're good to work tonight?"

"Yeah, love." Micki breathed out a sigh. "Tending bar is second nature at this point. What happened to Simon was awful, but I'd rather keep busy than sit at home and marinate in it. I wish I could take the same attitude with singing for the public."

"How can you? Bartending is just something you do. Singing is who you are," Jem said. "As for Simon, we need to think positively. The EMTs started a blood transfusion on-site. By the time they loaded him into the ambulance, his pulse was strong again. And I heard one of them tell the driver he was breathing adequately through a tracheotomy. Simon not only lived through the attack, he might actually recover from it."

"Hell of a way to silence somebody. Think he'll ever speak again?"

"I don't know. I suppose it depends on how deeply his throat was cut. But remember Hermie? Poor sod was virtually decapitated. That probably would've happened to Simon if the knifeman hadn't been interrupted."

Micki sighed. "I don't get it. We talked to Jimmy because we thought maybe he had it in for Georgia's new husband. But I don't think he forced Simon to lie about Rhys threatening Hermie. And I definitely don't think he had anything to do with the attack. You saw him. If he wasn't a hundred percent sincere, give him the Oscar and be done with it."

"Jem! Micki!" a man called down to them from the promenade just above the quay. It was Hack. "Don't board yet. I'm on my way down."

When he made it down to the quayside, he looked as if he were running on too little sleep. Although it was only twelve o'clock in the afternoon, as he advanced on them, he covered a yawn. He was in uniform, his specs dark against the sunlight, giving him that blank, inscrutable stare.

"What were the two of you doing at Franks All Marine?" he asked without preamble.

"Making inquiries," Jem admitted. In mixed company she would've pretended to be shopping for boating accessories, but there was no one around to overhear. This was prime time on the water. Virtually every craft was out to sea for either business or pleasure, sails up or engines humming.

"Learn anything?" Hack asked.

"Only stuff you probably already know. DS Conrad had *Family Man* brought to Jimmy Franks for an expert opinion on why it sank. The short answer is sabotage. I asked him about Conor Dupree, and he admitted that Dupree beat him up. He also confirmed that he broke up with Georgia over the beating."

Hack nodded. "I have yet to find any evidence that Conor Dupree has ever been to the Isles of Scilly. Of course, he might have come under an alias. Or he might have been dropped off by a friend with a boat instead of traveling via the usual avenues, like the *Scillonian III* or a plane."

Micki looked from Hack to Jem in happy astonishment. "We're sharing openly now? No more skullduggery?"

"I've given up," Hack admitted. "In this case, at least. Besides, I'm not much better than Jem. I opened a parallel investigation to DS Conrad's. Yesterday, I brought Simon into the station for a little chat. Sure enough, he fabricated the whole thing about Rhys arguing with Hermie. Another witness account is completely disproven. And by itself, Roddy Levitt's doesn't count for much."

"But why did Simon single out Rhys?" Jem asked. "He did his best to make him sound like a psycho."

"You know why. One lying eyewitness could be malice or stupidity. Two lying eyewitnesses is a conspiracy."

"What made you decide to do this for a living, Hack?" Micki asked. "Love of frustration? The joy of sifting through haystacks, looking for needles?"

That cracked his professional façade. "Not as easy as it looked on *Murder, She Wrote*, eh?" He grinned. "I need to get back to the station. We're starting a second sweep of Hugh Town for the knife-man. Putting a man on the water to buzz the other islands, too."

"There's still a good chance of finding him, right?" Jem asked. "I mean, he ran away from the scene in broad daylight… dressed in black… knife in hand and wearing a balaclava and silver anti-cut gloves…"

"You know how to make a man feel small. I'm surprised no one tackled him, but it's a weekday. Most people seem to be out on the water," Hack said somewhat defensively. "I have PC Robbins reviewing local CCTV footage. There isn't much of it, since Hugh Town has so little crime, but maybe we'll get lucky. In the meantime, PC Newt is going door to door through the neighborhood with one of our part-timers, looking for witnesses or someone who might be harboring the perp."

"If you catch him, can you let me know? Text me a check mark or something?" Jem asked.

"Sure. But in the meantime, take every precaution. Keep your eyes open and lock your doors. If you see or hear something that seems relevant, don't try to play Angela Lansbury. Just call my mobile direct. Got that?"

"Aye-aye, Captain," Jem and Micki said together.

*

Jem was in the habit of mooring *Bellatrix* just off the coast of St. Morwenna and wading the short distance to either the Square or Crescent Beach, depending on which bay she chose. Today, however, she was surprised to see a RIB shadowing her from St. Mary's to St. Morwenna. It bore the emblem of the Royal Mail. When she dropped anchor, the postie, a young man with the glossiest head of black hair Jem had ever seen, looped back around *Bellatrix*. He offered her a lift to shore, which she gratefully accepted.

"I love being a water postie," Pranav Dhillon declared, shaking her hand after helping her aboard. "Most days, a pilot takes me out by helicopter and I drop the mail at each island's individual post office. But on days when the tides throw us a curveball, I get to take this baby out."

Jem, who found the young man's enthusiasm contagious, was sorry the trip was so short. Thanking him, she disembarked at the green-tinged water stairs of St. Morwenna's Quay while he remained in the RIB, double-checking his mail parcels. She couldn't help noticing that the left hand rifling through the mail was 100% wedding band-free.

Of course, it was none of her business that Pauley hadn't had a date in ages. For all Jem knew, this friendly, attractive stranger was already in a committed relationship. Still, she made note of his name and the fact that he briefly visited St. Morwenna's post office each day, usually by helicopter. She and Pauley didn't have to go collect the post; in the Scillies, each inhabited island received home delivery via bicycle. But if Jem timed lunch just right, she might "accidentally" find herself in a position to introduce Pauley to Pranav. After that, who knew what might happen?

That was a sunnier mental image than Simon Weatherby lying on his back in a puddle of blood. Therefore, Jem cultivated the notion as she followed the Byway to Lyonesse House, cooking up various scenarios to get Pauley to the post office without her friend sensing a set-up. Jem herself despised blind dates and arranged meetings; resistance was only to be expected. If she wanted Pauley to give Pranav Dhillon a fair shake, she had to make sure Pauley believed she'd discovered him entirely on her own.

At Lyonesse House, Jem bypassed the front entrance as usual, following the stone path around the small wing to the back door, which opened onto the kitchen. As she approached, she felt for her keys, located them, and put her hand on the knob. It turned easily at the light touch.

"Pauley!" Jem bellowed. The kitchen lights were on, but the room was empty. Down the hall, manic barking echoed off the walls. Buck sounded like he was having the best doggy day of his entire doggy life.

"Pauley! The back door was unlocked!"

"Sorry, Jemmie," Pauley called. She sounded almost as happy as Buck. "Come here."

Jem obeyed without much enthusiasm. Pauley had probably bought Buck a new toy. They'd be playing together happily, and then Jem would ruin the fun by bringing the grim news about Simon. Steeling herself to be the bearer of bad news, Jem rounded the corner, looked in the sitting room, and saw Rhys.

He was down on one knee playing knotted rope with Buck, who had to pause frequently to nuzzle Rhys's hand or lick his face. He looked up, eyes meeting hers, and his smile was like the sunrise.

"Hiya, Jem."

"Hiya, Rhys."

CHAPTER TWENTY-FIVE

Stardust

It was too early for dinner, but Rhys was hungry—he hadn't cared for his food in lockup—so Pauley did a quick fry-up. While he ate, Jem and Pauley had tea and bombarded him with questions. Pauley had never been arrested; Jem had, but her situation had been more a case of police harassment than a serious criminal proceeding. They demanded a complete accounting of the experience from Rhys, who'd spent six days and five nights in police custody until the murder charge against him fell apart.

"They took me to the mainland by helicopter," Rhys said. "The way it works is, they sort of marry you to one officer. Not a bigwig—a PC Newt type, who has to stick with you while you're in the queue to be processed. The Exeter Police Station was so busy, we waited in this bloke's Ford Focus for three hours. Discussed football, surfing, and cricket, of all things.

"Then we were finally allowed to come inside, and I was handed over to the custody officer and his minions." As he spoke, Rhys absently petted Buck, who'd risen from a doze to demand another reassuring pat on the head. The little dog was obviously worn out, but every time he settled down on a cushion to snooze, he suddenly remembered Rhys was back, and the urge to be petted overrode his sleepiness.

"Were they horrid?" Pauley asked.

"No. Very professional. It was a bit like checking into the hospital. I had the notion I'd be given one phone call, but I wasn't.

One of the custody officer's people placed the call for me. I picked Lissa, since Hack promised to tell you two, and I wanted Kenzie to hear it from her mum, not those old men who hang around the Duke's Head Inn all day.

"Then I had to fill in forms and answer health and safety questions. Just when I thought being arrested was actually much easier than it seems on telly, they strip-searched me."

Pauley made an affronted sound.

"I know. But it didn't get too icky. Take your shirt off, check upper body. Given a fleece top to replace it. Take your trousers, shorts, and socks off. No, sir, keep your fleece top on," Rhys said with a grin. "Which made me feel so much better, bare-arsed with my bits in the wind, to have my chest covered."

"Did they ask you to bend over?" Pauley asked, voicing what Jem couldn't bring herself to.

"No. Just had a quick look and gave me trousers to match my top. Flip-flops for my feet. Phone, cash, keys, everything I came in with was taken away and put into storage, obviously.

"After that, they scanned my fingerprints—no ink!—and took my picture and did a cheek swab. They asked for a blood test to rule out drug use. I agreed, and when my solicitor arrived, she told me off about that. Said I must never give the police anything they can't compel, but it was already done."

Rhys paused, eyes flicking to Buck, who'd settled under Jem's chair—the better to see Rhys—and finally seemed to be settling down. "I can't tell you how much I missed that little mutt. Because after all the forms, and tests, and a second interview where my solicitor didn't let me say a single word, there was nothing for me to do but go to my cell."

"Did you have a cell mate?" Jem asked.

"No. My cell was tiny—I think they all were. There were other prisoners held on either side of me, and across the hall from me, and they never shut up. Literally never," Rhys said with a groan. "The first night, I didn't sleep at all, because one bloke kept calling for his mum. Another drummed on his bunk, night and day."

"You had a telly, though, right? Or books from a library cart?" Jem asked.

"No TV. No books or magazines. I had a toilet, a bed, and an overhead light. Plus a slot in the door so they could pass me trays at mealtime. Nothing too hot, and nothing that required anything sharper than a plastic spork to eat. I was bored out of my skull and hungry the whole time."

"Yikes. It sounds bloody awful," Jem said.

"It was. The high point was talking to my lawyer by phone. I was supposed to be remanded to HM Prison Exeter on Monday, but they were backed up, too. It would've been tomorrow, if they hadn't dropped the charges and released me."

"Dodged a bullet," Pauley said.

Rhys nodded. "I did it to myself. I went out to Candlewick Castle to paint. That's all. When I took a break and climbed down from the round tower to stretch my legs, the tide had gone out and there was Hermie, stone dead. The dry canister with the drugs and money had floated ashore, too. I opened it up and…" He sighed ruefully. "I gave into temptation. Hermie cleaned me out. I thought I had a chance to recoup all my losses and put the whole thing behind me. I counted out what he owed me, put the rest back, wiped the canister down, and tossed it back in the water."

"You should have taken it with you," Pauley said. "Oh, Jem, don't look at me like that. I know it's evidence. And I know the so-called right answer is, he should have left the money alone and called it in. But Hermie cheated him. No one in the islands can afford to be fleeced."

"I was going to say, I wish you hadn't deposited it in your bank," Jem admitted. "Better if you'd just kept a stash of euros under your mattress for the next year or so."

Rhys laughed. "No. I appreciate the loyalty. I really do. But I was stupid to take it and doubly stupid to deposit it. Maybe I was trying to get caught. One of the A.A. principles is rigorous honesty. I felt guilty about not living up to it."

"So what happens now?" Jem asked.

"Well, that depends on Hack, or maybe Devon & Cornwall. Maybe they'll charge me with theft, or tampering with a crime scene. Maybe they'll decide I was punished enough." Rhys shrugged. "A problem for tomorrow. Today I just have to worry about today."

"All this A.A. stuff is making you a better person. I'm not sure I like it," Pauley said, wagging a finger at him until he grinned. Jem realized she was grinning, too. For the first time since Rhys's arrest, she felt truly happy, as if something she couldn't do without had been restored at last.

"Don't worry," Rhys said. "Give me a day or two and I'll snap back to my usual arsecockle self."

"Tell me about the call," Jem said. "Was the speaker a man or woman?"

He shrugged. "The person who rang spoke through a voice spoofer. I picked up and someone who sounded like Darth Vader said, 'I saw you on the beach with Castleberry. You killed him and stole his money. Now you'll pay.'"

"Just like that? Melodramatic?" Pauley asked.

"Yeah. If I'm being honest, it sounded like a joke. But I called the number back, and no one answered. After a while, I decided I'd better not risk it."

"Do you think this was a personal campaign against Rhys?" Pauley asked Jem.

"I did at first, after talking to Roddy Levitt. But now I think he's just a jerk, not a would-be mastermind," Jem said. "Whoever killed Hermie got themselves aboard a boat with a boning knife and a pair of anti-cut gloves. They must have known that most knife killers end up with cuts on their hands."

"Do they?" Rhys asked.

Jem nodded. "I looked it up. Okay, these are the facts. We have a killer who planned to either murder Hermie, or threaten him with murder. And took the precaution of protecting his or her hands. But after Hermie's throat was cut, reality set in. There was a dead man on a boat in the channel between Tresco and Bryher. I think the killer panicked and made two stupid decisions—first, to sabotage the boat and sink it, and second, to try and keep Hermie's body hidden underwater."

Rhys and Pauley were listening attentively. Jem felt as though the puzzle was finally starting to come together.

"After that was done, and the killer was safe and calm, I think he realized his clean up efforts weren't very good," Jem continued. "He was watching the scene, somehow. Either hiding somewhere on the beach, or watching from a safe distance, perhaps with binoculars. Waiting to see if the wreck was discovered. That's when he saw you going to Candlewick Castle," she told Rhys.

"You're back to just saying 'he' again," Pauley said.

"I know. Sorry. Anyway, I think the killer rang you up to scare you, Rhys. Obviously, it worked," Jem continued. "Then he lined up a couple of fake eyewitnesses to incriminate you. One said he saw you on the beach with Hermie, and the other said he saw you threaten his life."

"Do you think he bribed them?"

"Maybe. Or maybe they're just friends who were willing to help," Jem said. "Hack reluctantly confirmed it was Noah Atwell who claimed Rhys killed Hermie on the beach and the other witness was Simon Weatherby. Remember last Thursday, when we met them both coming from Crescent Beach? Maybe they went there early to plant the gloves and knife, then hung around to see what happened next."

"I hate to think of Simon doing such a thing," Pauley said, shaking her head. "I wonder if an adult twisted his arm. Jimmy Franks, maybe?"

"I don't think so. Listen to this." Jem filled them in on her and Micki's conversation with Jimmy and the interview's shocking end, when someone with a black knife and silver anti-cut gloves had attacked Simon.

"When I was in lockup, I racked my brains to think of who might have actually killed Hermie," Rhys said. "I know I can't be the only artist Hermie cheated, but do you think money was the motive? What about love? The manager at The Ruin obviously thought Hermie was toxic for his sister."

"There's someone else." Jem told them about the attack on Jimmy and what Hack had learned about Georgia's ex-husband, Conor Dupree. The possibility that he had stealthily made his way to the Isles of Scilly, slipped aboard *Family Man*, and murdered Hermie in a jealous rage was simple and elegant. Dupree clearly wasn't the sort of man who weighed the consequences before he acted; judging by his police record, he drifted from fight to fight and fix to fix. But the killer's efforts to implicate Rhys suggested a devious and determined mind trying to clean up the mess.

"What are you thinking?" Pauley asked.

"That maybe we're looking for more than one person. The killer definitely has at least two accomplices—Simon and Noah. If I hadn't watched Georgia progressively fall apart, I'd think her and her ex might be in this together. She did seem especially distraught over the cottage not being hers free and clear after Hermie's death. She mentioned other financial hiccups, too."

"I think Georgia's genuinely heartbroken," Pauley said. "But she could still be trying to help Conor get away with murder. Maybe she's afraid for her life, and her son's."

"She could believe she must help Conor, or he'll kill them, too," Rhys put in. "That spoofer device could have made anyone, even a woman, sound like Darth Vader."

"True. I've been assuming Simon's friend Noah made the call, but there's no proof yet," Jem said thoughtfully. In the depths of her mind, some notion or memory was on its way up, making its way toward consciousness. She could feel the process happening, but there was no rushing it. All she could do was wait, and hope it surfaced in time to help her uncover Hermie's real killer.

"We've chewed over murder and knife crimes long enough," Pauley declared. Rising, she leaned over Rhys, who was still seated, to hug his neck. "God, I'm glad you're back. Never scare us like that again. Oh—look at Buck. He's dreaming."

Jem slipped silently out of her chair so she could look beneath it. Pauley was right. The little dog was curled in a ball, ears trembling, making soft whuffling noises as his dream-self frolicked.

"Look at that." Another slow, gorgeous grin spread across Rhys's face. "It'll be a long time before I take him for granted again. Or you two." He looked first at Pauley, but then his gaze shifted to Jem's face and stayed there.

"Is that the time? My program's on. I always watch," Pauley announced, as shamelessly fraudulent as she'd been two nights ago, when it had been Jem and Hack who needed some alone time in the kitchen. "Must dash."

"As if there's anything on at half-three in the afternoon," Jem muttered as Pauley disappeared into her bedroom and shut the door rather loudly.

"My idea. I asked her to give me some time with you." He stood up, looming over her despite her not-inconsiderable height. She still hadn't quite got accustomed to the sheer size of adult Rhys, not just in height, but in the width of his chest and shoulders.

"You're so beautiful," he said, sounding faintly amazed. "I can't quite get used to it."

Before Jem could scoff or deflect the compliment with a smart remark, Rhys reached out and took her right hand, then her left. He held them rather formally, as if they'd entered a ceremony requiring them to clasp hands and make a vow. Part of her wanted to pull away, to make light of his sudden earnestness. But his hands were big, warm, and familiar. After a split second, she felt poised on the tip of a blade. Then she no longer wanted to let go.

"Lockup was torture," Rhys said simply. He wasn't looking for sympathy, just stating a fact. "By the end of the first day, my brain was trying to eat itself. I slept as much as I could. I did sit-ups and push-ups and some of Pauley's yoga moves. If that doesn't prove I was desperate, nothing will. I thought I was losing my mind.

"Then I thought, I'm going to go through my memories. I'll call up every good thing that ever happened to me and relive it again. My sponsor in A.A., Sharon, calls it making a gratitude list: going over every single thing we've ever possessed or experienced that makes us feel grateful."

Jem nodded as Rhys stared directly into her eyes. She knew he didn't want her to interrupt him, and even if he had, her feelings were purely visceral, impossible to distill into mere words.

"I remembered being nine years old and trying to force you to notice me. I was such a prat. Trying to outrace you, out-climb you, out-spell you on one occasion." He chuckled. "That one went down in flames. Then we were friends and the world was our oyster. You, me, Pauley, and Cam," he said, referring to his late brother.

"So much of it was nothing special, really," Rhys continued. "Pretending we were knights, pretending we were running from sea monsters, building a tree fort that fell apart the first time a gale blew in. But when I was alone in the cell, it *did* seem special. Most of my childhood was incredibly happy. Not everyone is so lucky."

Jem nodded. The bond between her, Pauley, Rhys, and Cam had always loomed large in her consciousness, even when it caused her pain. She had no idea who she'd be if she hadn't grown up with such daring, inventive, irrepressible friends.

"Then we started to see one another as more than friends," he continued, dark blue eyes still locked on hers. "Do you remember that time you told me about stardust?"

"Not really," Jem admitted. As a girl, she'd talked endlessly about the constellations, planets, and celestial phenomena; she might have said a hundred different things on the topic.

"I was upset about something. I don't even remember what. And to distract me, you started telling me about the stars. How the Big Bang created the first generation, which were huge," he said, smiling at the memory. "Then they went supernova and created a different generation of stars…"

"With new elements," Jem said, remembering. "Carbon and magnesium and so on."

"Right. You said every human being was made from stardust—from the elements formed as the oldest stars went supernova and created new ones. You said, 'Parts of you went through a supernova. That means you can stand up to anything.'"

"It's still true," Jem murmured.

Gently, Rhys released her hands. His smile faded. "When you needed help, I wasn't there for you. Not like I should have been. But when I got banged up, you tried to clear my name. You snooped all over the islands and even Penzance. All because you refused to believe I was a murderer, no matter how stupidly I behaved.

"About—you know. What happened when we were kids," Rhys continued, seeming to reach deep within himself. "I *was* deliberately keeping you at arm's length, but not because of a grudge. I just didn't want to complicate my life. To risk feeling it all again," he admitted.

"Rhys…"

Before she could say more, Rhys's arm hooked around her, drawing her body against his in one swift, irresistible motion. He kissed her hard, with an urgency that said much more than words. Then he pulled back, his big hands settling on her cheeks as he cupped her face in his hands.

"All the best parts of my life were down to you. Just you, Jemmie." Slowly, he moved in for another kiss, as if giving her time to object. When his lips touched hers the second time, she sensed that Rhys was holding himself in check, commanding himself to be gentle rather than demanding.

Jem felt as if she were fourteen again, seized by the throes of first love, every inch of her skin tingling with excitement and fear. But while her emotions reverted to a girl's naïve, simpler state of mind, her now-experienced body responded like a woman: eager, tantalized, ready for more.

Am I ready for this? Am I sure?

"Wait," she gasped, pulling away.

"Sorry. I'm sorry," he muttered. His pupils were dilated, his face flushed. "I shouldn't have grabbed you like that. But for so long I've wanted to—"

"I know. Me too. It's just…" Jem faltered. The emotions were big, much too big, and expanding all the time, spiraling out like the Big Bang toward some conclusion she couldn't foresee.

"I should have asked first."

"No, really, it's all right. But I need time to make sense of this, you know?" Jem smiled at him weakly. "I haven't even decided if I'm going to keep my flat in Penzance, or move in here with Pauley. Besides…" Taking a deep breath, she forced herself to add candidly, "You aren't the only one protecting yourself. Or the only one afraid of… of feeling it all again. All of it… including the end."

Rhys seemed about to answer, but a loud, sharp bark made both of them jump. Buck, now awake, was struggling up from his spot under Jem's chair. He regarded them grumpily.

"Sorry, buddy," Rhys said. To Jem, he said, "I should get him home. But… we'll talk some more, right?"

Jem nodded. Of course they'd talk more. What did he want? Just one night together? A one-time rekindling of what they'd long desired, but never actually shared? Or did he want more, the way Hack wanted more?

What do I want? she thought, annoyed with herself. *Shouldn't I work that out first? I'm supposed to be avoiding men altogether. That's going really well.*

"He probably misses his own bed," Rhys said, scooping up Buck, who was accustomed to being carried. "As for me, I want a run on the beach. Feels like I've been caged for a year."

"I'm glad you're back," Jem said.

"Me, too. Thanks again for everything you did. Micki and Pauley, too." Halfway out the back door he turned, saying, "Be sure and lock up behind me. We don't know exactly who we're dealing with. But if they had it in for me, they might have it in for you, too."

CHAPTER TWENTY-SIX

"No Faffing, No Fear"

Pauley made it all the way to dinner before asking Jem what had happened between her and Rhys. Just as Jem settled in at the kitchen table with her chicken, rocket, and tomato salad in front of her and an inviting glass of Chardonnay at her right hand, Pauley said, "You seemed as if you needed space, so I gave you space. It's been four hours. Enough. Tell me what happened between you and Rhys."

Jem tossed her head. "I don't interrogate you about your love life."

"You would if I had one," Pauley retorted. "I'm surprised you haven't pounced on some lonely fisherman, or a bloke on a paddleboard without a wedding ring, and dragged him home for my inspection."

Remembering the water postie, Pranav Dhillon, who'd struck her as a good potential match, Jem decided to forgo denials and answer the question. "He said he thought about me a lot while in custody. That all this time, he's been protecting himself. Then he kissed me."

"Finally! You wanted him to, didn't you? Admit it."

Jem sipped her Chardonnay to give herself a moment. Then she said, "Of course I did. I've wanted it—and not wanted it—ever since I came back."

She half expected Pauley to badger her as she might have done when they were teens. "What do you mean, not wanted it? Don't you still have feelings for Rhys? Don't you want to find out how it could be now that you're both grown up?"

But Pauley didn't pepper Jem with breathless follow-up questions. From her expression, it was clear she'd already formed a theory about her friend's reluctance.

"What?" Jem demanded.

"Nothing. I don't have a dog in this fight. I'm a neutral party. I'm Switzerland," Pauley declared, pausing to taste the salad. "Oh! Very nice, if I do say so myself."

Jem forced herself to eat a few bites. It *was* good, but Jem couldn't focus on the flavors, not even the ripe red tomatoes, while her emotions put on an Italian opera behind the scenes.

"You're thinking about Hack. That I'm more interested in him," she told Pauley.

"Well, Hack's an interesting man," Pauley said. "A bit quirky. A bit mysterious. With the gaps in his history and his forbidden first name and all that. Sexy, if I'm being honest," she added with a grin. "But as a completely neutral party, I should point out that Rhys is crazy sexy, too. Even if it's a bit gross for me to say that, since I think of him more as a brother."

Jem went back to her Chardonnay. To her surprise, the glass was already half empty.

"Pace yourself," Pauley giggled. "After we eat, we still have to do the washing-up and arrange the vintage clothing so my interested parties can browse the pieces. The sale is tomorrow. I thought we might use the large wing's blue bedroom. I already pulled the dust cloths from the furniture and aired it out a bit."

"I saw your placard. Most of the tear-off strips were taken," Jem said. "How many people actually agreed to look at the clothes?"

"Four people. Four *thespians*," Pauley said, mimicking Clarence's pronunciation. "Speaking of that, did you know Clarence himself has been promoted to thespian?"

"Yes! I saw him playing the king in a skit about Puss in Boots."

"That's it. He has three lines in the new show. If he delivers them well, he'll be assured a speaking part in the next production." Pauley had a sip of wine, then asked, "You're going, aren't you? I already bought tickets. I just assumed."

"Of course," Jem said, relieved that Rhys had been released in time to participate. She really wanted to see him riding that hobbyhorse. It would provide ammunition for the next time he needed a telling off.

"But about the clothing sale. You don't think it's foolish, do you, Paul?" Jem asked. "Inviting people into your home when Simon was attacked and nearly killed just this morning?"

Pauley appeared to ponder the question. "Maybe. But three of the people are women. I know all of them, at least in passing. There's only one man. Roger Pinnock. Never met him, but I asked Clarence to give me the lowdown. He described him in one word. Harmless."

Jem sighed. "I'm sure he is. Still, we shouldn't take chances. I should at least be with you while you show the clothes. Is everyone coming at once?"

"I scheduled them each separately," Pauley said. "That way if one asks about the Romeo breeches and hose, I can try and steer them into confiding in me. If a fellow actor is present, I'll have no chance of winkling out the truth."

"All right. I'll work in the library until just before Roger Pinnock is scheduled to arrive," Jem said. "Two is always better than one, and we'll have our mobiles if we need to call for help. Clarence is just down the Byway." In a previous scrape, Clarence had already proven himself brave and reliable. Jem had no doubt that if she rang him asking for help, he'd come running to Lyonesse House, long gun in hand.

"Perfect. It'll be fun. I'm looking forward to showing off the furs and dresses," Pauley said. "Even if I don't learn anything interesting,

I might still earn some pocket money. And I'm giving Clarence a ten percent commission."

"You enjoy his company, don't you?"

"I do. Sometimes I wonder if…" Pauley stopped, waving away the remainder of the sentence. Her features drooped into that sad, guarded look she'd worn ever since Mrs. Gwyn died. "Never mind."

"Well, I for one love to see you so enthusiastic. About anything," Jem said pointedly, trying to keep her friend from slipping into gloom again. Nothing about what Pauley proposed seemed to fall into the category of playing Angela Lansbury, which is what Jem had promised Hack they wouldn't do. Besides, even though the rediscovered Oscar Wilde poem had temporarily improved Pauley's bottom line, she could still use the extra cash.

And we still have the mystery of those antique spectacles I found near Hermie's corpse, Jem thought. *Maybe one of the thespians can shed some light on the specs, if nothing else.*

*

On the next day, Wednesday, Pauley received the three female prospective buyers at eleven, twelve, and one o'clock. Unable to repress her curiosity, Jem couldn't resist dropping in on all three visits. The women all seemed genuinely interested in examining the vintage clothes and paid her little attention. None of them asked about silk hose or Romeo breeches. Nor did they show much interest in the small box of costume jewelry, including a broken pair of spectacles, that Pauley placed near the furs. They *did* each buy several items, and by the time the last woman left, Pauley was over the moon.

"You know what outrageous, sexy, crazy thing I'm buying with this money?" she asked Jem.

"Wine fridge? Jacuzzi?"

"Paint! I've earned enough to liven up the kitchen. If I do the work myself, I mean."

"If *we* do the work," Jem said, hugging her friend. Whether she ultimately chose to remain in Penzance or not, she'd still be spending plenty of time in Lyonesse House. Offering to help transform the kitchen from bosh to posh was the least she could do.

Someone knocked at the back door. "Excuse me? Ms. Gwyn?"

Pauley whispered, "There's Roger Pinnock. Let's go meet him together."

After the introductions were made, Pauley led Roger to the large wing, which entailed passing through Captain Mortimer Gwyn's original building. Jem tagged along behind them, feeling rather like paid security. Though from the moment she beheld Roger, a little man with a round face and a forelock that continually flopped into his eyes, she understood why Clarence had pronounced him harmless.

"You live here? It's like a museum," he said, looking at the seventeenth-century furnishings as if he wanted to examine each and every one.

"That was the idea. Then life happened, and it just keeps happening," Pauley said, beckoning him through to the large wing. The blue room was the first bedroom on the left. Inside, about half of Pauley's vintage sale inventory remained, laid out on bits of furniture or hanging over the backs of chairs. If Roger was disappointed by the limited collection, he didn't show it. Instead, he made a beeline for a lady's red velvet snood, clapping his hands with delight.

"We're going to put on a murder mystery set in the 1920s," he explained. "We being the Tidal Pool Players, of course. A hat like that would be perfect for whoever plays the intimidating dowager."

Pauley, glancing over her shoulder at Jem, mouthed, *Clarence.* Then to Roger she said, "You're not a Scillonian, or even Cornish, are you? Where do you hail from, Roger?"

"Slough. Just like *The Office*," Roger said. "I mean, not quite like *The Office*. Not as electrifying. Not as glamorous and deeply rewarding, either."

That reply, and the sly way Roger delivered it, startled both Jem and Pauley. A dry wit was a nice surprise. Perhaps there was more to him than met the eye.

"What brought you to the Isles of Scilly?" Pauley asked.

Roger gave her an impish smile. "Would you really like to know? It's not a long story, but not everyone seems to get it. Bit of a mixed reaction."

"Fire away," Jem said, forgetting she was there to prevent Pauley from being knifed to death, not to steer the conversation.

"By all means," Pauley said.

"Well. It all started with my sister. She was born with disabilities." Roger picked up a pair of woolen trousers, measuring its long leg against his far shorter one. "Mum decided the best thing would be to homeschool her, so she kept me home, too. It was easier for her, and that way, I could help out. I don't blame her," he said, returning the trousers to their place and moving on to the next item, a white silk blouse.

"I think I would've quite liked going to school, actually," Roger continued. "Running about with the other kids. Having different teachers each year, and all that. But it wasn't to be. Then, when I was eighteen, my mum died. Very sudden. An undiagnosed heart ailment. That left me alone to care for my sister. I could've put her in one of those places. You know what I mean. Except she didn't mix well with new people and was accustomed to being with me. Instead I took a factory job, working nights, and stayed home with her during the day."

Pauley was staring at Roger. Jem thought that if he'd looked up from his careful evaluation of each item, he would've been unnerved by the degree of attention she was giving him. But he didn't look up, just kept on telling the story in his quiet, matter-of-fact tone.

"My sister did well with me. She lived to be forty-seven years old. The doctors used to say she'd be lucky to see thirty. I think she had a good life. Different, but good." Roger returned to the crimson snood, which he seemed to find irresistible. "But after she was buried and the house was empty, I took stock of my life and I didn't like what I saw. I never had what I would call a proper education. I made a decent wage at my job, but it was dull, and by the end I hated it. Never got married. Never even went on a date in the whole of my life. Can you believe it?" He gave Pauley a sidelong glance, as if assuring himself she wasn't asleep.

She nodded, still listening avidly.

"One day I woke up and thought, right. What's the point? I might as well end it. The only person who ever needed me was my sister, and she was dead. Time to pull the plug." Sighing, he turned to the little box of costume jewelry, pawing through its meager contents. "That's when a little voice in the back of my mind said, 'Roger, with you it's all faffing about, and it's all fear. You'd rather die than be free. You have the whole world in front of you, and you can do anything you want. Anything that strikes your fancy.'

"I don't know if that was the voice of God, or an angel, or just myself speaking the plain truth. But I took it to heart. Sold my house. Quit the job. Packed my bags and went on a vacation to the only place in England I knew absolutely nothing about—the Isles of Scilly. And I loved it. Bought a tiny cottage in Hugh Town and made it my home."

"Good for you," Jem said. Because Pauley looked on the brink of sobbing, she felt it was her duty to provide cover by attracting Roger's attention.

"I changed my whole way of living," the little man continued, turning to look at Jem, pleased by his story's reception. "No faffing, no fear. That's my motto now. I was terrified of public speaking, or being the center of attention for any reason, so I joined the Tidal Pool Players. The first time I was meant to say a line in front of a real audience, my mind went blank and the assistant director had to feed it to me. But after that, I grew steadier. Now I get all the best character roles. And I never freeze or forget a line."

Pauley, who'd dashed away her tears, applauded. Beaming at her, Roger plucked the broken specs out of the costume jewelry box and held them up. "I don't suppose you have more like these? Wire-framed?"

Pauley caught her breath. "No, I'm afraid I don't. But I found a pair, not long ago, that probably would've been perfect."

"I found them, actually," Jem said, stepping closer to Roger. "Right after I found the body of Hermie Castleberry near Candle-wick Castle."

Jem had met a few cool liars in her time, but Roger Pinnock wasn't one of them, despite the skills he'd acquired onstage. At the mention of Hermie, he blanched and promptly dropped the box, spilling earrings, paste necklaces, and cocktail rings all over the carpet.

"Calm down," Pauley said, bending to pick them up.

"We just want to know why you were there," Jem said. "I don't suppose you want to tell us about some missing silk hose and Romeo breeches? We know they disappeared around the time of the murder."

Roger groaned. "I can't believe I was just bragging to you about my motto. No faffing, no fear? The moment I saw that poor man dead, I reverted to type. Bang. All my progress, gone in an instant."

"Don't beat yourself up. Just tell us what happened," Pauley said, rising with the refilled box in her hands. "You went to Candlewick Castle in costume, didn't you?"

Roger nodded. "I didn't think anyone would notice if I borrowed some of the Florentine pieces for a couple of days. It was for an outside audition, which is against the rules. But I didn't want to compete with the Tidal Pool Players," Roger said, wringing his hands. "Just expand my horizons a bit. There's a theater company on the mainland that travels all over the West Country. They perform at all the best venues, like the Minack and Pencarrow. I wanted to do a sort of immersive outdoor video audition, like Elijah Wood did when he wanted to play Frodo Baggins."

Roger seemed to expect Jem and Pauley to know what he referred to. At their blank looks, he added, "Elijah Wood dressed up like a Hobbit and filmed himself doing a *Lord of the Rings* monologue in the woods. So inspirational! He made a bold, decisive stab at his goal and succeeded. Of course, he was already a film actor and somewhat well known. But still.

"After the storm, I thought the coast would look a bit wild, so I dressed up like a Cavalier in a smart frogged coat, the velvet breeches, white hose, and a pair of antique specs. Using my selfie stick, I was just filming myself delivering a monologue from *The Lion in Winter* when the tide went out.

"That meant I could reposition myself where the castle would figure more prominently in the background," Roger continued. "So I switched off the recording and picked my way down the rubble. That's when I saw poor Mr. Castleberry, white as bone, dead on the beach." Roger began to blush deeply, coloring from the hollow of his throat to the roots of his hair. "And that's—that's when the catastrophe happened. I—I did a poo. I didn't mean to," he cried, looking from Jem to Pauley. "It just burst out of me. Like a scream. An intestinal scream."

Despite his evident mortification, Roger seemed so staunchly determined to make a clean breast of it, Jem wanted to bundle the little man in her arms. "You poor thing. What a shock. It's completely understandable."

"Did it happen to you, too? When you found the body, I mean?"

Pauley said, "Never mind how *she* reacts. Finding dead people is kind of her thing. But I understand completely. I guess the Romeo breeches didn't wash up too well?"

"Oh, goodness, no. A wash was out of the question. You must understand—they were *desecrated*. The silk hose, too," Roger said. "I must've dropped the specs around that time. I don't remember. All I know is, I was climbing uphill, trying to think of what to do, when a man climbed down from the round tower. Rhys Tremayne—do you know him? Of course you do. Such a handsome fellow," Roger added, shaking his head sadly. "Of course, I couldn't bear to let him see me, or smell me. So I hid behind some rocks.

"When I was sure he was gone, I took off the breeches and hose, bundled them up, and flung them into the sea. My frogged coat saved me. Because it was so long, and because I'm not very tall, it covered my bare legs past the knee. I looked odd, but not indecent.

"I made it home and got the coat back into wardrobe the next day. I thought perhaps no one would ever know, but then Clarence sounded the alarm. People started accusing each other of stealing. That's when I got the idea that perhaps if I hunted through some vintage shops, I could find similar items to replace them."

"Pauley and I know Rhys well. We think if we can work out who tried to fit him up, it might lead to Hermie's killer," Jem said. "If you were the very first person to discover Hermie on the shore, why didn't you call it in?"

"I was too concerned with getting rid of the evidence and finding a way home. Besides, I thought surely Rhys would do it. When he didn't, and I saw him pick up some flotsam and take a handful of banknotes out of it, well…" Roger regarded Jem and Pauley apologetically. "I wasn't sure what I was seeing. I concentrated on getting away."

Jem and Pauley looked at one another. In light of the circumstances, Roger's conclusions weren't hard to fathom.

"Never mind all that," Pauley said cheerfully. "Hermie swindled Rhys out of a lot of money, but there's nothing to be done about it now. The police recovered the cash from the dry canister. Rhys learned his lesson. And as far as the missing bits of costume go, your secret dies with us."

"That's right," Jem agreed. "We promise never to tell a soul."

Roger Pinnock left Lyonesse House a happy man. His conscience was relieved, and while he hadn't discovered replacement breeches and hose, he did pick out several very nice items to donate to the Tidal Pool Players, including the crimson snood.

"A red hat for a red herring," Pauley said. "That's what this sort of thing is called, right?"

Jem nodded. She'd noticed a gold-edged white bundle placed off to the side, away from the other vintage pieces. A Post-it stuck to it read, NOT FOR SALE.

"What's this?"

"Oh, I pulled it before the sale started. It's a formal tablecloth," Pauley said, shaking it out to show Jem the richness of the fabric. "I'm going to sew it into the perfect cape for the Pransom Hence to wear this Saturday night."

CHAPTER TWENTY-SEVEN

In the Trap

On Saturday afternoon, Jem and Pauley decided to leave *Bellatrix* moored on the outskirts of St. Morwenna and take Bart the Ferryman's vessel, *Merry Maid*, to Hugh Town for a late lunch, followed by the fairy tale comedy's opening night.

They were both glammed up for the occasion. Pauley wore a black lace dress with baby-pink accents; Jem wore a backless blue sundress that showed off her tanned arms and long legs. Pauley's hair was styled into waves, and Jem had gone for a chignon. She'd even dug into her friend's cosmetic arsenal and made up her face. Some mascara and matte red lipstick could work miracles.

The plan was to eat supper at the Kernow Arms and linger over drinks. When Micki's shift ended, she would do a quick change in the employee lavatory, changing into a dress and fluffing her curls. Then the three of them would make the short walk to the Empire Theater together.

Having recently resurfaced, Bart the Ferryman showed no signs of contrition. He told anyone who'd listen that the First Annual Pirate Extravaganza had been an unqualified success. It had been so good, in fact, there would be no Second Annual Pirate Extravaganza.

"When you've reached the pinnacle," he said solemnly, "you have to know when to quit. Once you top the summit, there's nowhere to go but down."

To Jem and Pauley, Bart was slightly more forthcoming. "No, Tresco is no longer available to me for future schemes," he said, shrugging as if no one could fathom the ways of councils and landlords. "People are monstrously jealous of success, and I'm at the top of my game.

"You, on the other hand," he continued, pointing at Jem, "are in a bit of a slump, now aren't you? I bet some mates you'd solve the Castle murder case in three days. But today marks two weeks, doesn't it? Thanks for nothing. I can't show my face on land again until I earn enough to cover my losses."

"Go back to your wheelhouse," Jem said sourly. "I don't trust this bucket's autopilot."

"Ignore him," Pauley said as Bart shambled back to where he belonged. "At this point, I'm rooting for Hack. Maybe if he has a big win, he'll be magnanimous enough to tell us why he was transferred from Exeter. Or clue us in about his first name, at the very least."

"It's driving me barmy," Jem admitted. "I feel like I've overlooked something."

"I think it comes down to a lack of resources," Pauley said loyally. "Only the police can scour the islands for any trace of Conor Dupree. Even if Simon Weatherby got his voice back tomorrow, you wouldn't be allowed to question him. And if you think Georgia really might be an accomplice, the next logical step would be to try and catch her admitting it by coercing her into confessing or intentionally catching her in a lie. Even tapping her phones and monitoring her internet use. All things illegal."

"I know." Jem had told herself all those things, but it didn't make her feel any better. She hadn't spoken to Hack since Tuesday, not long after the near-fatal attack on Simon Weatherby. His balaclava-wearing, silver-gloved attacker had not been found. Fortunately, Simon was now expected to recover, although it would take months, perhaps years, for him to regain full use of his voice.

As for the police, they showed no signs that an arrest was imminent. Every morning, the IoS PD deferred all media inquiries to Devon & Cornwall, who replied with some version of, "We are working diligently toward a resolution and will advise the public when appropriate." Meanwhile, all over the Isles of Scilly, doors and windows were locked, and even the emmets looked over their shoulders once in a while. It was a strange situation, all the more uncomfortable because it seemed so foreign to their normally peaceful, unhurried way of life.

Jem asked Pauley, "You don't think this is destined to be an unsolved murder, do you?"

"I hope not. I'd like to have at least one more conversation in my life with you that doesn't revolve around murder."

*

The Kernow Arms was busier than Jem had ever seen it. Micki, stuck behind the bar serving drinks and making change, had no time to hobnob with friends. Taking a table near the back so as not to distract her, Jem and Pauley ordered fish and chips along with their favorite local beer, Double Drowned. When their plates were clean, apart from the odd burnt chip, Jem's mobile rang. It was Hack.

"Hello?" she said eagerly.

"Why, hello to you." He sounded pleased by her enthusiasm. "I wish it was just the sight of my name on your screen that put that lilt in your voice. But I'll bet you're hoping I have news."

"News would be nice."

"First, there's Simon. His mum still won't allow us to interview him. Because of his age and condition, he's considered vulnerable," Hack said. "In the old days, a detective could've shooed his mum away, planted himself by the kid's bed, and refused to leave until he scrawled a name on a notepad. Nowadays, that's the sort of tactic that leads to an ethics inquiry, or overturns a case on appeal. But if we're patient, we'll get there. He'll come clean in the end."

"Fine," Jem said, unable to feign enthusiasm. Pauley looked curious, so she made a dismissive gesture to indicate nothing worthwhile had yet been said. She couldn't put the call on speakerphone. There were too many patrons seated around them, and that would risk getting Hack into trouble.

"Second, there's Georgia's ex-husband, Conor Dupree. I have bad news, and I have worse news," Hack said.

"Hit me."

"The bad news is, there's no evidence that places him in Hugh Town, or the West Country in general, during the week Jimmy Franks was assaulted. It's not impossible that he was here, but there's not a shred of evidence to justify formally raising the possibility."

"And the worse news?"

"Conor Dupree entered a residential drug treatment facility three weeks ago. It's one of those intensive programs that don't permit the patients to leave campus or be unsupervised at any time. Not even while sleeping. While Hermie Castleberry was murdered, and Simon Weatherby was attacked, Mr. Dupree was in Norwich, theoretically kicking the habit and definitely surrounded by witnesses."

Jem let out the verbal equivalent of a shrug.

"You sound completely beaten. I expected you to argue about Conor Dupree," Hack said. "As shiny objects go, he positively sparkled."

"I've gone over Jimmy Franks's story a dozen times," Jem said. "How he described the attack just doesn't make sense. He was alone at the office after hours. Someone attacked him from behind. He was sucker punched. As he lay dazed on the floor, the attacker said, 'I'm Conor Dupree, stay away from Georgia.' Or something to that effect. Why would a man dressed all in black, wearing a balaclava, start his threat by introducing himself?"

"Do you think Franks was lying?"

"No. I mean, I probably would, except later the same day, Simon was attacked from behind by a person all in black, wearing a balaclava."

"Hermie's throat was cut from behind, too, according to the post-mortem," Hack said.

Jem closed her eyes and pinched the bridge of her nose. "I can feel the answer floating around inside my skull. I just can't grasp it."

"Take a break. Enjoy the play. Your brain will cough up the answer when it's ready," Hack said kindly. "I'd better wind this up. I expect to be back to regular shift hours next week. What would you say to dinner? Next Saturday, maybe?"

Jem thought about that. Whenever she tried to focus on the possibilities with Hack, she saw Rhys's face. And whenever she tried to imagine a grown-up affair with Rhys, she thought of Hack.

"I'll let you know. Thanks for the news."

"My pleasure," he said, and rang off.

"I'm Conor Dupree," Jem muttered.

"Excuse me?" Pauley looked amused.

"Who would introduce themselves as Conor Dupree? He isn't well known in the Scillies," Jem said. "Jimmy Franks wasn't frightened by the name, just by the sucker punch. The only people who might know about Conor, and think of him as a threat, are Georgia and…"

Her phone buzzed. It was Kenzie.

"Hey, Kenzie," Jem said. "Only a couple of hours to showtime."

"Jem." The girl's voice was a bare whisper.

"Speak up, Kenz."

There was no reply.

"Kenzie. I'm putting you on speaker. Talk louder."

"I'm in the trap," Kenzie whispered, the words barely registering in the middle of the Kernow Arms's busy dining room.

"What?"

"What do you think you're doing?" a male voice asked in the background. The line went dead.

Jem's stomach dropped. She tried to call Kenzie back, but it rang six times and rolled over to voicemail.

"What's happening?" Pauley demanded, voice rising as it always did when she was seriously afraid.

"Leo Dupree killed Hermie Castleberry. Then he tried to fit up Rhys," Jem said. "I think Kenzie must've gone to the Empire Theater and found Leo in the room beneath the stage, under the trapdoor. They call it the trap."

"What? Why?"

"I can't explain. Call Hugh Town Station. Tell them what I just said. I'm going to get Kenzie."

"Me, too," Pauley said, but her face was white.

"No, you're going to stay here. Do whatever Hack tells you. I can take care of myself."

"But if Leo did these terrible things, he's sick. Dangerous."

"Yes," Jem said grimly. "But he's also a teenage boy."

CHAPTER TWENTY-EIGHT

Chip Off the Old Block

Hurrying uphill toward the Empire Theater, she saw the double entryway was secured with a padlock and chain, just as it had been the first time she visited. The performance was still two hours away, and most of the actors probably hadn't arrived. As she paused on the corner to let one of Hugh Town's many golf carts go by, Jem saw the theater's side door open. Out came a slight teen girl with a blue buzz cut that made her look like a ballpoint pen. Behind her came Leo Dupree, taller, stronger, and three years older, the fingers of his right hand digging into Kenzie's shoulder.

Jem drew a sigh of relief. It probably would've been wiser to search for some place to hide, like behind a parked car or inside a shop. But she was too angry to do anything but clench her fists and glare at the boy as he marched Kenzie toward the intersection of Shipyard Road and Caraway Street. Fortunately, Leo didn't turn to look behind him. He wasn't carrying a knife or wearing the anti-cut gloves, but there was a satchel slung over his shoulder.

Georgia scolded him about keeping things in the trap. Leo must've been using it as a bolthole, Jem thought. *Franks All Marine is only a hundred yards down Sailmaker Street. After Leo tried to kill Simon, he probably tore off the mask and ran for the theater. That's how he got away so quickly. He had a hiding place with a secret room even the theater people don't think about.*

As Jem followed Leo and Kenzie up Caraway Street, she wondered what Leo had in the satchel. Another scenario occurred to her. The former Chief Anderson, aka Randy Andy, had a flat here, and Lissa stayed over with him as much as he visited her on St. Morwenna. Assuming Lissa and Randy Andy had made up, she and Kenzie had probably stayed overnight at his flat to make attending the theater easier. Kenzie had probably wandered to the theater, perhaps to watch preparations for the comedy, or perhaps even with the intention of meeting Leo, an older kid she looked up to.

Of course she did. He does what he wants, without the slightest regard for the rules, or other people's feelings. To a rebellious girl, he looks like a free spirit. To me, he looks like a budding psychopath.

If Jem's scenario was correct, Kenzie had at some point found herself inside Leo's hidey-hole, the trap. After arranging to have the weapon and anti-cut gloves from Hermie's murder planted on Rhys's property, probably by Simon and Noah, Leo had obtained replacements for his subsequent attack on Simon. Were they inside the trap? Had Kenzie seen them, guessed that Leo was the killer, and rang Jem in desperation?

I hope she rang 999 first, Jem thought. But it didn't matter now. She knew what she had to do, and the die was cast.

Leo half-guided, half-pushed Kenzie toward number 6 Caraway Street. The first time she saw that sweet little cottage, with pink roses climbing its stone walls and a rustic front door with heart-shaped brass hinges, Jem had thought it adorable. Now it made Jem's upper lip curl. It looked like the perfect love nest, and for Hermie and Georgia it had been, at least for a little while. But the woman who'd tearfully begged Jimmy Franks on her knees not to call the police about "Conor Dupree" must've known the real assailant was her son, Leo. She'd protected the boy after a serious offense, and the next episode had been murder.

At the door, Leo opened it without need of a key and pushed Kenzie roughly over the threshold. Jem lurked close to someone's vine-covered obelisk until the door closed behind Leo. Then she sprinted across the street and paused near the cottage's stone birdbath, checking the house for CCTV cameras. There weren't any.

I need the element of surprise, Jem thought, briefly considering the front door, which was probably still unlocked. Why wouldn't it be? Leo had no reason to lock it behind him. He was the one person in the entire Isles of Scilly who had nothing to fear from the killer at large.

Deciding to check for a back door, Jem hurried around to the rear of the cottage. There was a neat little subtropical garden in the back, with clumps of spiky bushes and an obelisk thick with yellow clematis vines. In the kitchen, the curtains were parted to let in the sunlight. By standing on a low stone wall, Jem could see through the empty kitchen and dining nook, straight into the hall which led to the front room. In that room, a figure was pacing, but she couldn't tell who.

Refusing to second-guess herself or look over her shoulder, Jem tried the door handle. It, too, was unlocked. She slipped inside the kitchen and after the briefest of hesitation, locked it behind her. After attempting to murder Simon Weatherby, Leo had proven his ability to do a runner. A locked door might slow him down for only a couple of seconds, but that might be enough to get him caught.

Georgia's kitchen had gleaming quartz counters and sleek black cookery tools. From eight pegs on the wall hung a slotted spoon, two whisks, a masher, a grater, a pair of spatulas, and a meat tenderizer. Everything was in its place except for the knife block. There was an empty space.

"Leo Dupree," Jem shouted, marching down the hall to the front room. "I'm here for Kenzie."

The once-cheerful living room Jem recalled from her first visit was now gloomy. With the blinds closed and the curtains shut, the striped wallpaper looked gray, and the room seemed best suited for a wake.

Three people ranged around the room. Leo, standing in front of the TV, looked faintly bemused to see an angry librarian storming into his midst. Kenzie, sitting on the sofa with her knees drawn up to her chest, was dead white and rigid with fear. Georgia stood beside what had once been a wall of family portraits. The pictures were off their frames and on the floor, while Georgia looked like she'd died and woke up in hell.

Her eye make-up was smeared, her blonde hair uncombed. Instead of her usual shapeless dress, she was still in her bathrobe. "I didn't know," she quavered to Jem. "I swear to you, I didn't."

Leo was now wearing his silver anti-cut gloves. The all-black knife mentioned by one of Jimmy Franks's employees was in his right hand. Lifting it higher, he made a comedy stabbing motion, like a weak comedian pretending to be a slasher.

"Who's first?" he asked Jem pleasantly. "Nosy?" He pointed at Kenzie. "Stupid?" He pointed at Georgia. "Or you?" Leveling the blade at Jem, he took a step closer.

"Leo, you've made a mess of it. Don't you want to end this now, before you make things even worse for yourself?"

"What are you on about? I'm sixteen," he chuckled. "I won't be in any real trouble no matter what I do. I learned that at home in Norwich."

"My son isn't well," Georgia began in a high, hysterical voice. "The psychologist said—"

"To hell with the psychologist. People like him are jealous of people like me," Leo said evenly. If he was upset, he gave no sign. This was a game to him, an afternoon diversion that had only become more interesting with the appearance of Jem.

"It's the same with my dad. People are bloody terrified of him," Leo said with relish. "He does what he wants. So do I."

"You killed Hermie while you were at camp on Bryher," Jem said. "In the middle of your Sea Guides program, when Mr. Mourby did a vanishing act, you did, too. You told your friends you slipped out for a swim in the heated pool. But you really swam out to meet your stepfather's boat in the channel. Was it on the spur of the moment?"

"Of course not. Mourby always pulls that crap. He thinks because he once trained for the Olympics, we should just be grateful for his presence," Leo said. "I knew he'd put on a film and go down to the pub. I told Hermie when to bring the boat round. He was expecting me."

Without taking her eyes off Leo, Jem said, "I noticed something when I passed through the kitchen."

"What? This knife? Well done you." Leo's tone was scornful as only an adolescent boy's could be.

"No. I think the photos on the fridge had been taken down. The magnets were all by themselves, spaced oddly. It's a bit like those portraits on the floor near Georgia's feet." For a fleeting moment, Jem studied the wretched woman. "You've taken off your ring."

Georgia nodded pathetically.

"That reminds me of the platinum ring on Hermie's finger. The one Vera Vet retrieved," Jem continued, still speaking to Georgia, though her gaze was locked on Leo again. "Did you start to doubt him then, or did you still believe? At The Ruin, you told me he was away a lot. That he worked all the time and had a yacht he never told you about. Meanwhile, he told Jimmy Franks he was burning the candle at three ends. It's almost like the family man had more than one family."

"He had three families," Leo spat, clearly disgusted with his stepfather. "I confronted him about it just before Sea Guides Camp. I told him my price. He didn't want to pay it, but he was scared I'd spill the beans to Mum. We kept up the negotiation by phone even while I was at camp. Then I told him to come get me and we'd shake on a deal." Leo grinned his boyish, disturbing smile. "But what I really intended was to put the fear of God into him."

Jem nodded. Had she imagined a faint sound on the front porch? It was impossible to tell. She just had to keep Leo talking, and prevent that deadly looking black knife from coming anywhere near Kenzie's throat.

"I liked Hermie at first," Leo continued. "I thought he was generous. Much better than that prat Jimmy Franks, who made Mum work and never bought me so much as a Cornetto. I didn't try to get rid of him the way I got rid of Jimmy. I even danced at the wedding, and I hate dancing. Hermie bought me an Xbox and a bicycle and everything was fine.

"But he worked all the time, and stayed gone for days at a stretch. Some of the excuses he gave Mum didn't add up," Leo continued. "I started following him. Listening in to his phone calls. One day, when he thought no one was looking, I saw him switch his gold wedding band for a platinum one. Later, I saw him switch it to a bigger gold one with diamonds."

"But why didn't you come to me?" Georgia wailed.

"Shut up," Leo said savagely. "This isn't about you. You're too stupid to hear the truth about anything, Mum. Look at the state of you! You believe what you want to believe. You're better off in the dark."

"You thought he was holding out on you," Jem said to redirect Leo back to his self-aggrandizing version of events. Until the moment she'd seen the front door knob turn slightly, she'd felt almost supernaturally calm. Now her heart pounded in her ears and she felt slightly sick. It wouldn't be long now.

"Of course he was holding out on us," Leo snapped. "He had a wife in London and another in St. Ives. Do you know how much it costs to keep three wives? And Mum and I were a distant third. We got the smallest slice by far."

Suddenly Kenzie, who must have been working herself up to something while Jem confronted Leo, shot to her feet. "I have nothing to do with this! Let me go!"

Leo brandished the knife at her, making her quail. "You're a hostage, you stupid little bint. I'm going to work out the best way to get off the island. You're coming along for the ride. I'll let you go home once I'm safely away—unless you get on my nerves." He flashed Kenzie a smile that chilled Jem's blood.

Every fiber of her being wanted to throw herself at Leo, wrestle away the weapon, and see how he liked eight inches of sharpened steel waved under his nose. Instead, she redirected him again, certain she, Kenzie, and Georgia weren't the only ones listening.

"You said you got a chance to swim out to meet Hermie on *Family Man*," Jem said. "You must have brought the gloves and knife with you in a dry bag. Did you buy them on Bryher?"

"Took them out of the hotel kitchen," Leo said. "There was so much gear in there, I doubt they ever noticed."

"What did Hermie do when you threatened him?"

"Well… in real life, that went a little different than I imagined," Leo said, again flashing that wolfish grin that was far more disturbing than his usual coldness. "The plan was to show him the knife and give him a good scare. But when he wouldn't see sense, another idea came to me. I said I was swimming back to Bryher.

"I jumped overboard to make a splash. Then I crept up the ladder to the aft section, stripped naked, put on my gloves, and came up behind him with the knife. I put the knife to his throat. I thought I was just going to scare him. But the minute I heard him gasp, I knew I had to do it."

"Tell me he didn't suffer," Georgia pleaded.

Leo shrugged. "I couldn't say. He was dead by the time he hit the deck. Blood was everywhere. But not on my swim trunks, because I was clever enough to keep them safe," he added proudly.

Jem wanted to vomit. It wasn't the details of Hermie's death. Leo's glee turned her stomach.

"My son isn't well," Georgia whispered. "It's my fault. I fell in love with Conor. I chose to have his baby."

"There's nothing wrong with me," Leo burst out. "I'm smart. You wish you were as smart as me!"

"No, you're not. You made a total shambles of hiding the body," Jem said, again clenching her fists to keep from launching herself at him. "Tying his feet to an ice chest was stupid. Sinking the boat was stupid, too. Your mum might have sold it."

Leo's mouth contorted. For a second, she thought he would lunge for her, knife raised. Instead, he said, "You're just upset because you couldn't work out what really happened. I shifted all the blame to Rhys Tremayne. If Noah and Simon hadn't lost their nerve and recanted, it would've been perfect. Noah wouldn't grass if you threatened to draw and quarter him, but Simon gave in right away. That's why I had to cut Simon's throat—to keep him from telling all."

The front door opened. Jem, who'd been awaiting this moment, had expected it to burst open, like in some American cop drama. Instead, Hack opened it calmly and strolled in, thumbs hooked in his duty belt as if he'd paused to pass the time of day. Behind him, PC Robbins and PC Newt entered, Tasers held at the ready.

"I think we've heard enough," he announced to the room at large, giving everyone a tight, humorless smile. Leo could only gape at him, momentarily a child again.

"Kenzie, come here," Jem said. The girl jumped up and ran to her, burying her face against Jem's chest.

"Leo, it's over," Georgia said. "Put down the knife. They're here to help you."

Instead of releasing his weapon, the teen launched himself at Hack, all arms and legs and a long, sharp knife. The action happened too fast for Jem's eyes to follow. One moment, Leo was a deadly threat. The next, Hack had knocked the weapon out of his hand like a man swatting a fly. In two blurring moves, he had Leo spun in the opposite direction, both arms twisted behind his back and his face pressed into the carpet.

While PC Robbins covered him with her Taser, PC Newt snapped on handcuffs. Turning his back on Leo as if the boy no longer merited the slightest consideration, Hack approached Georgia, who'd collapsed in a heap.

"Are you injured, Mrs. Castleberry?"

Shaking her head, she stared up at him with wide, desperate eyes. "It really is all my fault. I took him away from Norwich for putting floor cleaner in another boy's drink. He saw different psychologists. They tried to pretty up his diagnosis with fancy jargon, but in the end it was always the same. Psychopathy. Just like his father."

"You knew all along that Leo attacked Jimmy Franks, didn't you?" Hack asked.

"Yes. When Jimmy said the man who hit him called himself Conor Dupree, I knew."

"Did you suspect Leo killed your husband?"

Georgia's mouth worked. "He's sixteen years old. He was away at camp. Under the supervision of professionals. And it was such an awful thing, a brutal, unforgivable thing…" She tailed off, unwilling to admit more, at least aloud.

"Georgia," Jem said. "When did you notice a kitchen knife was missing?"

The woman's eyes filled with tears. "I… I think I need a lawyer."

"You'll have one," Hack said. Returning to where Jem still held Kenzie in her arms, he asked, "She's okay, isn't she?"

Jem nodded.

"What about you?"

"I'm fine." Jem waited for him to berate her for entering the Castleberry home. He'd been angry enough when she phoned his mobile to say she was heading for the Empire Theater, insisting that she wait outside the venue for him to arrive. While he mentioned Leo would probably go home before trying to flee the island, he'd cautioned Jem not to try and rescue Kenzie on her own. When push came to shove, she hadn't been capable of waiting outside the cottage while Leo held Kenzie at knifepoint inside. After seeing Hermie's corpse and Simon's mutilated body, Jem had been unable to leave the girl to her fate.

A *crack-BOOM* from the vicinity of the kitchen made everyone jump. Hack drew his Taser and bellowed, "Police! Stay where you are!"

The intruder didn't obey. From out of the kitchen strode Rhys, red-faced, eyes snapping, fists clenched at his sides. He was in full costume as the Pransome Hence, including riding boots, a purple tunic, and the white and gold cape Pauley had made out of an old tablecloth. The gold paper circlet on his brow confirmed his princely status.

"Kenzie! Is she all right?" he demanded of Jem.

"Fine. What are you doing here?"

"She texted me," he said, taking a deep breath and visibly trying to calm himself. "Look at this."

He passed over his mobile. The text, probably sent just after Leo interrupted Kenzie's call to Jem, read,

Leo killer taking me to 6 Caraway

Hack, who'd peeked into the kitchen to view the cause of the *crack-BOOM*, returned to have a look at Kenzie's text. He gave a low whistle.

"Was the back door locked?"

"What do you think?"

"Kicked the ruddy thing off its hinges. Impressive. But I must remind you, there's such a thing as calling the proper authorities."

"I'll try and remember that," Rhys said through gritted teeth.

"And you're, erm, stepping on evidence. Just there." Hack pointed. "That knife is lying under your boot, your highness."

Taking a deep breath, Rhys moved aside. He now looked redder and angrier than when he'd burst in to save Kenzie's life.

Kenzie, who'd pulled away from Jem at last, regarded Rhys with bemusement. "Why did you come here dressed like that?"

He stared at her with raised eyebrows.

"Never mind," she said. Then whispered to Jem, "Only it's embarrassing."

CHAPTER TWENTY-NINE

Pirates Hideaway

"I like the new name," PC Newt told Jem.

"You like everything," PC Robbins retorted. "I preferred the old Cornish, myself."

"*Gwin & Gweli* was my idea," Clarence said with a sigh. He was sitting on the front row of folding chairs, fanning himself with one of his own flyers. There were only three rows of chairs, signaling an intimate affair. Jem and Pauley were in the middle; PC Newt and PC Robbins were in the back. It was a lovely Saturday, typical for late summer in the Scillies: soft breeze, clear skies, and the mingled scents of sea and lush green growth. The grass beneath their feet had been recently cut, and Clarence had given the B&B a pale blue trim to make it prettier for next season's listings.

"Anyway, I think it put people off. No one likes to discuss a place when they're not sure how to pronounce it," Clarence continued. "So good riddance! Pirates Hideaway sounds fun. It conjures up images of a romantic island getaway, not a second language textbook."

Pauley, who'd suggested the name change, beamed at Jem. After giving Clarence his percentage of the vintage clothes sales she'd made to members of the Tidal Pool Players, she'd made him a business proposal. Now she was part owner of the B&B, which lent the operation new gravitas.

"No faffing, no fear," she'd said, quoting Roger Pinnock, whose personal story had inspired her to take the plunge. When Clarence had nearly cried for joy, Pauley had insisted it was good business, not charity.

"I spent so long caring for Mum and Dad, I completely lost sight of myself. I need to get back in the world," she'd said.

As far as Jem could tell, the world was responding well. Until that point, Clarence's B&B was just another venture from a recent transplant, liable to disappear as quickly as it had sprung up. Now Pauley Gwyn, scion of one of the islands' oldest families, was involved, and Pauley wasn't going anywhere. Other merchants and hoteliers who'd previously given Clarence the cold shoulder were suddenly taking his calls.

"Here we are. Are we late? She's not on stage, so we can't be late," said Kenzie, appearing on the Byway and dragging Rhys by the hand. "He was so excited that the police had recovered his paintings, he had to pry open all the crates right away. I thought I'd never get him to leave off."

Dropping into the seat behind Jem, Kenzie leaned close to her ear and asked, "Have you seen them?"

"No. I look forward to being asked," Jem said, smiling at the girl.

"They're completely incomprehensible. It's amazing," Kenzie burbled. "That's how you know when it's really art, when you can't make heads or tails out of it. Forget Hermie. It won't be long before Rhys gets a real agent and everyone knows his name."

Rhys took the seat beside Jem, easing into the space so that he didn't kick Clarence out of his chair simply by extending his legs. "Honestly, they're crap. But I see what I did wrong. Why they never quite expressed what I wanted to say. The next set will be better."

"Your sunsets are still selling."

He rolled his eyes. "Don't damn me with faint praise."

"Hello, Rhys," Clarence said shyly. For all his swagger and bravado with Jem, Micki, and Pauley, when he actually addressed an attractive man, he took it down a notch—way down a notch, making himself almost invisible. "I hope there's no hard feelings."

"Are you kidding? You killed it. The role was made for you," Rhys said.

On opening night, at the moment the Pransome Hence was meant to ride his hobbyhorse into the audience's hearts, Rhys had been at Hugh Town Station with Kenzie, providing moral support while she gave her statement. Therefore, Clarence had stepped into the breach, shocking the almost entirely local crowd, who fully expected Rhys. A smatter of confused laughter followed, prompting Clarence to glare at the audience and ad lib, "You *wish* you had a prince like me." The people had roared, and from that moment, the role was his.

"Is Hack coming?" Pauley asked in a perfectly neutral voice. She was still committed to being Switzerland.

"Working. So Newt and Mel could have an evening off."

"Good man."

Rhys, frowning slightly, brushed Jem's hand with a fingertip. The smallest of touches, it felt wonderful, but just at that moment, her mind was on other things.

"Pay attention," she whispered.

The Pirate Hideaway's first Saturday evening concert began with the chanteuse, dressed from head to toe in flowing white, sticking her head out the B&B's back door. Slowly, the rest of her followed.

Stiff with stage fright, Micki gamely made her way to the microphone. Slipping her guitar strap over her shoulder, she began to pluck out the melody of a familiar Cornish air.

"Jem…" Rhys began, but she silenced him with a smile.

"Hush. She sings like an angel. I don't want to miss a note."

A LETTER FROM EMMA

Thank you so much for reading *A Death at Candlewick Castle*. If you enjoyed it, and would like to be informed of my future releases, please sign up at the following link. I promise never to sell or reuse your email address in any way, and you can unsubscribe whenever you choose.

www.bookouture.com/emma-jameson

In Jem Jago's second amateur sleuthing adventure, I expanded the playing field a bit, setting some of the action on lush, luxurious Tresco. If you found yourself smiling as you read my descriptions of the island, I have good news: The Ruin is an actual establishment, and so is Candlewick Castle—though in our reality, it's called Cromwell's Castle. I also gave Jem her own little boat, *Bellatrix* (the name means "female warrior"), to assist with her adventures around the Isles of Scilly and the coast of Cornwall.

In this book, I tried to deepen some of the supporting characters. Pauley and Micki both have their own ambitions, and in future books those dreams will be explored. I made Micki a folk singer because people have recently rediscovered the magic of sea shanties (traditional work songs sung on sailing vessels) and because the lyrics of folk music reveals a great deal about the character and identity of a people. As for her stage fright, I based that a little bit on myself. There's a lot of anxiety that comes with writing a novel and sending it out into the world. Micki is realizing that there's no shortcut—the only way out is through—and I've eventually come to realize that, too.

As for Pauley, I teamed her up with Clarence because he amuses me, and I think Pauley will play off him quite well. They're both single, they both have an entrepreneurial flair, and they both appreciate fashion. It should be fun, watching their friendly partnership develop.

Of course, if you're curious about Jem's love life, there's much more to come. Hack gave her that sizzling kiss, while Rhys relied on his memories of Jem to endure a difficult situation. In book three, both men will try to up the ante. What will Jem do? I very much hope you'll come back and find out.

One last thing. I often say the difference between a book that finds its way and a book that sinks like a stone is simple: reviews. Honest reviews are the lifeblood of books in today's competitive digital sphere. If you enjoyed *A Death at Candlewick Castle* and would be willing to write a review, I would be eternally grateful. Thank you for that, and thank you for being a reader. The world is full of amusements and distractions, but reading is a special act. It requires as much from you as from me; your capacity to envision, empathize, and enjoy is what turns keystrokes into a memorable experience. I'm grateful you took the time to visualize Jem, feel for her situation, and hopefully laugh and smile as the story unfolded.

Until next time,
Emma Jameson
2021

emmajamesonbooks

@msemmajameson

emmajamesonbooks.com